PRAISE FOR *THE*

"Kimberley Woodhouse is a master at historical romance. It's nearly impossible to find her equal."

–Colleen Coble, *USA Today* bestselling author of
The View from Rainshadow Bay and the Rock Harbor series

"Once again Kimberley Woodhouse spins a charming story of love, mystery, and adventure. Set against the backdrop of the gold rush in California, Kim shows us the life of greed and corruption so evident in the desires of man to get rich quick, while giving a beautiful example of God's mercy and truth. I encourage my readers and anyone else who enjoys a fun and inspiring read to get their hands on a copy of *The Golden Bride*."

–Tracie Peterson, bestselling author of
the Golden Gate Secrets series and many others

"Kimberley Woodhouse is a must-read for me! Her grasp on historical fiction is delightful, and the stories she weaves leave me eagerly anticipating her next tale!"

–Jaime Jo Wright, Daphne du Maurier and Christy Award-Winning
author of *The House on Foster Hill*

"Kimberley Woodhouse does it again. *The Golden Bride* is filled with mystery, history, and intrigue that will keep the reader glued to each page from cover to cover."

–Darcie J. Gudger, author of the Guarded series, *SPIN, TOSS,*
and *CATCH* (spring 2019)

"Kimberley Woodhouse's commitment to historical integrity, paired with her luminous storytelling, makes her an author to both trust and cherish. Any book with her name on it is a book I need to read."

–Jocelyn Green, award-winning author of *Between Two Shores*

The Golden Bride

The Daughters of the Mayflower

KIMBERLEY WOODHOUSE

BARBOUR BOOKS
An Imprint of Barbour Publishing, Inc.

Cover Image: Ildiko Neer / Trevillion Images

Published by Barbour Books, an imprint of Barbour Publishing, Inc., 1810 Barbour Drive, Uhrichsville, Ohio 44683, www.barbourbooks.com

Our mission is to inspire the world with the life-changing message of the Bible.

ecpa Member of the
Evangelical Christian
Publishers Association

Printed in the United States of America.

DEDICATION

This book is lovingly dedicated to Kayla.
I could gush about how beautiful you are inside and out and how
you inspire me every single day, but I'll try not to embarrass you.
Avid literature enthusiast, language student, and theology buff,
you never cease to amaze me with your love for the Lord and your
passion for learning. You've faced more adversity in your young life
than most people ever have to deal with in an entire lifetime, yet you
smile and shine God's love to everyone around you. I'll never be able
to tell you how proud I am of you and how very thankful I am that
God gave you to us. It's amazing to get to be your mom. I am so
excited for the journey you are on, and I miss you like crazy.

1 TIMOTHY 1:17 (scripture in Greek)

Τῷ δὲ Βασιλεῖ τῶν αἰώνων, ἀφθάρτῳ ἀοράτῳ μόνῳ Θεῷ,
τιμὴ καὶ δόξα εἰς τοὺς αἰῶνας τῶν αἰώνων· ἀμήν.

Daughters of the Mayflower

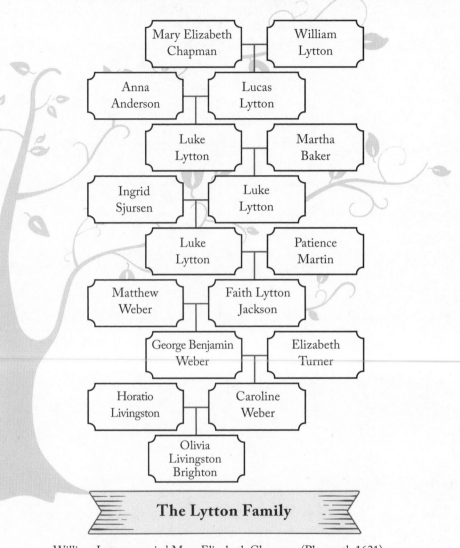

Mary Elizabeth Chapman — William Lytton

Anna Anderson — Lucas Lytton

Luke Lytton — Martha Baker

Ingrid Sjursen — Luke Lytton

Luke Lytton — Patience Martin

Matthew Weber — Faith Lytton Jackson

George Benjamin Weber — Elizabeth Turner

Horatio Livingston — Caroline Weber

Olivia Livingston Brighton

The Lytton Family

William Lytton married Mary Elizabeth Chapman (Plymouth 1621)
Parents of 13 children, one who was Lucas
Lucas Lytton (born 1625) married Anna Andersen (Massachusetts 1649)
Luke Lytton (born 1652) married Martha Baker (Massachusetts 1675)
Luke Lytton (born 1677) married Ingrid Sjursen (Massachusetts 1699)
Luke Lytton (born 1700) married Patience Martin (Virginia 1730)
Faith Lytton Jackson (born 1742) married Matthew Weber (Virginia 1775)
George Benjamin Weber (born 1776) married Elizabeth Turner (1798)
Caroline Weber (born 1799) married Horatio Livingston (1816)
Olivia Livingston Brighton (born 1829)

Dear Reader,

I'm so glad you've joined us for the next installment in the Daughters of the Mayflower Series, *The Golden Bride*.

In 1849, California was a wild and crazy place. Not only had the territory gone from Spanish to Mexican to US control, but crime and violence had taken over most of the area as people flocked from all over the world in search of their fortunes in gold. California's native peoples had been mistreated, many of them were brutally murdered, and the territory was in desperate need of government, all while it barreled toward becoming the thirty-first state in the United States.

San Francisco—formerly named Yerba Buena—quickly became one of the world's greatest ports. Tens of thousands of people descended on the area in just a matter of months. This is where we come to our story.

If you've read any of my other books, you know that I am a history buff. I love introducing true history to people through fictional stories in hopes of sparking interest in our great past. It has been a joy to receive the stacks of letters, emails, and Facebook messages from readers who are excited about our great country's history, and it encourages me to learn that I have done my job. It is my hope that this story will do the same for you.

While I did a lot of research into the background of San Francisco for this book, please remember that it is a work of fiction. I've used the names of some historical characters and streets, as well as included many historic events in the story, but please see the note at the end of the book for details about what truly happened and what I created for the world of *The Golden Bride*.

As always, I pray this story blesses you.

Enjoy the journey,
Kimberley

CHAPTER 1

*June 1849,
somewhere between San Jose
and San Francisco*

No matter how much he thought he deserved to be one, Olivia Brighton's husband of six weeks was *not* a king. Just because he'd been named after the thirteenth king of Judah didn't mean he was destined for greatness as well. Even if that's what his father had told him. And saying it over and over didn't make it come true either.

His namesake was a righteous ruler and godly man, but Hezekiah Brighton was neither. Nor was he rich, honest, or even smart, for whatever that was worth. And it wasn't worth much. *Hezekiah* wasn't worth much.

Shame washed over Olivia for a moment, and she grimaced at her thoughts.

As she stood beside their covered wagon and looked out toward the horizon, Olivia sighed. Guilt had been her constant companion these past few weeks. It seemed like every time she turned around she was having to repent. *Lord, I'm sorry. Forgive me for my horrible thoughts toward Hezekiah.*

No matter what kind of man he was, he was her husband. *She* was the one who had agreed to marry him after she'd only known him a day. He'd been so handsome, attentive, and charming. Even though she'd had plenty of doubts about him, his offer to help and promise to take her to San Francisco so she could be near her brother had made her jump in with both feet faster than she could say her new name.

She should have spent more time in prayer about it, but she missed her brother, Daniel, the only family she had left. It had been years since she'd seen him, and her heart ached for family. That was not a good excuse to marry a complete stranger, though, no matter how good-looking he was. But after Mama and Daddy had died so suddenly, her options had spiraled down to nothing. And there had been debts to pay.

What did she think would happen even if Hezekiah honored his promise and took her to San Francisco? It's not like all of a sudden she wouldn't be married to him anymore. And she *definitely* couldn't just up and leave and go live with her brother. Why hadn't she thought this through? It was so unlike her to grasp at straws. What would she tell Daniel? He was sure to be disappointed when he met Hezekiah.

If they ever made it there and the two men in her life actually met. . . That was a mighty big *if*. Her husband's detours were getting out of hand.

In the still of the morning air, Olivia shook her head of the negative thoughts. She'd made a mistake and would have to live with it. She needed to make the best out of the situation and pray that the man she married would eventually get them to San Francisco and provide for her. Or at the very least yearn to be a better man.

While worry had never been something she struggled with in the past, her new marriage had given her a fair share of it. Hezekiah hadn't stuck with the same thing for more than two days in a row. Almost every day he'd come up with a new scheme—his next get-rich-quick idea. They'd done little more than drive around in the wagon for six weeks, always looking for a new way to find his fortune.

The sun fully crested the horizon, its rays warming her face. Breakfast wouldn't make itself. Olivia wasn't sure they had enough food to last them through the day, but they could at least start off with a decent meal. Hezekiah had taken off with one of the horses an hour earlier saying something about his plans, but Olivia hadn't truly been listening. Every day it was the same. He'd get up and go off and come racing back with news of whatever they were about to plunge into next. They'd eat breakfast, and then they'd head out with the wagon. By the time they reached the destination, the jobs were gone, the money was gone, or Hezekiah simply had changed his mind and told her that the *next* day he would find whatever it was he was looking for.

Like clockwork, she heard the hooves of their horse running toward her. Wiping her hands on her apron, she realized that Hezekiah hadn't been late for one meal. See? At least he was dependable in one area. Maybe that was what she should do to turn her attitude around. Try to find one positive thing about her new husband each day. She could do that. Maybe.

"Olivia!" Hezekiah's shout broke through her thoughts, and she turned to him and pasted on her dutiful-wife smile.

"Good morning. Are you hungry?" She pumped enthusiasm into her words.

"I sure am." He hopped off the horse and tied it to the wagon. Placing his thumbs under his suspenders, he walked toward her and kissed her on the cheek. "I've got great news. We're headed to San Francisco."

The shackles of doubt and worry fell off her like a burdensome weight. "Really? We're finally going?" She could hug the man.

"Yup. The rumors are true. There's plenty of gold there, and I aim to get my share of it!" He sat on the ground and started wolfing down his plate of food.

Maybe he didn't deserve a hug after all. But what did it matter? They were headed to San Francisco! After she told Daniel the truth, maybe he could help. There was hope on the horizon. She doubted there was enough gold there to amount to much anyway. Hezekiah was always blowing things out of proportion.

"We're only a day or two away, and I need supplies, so we'll stock up as soon as we're done here. Then tonight or tomorrow we'll camp outside of town so that I can get started the first thing in the morning."

"That sounds like a good plan." Forcing her breathing to remain steady, Olivia kept her excitement at bay. She would show Hezekiah her support and allow herself to rejoice that she would finally see her brother again. As joy and relief mingled in her mind, another emotion swelled in her abdomen.

Grief.

Mama and Daddy were gone, and she didn't know if Daniel had received her letter. How would he take the news? What if she had to tell him in person? So many things had happened that had brought her to this place. What would he think of her decisions? Would he blame her?

"I'll need you to work at your brother's restaurant for a while to support us." Hezekiah broke through her thoughts. "Just until the gold starts coming in."

Of course he would. She shouldn't have told Hezekiah about Daniel's prosperous business, but she'd offered to get a job there, thinking it would motivate her husband to get them to San Francisco faster. "That's fine. I don't mind hard work." And it would keep her busy. Maybe that would help the ache of loss fade.

He slurped up the last of the gravy off the plate. "It's just for a little while. We'll be rich before ya know it, and we'll have a passel of kids." The tone of his voice sounded convincing, but Olivia knew better. "Let's get packed up so we can get supplies. It's going to be a great day." Hezekiah rubbed his hands together.

Yes, it would be. She was on her way to San Francisco.

Miles and hours later, Olivia stretched her legs beside the wagon. Foolish man. He'd spent every last penny on supplies for his gold digging but hadn't bothered to replenish any of their food stores. She had enough to make a pan of biscuits, and that was it, so Hezekiah had gone off to hunt something for dinner.

Olivia wouldn't hold her breath. The man had tried to hunt numerous times and never came back with anything. Looked like biscuits would have to do at least until they made it the rest of the way into San Francisco tomorrow. Looking in the direction of the town, Olivia could only hope it wasn't that much farther. Between getting stuck in the mud, Hezekiah spending entirely too much time buying supplies, and then his penchant for getting lost, she doubted they could even make it tomorrow.

Once again ashamed for her negative thoughts, Olivia plopped down onto the grass. This wasn't her. She'd never been such a negative Nellie. How had six weeks changed her so much?

Lord, I need Your divine help. I don't know how to deal with all this. I want to honor You with my thoughts and my actions. But I don't think I made a good decision marrying Hezekiah, and now that I've got to deal with the consequences, I'm a mess. Help my attitude. Help me be a good wife. Help us to find our way to Daniel's. And forgive me, Lord. Please.

As she poured out her heart to the Lord, Olivia felt a bit better. It didn't change the circumstances, but she knew she needed to get herself back on a more positive track. She couldn't continue down this path of negativity and complaining.

Daddy had always teased her about her skepticism and her partiality for sarcasm, but her life had been full of family, love, laughter, and quick wit back then. It had balance. Now there wasn't much to be happy about, and her pessimism had gone to an extreme. It wasn't good, and she knew it. But how could she fix it? Confessing it every day just made her feel worse and like more of a failure.

A shot rang out in the distance. Lifting her head toward the sound, she convinced herself to be positive. Perhaps Hezekiah had gotten them some meat for dinner after all. She could always hope. Standing up, she went back over to where she'd started to set up camp for the night. She should get everything going so that when he came back to their wagon, she could make them a meal. And maybe she could work on her attitude with Hezekiah and show him some encouragement and support. The Bible did say that a contentious woman was like a dripping rain. It also said that it was better to live in the wilderness than to live with a contentious woman. She didn't want to be that—even if her marriage was less than ideal.

Olivia just needed to find herself again. Starting now. Maybe God could still bless her marriage if she looked at it as a chance to make up for her mistakes.

When the biscuits were finished and she'd done all she could to tidy up and get everything ready for the night, Olivia looked off in the direction she'd heard the shot. Maybe he hadn't shot anything after all. But watching the sun sink in the western sky made her nervous. Hezekiah had never been late for a meal. Until now.

Maybe he'd gotten something large like a deer. That would take him a while to clean and drag back to camp, wouldn't it? Sitting down next to the fire, she was overtaken by weariness. She'd just sit down for a spell and wait for him to return.

The howl of an animal brought her awake in an instant. How long had she been asleep? The night sky was illumined by a canvas of stars with the moon shining high above. Rubbing her eyes, she tried to get rid of the cobwebs of sleep left in her mind. Olivia jumped to her feet and looked around. She'd been resting up against the wagon wheel this whole time, and the crick in her neck was proof. Looking around, she spied the pan of biscuits still sitting by the fire. But no Hezekiah. What if he'd gotten lost again? Or had been attacked by a wild animal?

The thought made her gasp, and she put a hand to her throat. As much as her husband wasn't ideal, the idea of anything happening to him sickened her.

With a quick cleanup of the camp, Olivia decided she had to find him no matter what. She placed a couple of hard biscuits into her apron pocket, grabbed the lantern, and climbed onto their other horse, Buttercup. *Lord, please let me find him. Please.*

She pointed the horse in the direction from which she'd heard the shot. Hezekiah might be well beyond that place now, but at least it gave her a place to start.

Time passed in the plodding steps of the horse. Afraid she might miss his prone form if he'd fallen asleep, Olivia didn't want to take any chances by going too fast. Sweeping the lantern back and forth, she searched. As the horizon began to light with the predawn hues of orange and gold, she didn't know what to do. Too many scenarios ran through her mind. Hezekiah killed by a bear, fallen from his horse and severely injured, wandering in the wilderness around them, dying of hunger and thirst. Her heart filled with compassion for the man she'd married, and once again guilt took up residence. Maybe if she'd been the wife he needed—the wife she should have been—he wouldn't be lost right now.

Another horrifying thought took root. What if he'd taken off without her?

Shaking her head, Olivia couldn't believe that was true. Especially not without all the supplies he'd just spent their last money on. But. . . would he?

Buttercup shook her head and whinnied, bringing Olivia's focus back to the trail in front of them. A shadowy form on the ground didn't appear to be moving. Buttercup took a step back and whinnied again. Something wasn't right, and the horse didn't like it.

Olivia took a deep breath and slid off her mount's back. She patted Buttercup's neck and spoke in a soothing tone. "It's all right. I'm going to go check this out. You just stay right here for me, all right, girl?"

A huff from the beloved animal wasn't very encouraging.

With tentative steps, Olivia moved forward until she realized the form on the ground was indeed a person. The buzzing of flies caught her attention right as she noticed the darkened grass. Blood. And lots of it.

With a gasp, she covered her mouth with her right hand but moved quickly to the body's side. It only took a second for her to recognize Hezekiah Brighton.

Her husband.

Dead.

Perhaps God hadn't given her a second chance after all.

CHAPTER 2

May 1849,
San Francisco

Joseph Sawyer shoved his hands into his pockets and walked to Livingston's Restaurant for lunch. It was hard not to feel utter sadness and shame at the depravity he saw around him as he took long strides through the dirty, raucous town. San Francisco had turned into a modern-day Sodom and Gomorrah with all the crazed gold seekers who flooded the streets each day.

He could say that with all honesty and without judgment because not too long ago, *he'd* been one of them. When he came to San Francisco by chance two years ago, he'd been a mess. He'd been lost, broke, always looking for a fight. But after gold had been found, he threw all of his energy into the hunt. Why God had chosen to bless him with a bountiful claim was beyond Joseph's understanding, especially when he had been a ne'er-do-well himself. But here he was. Grateful for grace, second chances, and a friend who had picked him up out of the pig sty.

Walking through the open door of the restaurant, Joseph headed to his regular table.

"I'll be there in a minute." Daniel Livingston waved from across the room.

Joseph waved back.

It amazed him to this day. If not for Daniel, Joseph would've been killed when he'd first found gold. The memory of that night rushed into his mind as he took a seat at the table and watched the restaurant continue to fill. Daniel had barely known him at the time but said for some reason God had placed Joseph on his heart. So Daniel had gone to find him that night and had dragged him out of the saloon. With his pockets full of gold nuggets that he'd been showing off, Joseph had been picking a fight. . .again.

He owed Daniel his life, and not just his physical life. If his friend hadn't taken him in, given him advice to lie low and keep his mouth shut, Joseph would certainly be lying dead in the street, his claim taken by someone else.

Over the next weeks, Daniel fed him, straightened him out, and introduced him to the Lord. Once Joseph had his eternal life in order, Daniel helped him figure out a plan. He'd spent days toiling with Joseph at the claim, found him suitable workers, helped him open a bank account, taught him how to study the Bible, and showed him how to give to others.

Thankful those difficult days had taken place but were now safely ensconced in his past, Joseph smiled. It all boiled down to the fact that God wasn't done with any of them yet. He was a God of second chances. Even so, on some days Joseph wondered why the Lord tarried. It had to grieve Him to see the way the world had gone.

Looking around the crowded restaurant, Joseph felt a bit of that grief. Nearly all of the tables—more than thirty if Daniel hadn't added more—were full. Full of men caught up in the lust and greed running rampant in this city. Plagued with stealing, prostitution, gambling, and murder, San Francisco wasn't a place most God-fearing people stayed. But his friend Daniel remained, stating that someone had to stand for what was right and be an example of Christ. His actions encouraged Joseph to do the same.

Now that he'd already made a small fortune for himself in gold and the claim was still producing, Joseph had funded the building of a church and, with Daniel's help, had purchased clothing and food for people in need. He longed to do so much more, but trying to keep his prosperity quiet was harder than he'd anticipated—to say nothing of protecting his workers and the mine. It was a good distance away from San Francisco, but that didn't stop thieves from trying to hijack it all.

So every day at lunch, he and Daniel discussed their plans. What they could do to help next. How they could shine a light for Christ in San Francisco. What better place to do it than from within the heart of the city? The restaurant was the most popular eatery in town. And not just because it had the best food, but because Daniel didn't believe in gouging the customers like everyone else did. That only made its reputation grow.

The Lord had truly blessed Joseph and his friend. They might be two of only a few upstanding citizens in San Francisco right now, but they could change that by helping one person at a time. It could be done. Just look at what God had done in Joseph's life.

A young, skinny boy came to the table. "Would you like the lunch special, Mr. Sawyer?"

The rich scent of roast beef filled the restaurant. "Yes, I would. It smells wonderful. Thank you very much." Joseph smiled at the kid and wondered where Daniel had found this one. Always soft-hearted for the needy, his friend hired a lot of the downtrodden to help them get on their feet.

The object of his thoughts—the owner and Joseph's friend— made his way to the table. "Sorry to keep you waiting." Daniel picked up his napkin and placed it in his lap. "We keep getting busier every day it seems."

"No matter how many times you apologize, it still doesn't need to be done. It's never a problem. I know you have a lot to do to keep this place running."

Daniel shook his head slightly. "It's definitely a wonder to me how fast this town has filled up—with more coming every day. I know God has me here, but some days I'm exhausted by it all and think of moving to a quiet place in the country—away from all this."

Joseph leaned forward and put his elbows on the table. "I've had the same thoughts, my friend."

"But you know I'm not going anywhere. I know God has me here." He swiped a hand down his face. "I'm simply tired."

"What can I do to help? You know I've got plenty of workers that keep things running—thanks to you—so let me help you here."

Daniel leaned back and appeared to be pondering the request. "You know. . .there is something that would really help me. But it's a lot to ask."

"It can't be more than what you've done for me, and besides, you rarely ask me for anything." Joseph tapped his finger on the table to emphasize the point. "Tell me what you need."

The young skinny kid brought them plates of steaming food and filled their coffee cups.

Daniel nodded and looked at the young man. "Thank you, Stephen."

The kid beamed a smile at his boss.

Joseph looked to his friend. "I'll say the blessing, and then you can tell me what you need." As he lifted a brief prayer of thanks heavenward, he also prayed for wisdom for them as they sought to do the Lord's work in their town.

With a bite of food lifted on his fork, Daniel cleared his throat. "You know I've opened that mercantile and restaurant in Sacramento?"

The smell of roast beef and mashed potatoes filled Joseph's senses and made his mouth water. He took a bite. "Mm-hmm. How's it going?"

"Well, I need to get a large load of supplies up there. They've been sitting in my storehouse in the back for way too long. I'm just short-handed and haven't had time to go myself. It might take more than a week for you to deliver them. Are you willing to do that?"

"Of course. I don't have a city council meeting for another couple of weeks, so I'm free to go. Anything I can do to help." A trip to Sacramento might be kind of nice. At least he'd get away for a little while.

"That would be a huge help to me." Daniel put his napkin down and took a deep breath. "And that way I don't have to leave right now. . . ." His friend let the words hang as if there was more to the story.

Joseph waited a moment and watched Daniel's face. "Something else on your mind?"

His friend sighed and looked out the window. "I received a letter from my sister that our parents have died."

The grief carried in the words hit Joseph in the chest. He leaned back. "I'm sorry about your parents. I had no idea—I thought they were doing quite well." He knew how close Daniel had been to his family. They were dear to him even though distance kept them from seeing one another.

"They were. But apparently, they caught some disease from the village they were ministering to. Olivia found them, but they died a few hours later."

"I'm sorry. That must have been devastating for her. How is your sister doing? How far away is she?"

"They all lived down near Santa Barbara. My parents had wanted to be missionaries there, but my dad ended up being a farmer for the most part and would visit the villages once a month. They didn't have much, so I'm sure Olivia has had to sell the farm. That's why I'm worried. I have no idea how she's doing. She's only a kid."

"How old is she?" Joseph's heart sped up. He knew firsthand what it was like to be on his own as a kid. And a girl being left alone and on her own didn't bode well.

"Let's see. She's ten years younger than me. . . ." Daniel gave a sad chuckle. "I guess that means she's twenty years old. So not a kid anymore." His words faded as he stared out the window again. "She was just a kid the last time I saw her." He shook his head.

Joseph noticed the sheen of tears in his friend's eyes, the weight of loss printed on his features. "Santa Barbara is a good ways from here. Do you need to go get her? Or do you need *me* to go get her?"

Daniel looked him in the eye again, his grief plain. "No, but thank you for offering. She wrote that she was going to make her way here, but I have no idea how or when. And that's what worries me. I feel helpless to do anything. What if something happens to her on the way?"

Thunk. Another shovelful of dirt and rocks landed on top of the lifeless body of Olivia's husband. As she peered down into the hole, tears blurred her vision. Sweat seemed to trickle from every inch of her skin, saturating her hair and her dress. What did it matter to add her tears to the mess? The digging had been grueling, but who else was there to do it? As she'd dragged his body into the hole, her back had tried to remain rigid against the sobs that threatened to overtake her, but it hadn't worked.

Utterly alone, she knew it remained her duty to give Hezekiah a decent burial. And with every shovelful of dirt, her shoulders weighed down with one very agonizing thought. She hadn't been a decent wife.

Oh, on the outside she had done her wifely duties. But inside? She'd done nothing but whine and complain. She hadn't respected him. She hadn't even truly loved him. While Hezekiah had been a handsome man, she could only admit to being drawn to him for his looks. And that made her very sad. How had she not seen more? Rather than nitpicking in her thoughts about all his flaws, she should have been looking for his good traits.

It all amounted to one fact: She wasn't deserving of the husband she'd had for a mere six weeks. God had deemed fit to leave her alone because of it. First her parents had died. Then her husband. On top of that, the blame for her husband's death rested squarely on her shoulders. What would Daniel think of her now? The thought made her feel even more alone.

She was left with a wagon and two horses and a load of gold-digging supplies. Not a penny to her name. Not an ounce of food left. And no idea how far she might be from town. Could she even drive the wagon? She'd never done that by herself.

As she neared the completion of her task, her heart ached worse than her muscles, which screamed in agony. She'd failed. Again.

By the time the hole was filled in and mounded with dirt, the day was almost over. Olivia covered the mound with rocks and hoped she'd done an adequate job. It was the best she could do. Standing at the edge of the grave, her hands on the handle of the shovel, she took a deep breath and realized she'd done nothing for a service. No prayer. Nothing. As she wracked her brain for words to say, the only thing that came to mind was her favorite psalm. Through her tears, she recited the verses:

"The LORD is my shepherd; I shall not want.
"He maketh me to lie down in green pastures: he leadeth
    me beside the still waters.
"He restoreth my soul: he leadeth me in the paths of
    righteousness for his name's sake.
"Yea, though I walk through the valley of the shadow of

death, I will fear no evil: for thou art with me; thy
rod and thy staff they comfort me.
"Thou preparest a table before me in the presence of
mine enemies: thou anointest my head with oil; my
cup runneth over.
"Surely goodness and mercy shall follow me all the days
of my life: and I will dwell in the house of the Lord
for ever."

Olivia felt like she was in the valley of the shadow of death at that
very moment. Perhaps she was doomed to stay here after all her
dark thoughts about her husband. Guilt filled her mind again. Tears
flowed down her cheeks. She stood at the edge of her husband's grave
thinking selfish thoughts. It was all about her.

About how she felt.

About what she would do.

About her loss.

Yet she'd just buried Hezekiah and hadn't given a thought to
whether her husband was with God. How awful was she?

There was so little that she knew about him. He'd never taken her
to church, and she'd never seen him open the Bible. His death must
have been horrible. He'd been all alone. Maybe he cried out to God in
the end. There was hope in that. *Oh God, forgive me again for thinking
only of myself. I pray that You drew Hezekiah to Yourself in the end.*

Poor Hezekiah. The thought of him suffering made her stomach
uneasy. The best she could surmise was that he'd shot himself in the
leg accidentally. Probably chasing an animal. All so he could provide
a meal for them.

Bile rose in her throat. He'd gone because of her.

Because she'd complained about him not buying foodstuffs.

She'd whined about only being able to fix a pan of biscuits.

Two tears slipped down her cheeks and dropped onto the grave.

Buttercup nudged her with a whinny that broke her thoughts. The sky was losing its light.

"You're probably thirsty, aren't you?" Olivia reached out to stroke the horse's mane. Where was their other horse? Poor Buttercup could never pull the full wagon by herself, could she? And she couldn't leave the other horse out here alone.

A sigh escaped Olivia's lips. She was covered in dirt and sweat. Hadn't eaten all day. Hadn't had anything to drink. And she'd just buried her husband. She didn't deserve to have her animals to take care of. She deserved to be all alone. Hadn't God proven that today?

Buttercup nudged her again, not willing to be ignored.

"Let's get back to the wagon. The creek will refresh us both." She swiped a dirt-covered hand at her cheeks and patted the horse, the only thing left from her parents.

Every step on the way back to the wagon, Olivia thought over her words and actions since she'd married Hezekiah. How many of them had been motivated by selfish desires? How many of them had been forced and faked? The answers only made her feel worse.

When they reached the wagon, the sun was sinking in the west. Olivia grabbed the other rifle and her dressing gown and took Buttercup down to the water. At least she could get cleaned up. But then what would she do?

Her heart lifted a bit when she realized they weren't far from San Francisco. She could go the rest of the way, sell all the gold-digging supplies, and find her brother.

As soon as hope and relief struck her, guilt swept in again. She shouldn't feel hope or relief. Not in light of her husband's death. At the edge of the creek, Olivia collapsed as she finally allowed the gut-wrenching sobs to take over. She couldn't fight it anymore—she was too tired. What had she done? What had she become? Was it her fault that Hezekiah was dead?

What was she supposed to do now? Her parents were gone. She'd gotten married, and now her husband was gone. What would her brother think of her actions if she found him? The very real possibility of being turned away and rejected filled her stomach with dread.

Stripping off her dress and shoes, Olivia couldn't see through the tears that continued to flood her eyes. She plunged herself into the creek and hoped the cold water could do a miracle in her heart and soul. If only the last six weeks could be cleansed from her mind like all the dirt caked onto her body was washed away by the water. But the more she cried, the harder the sobs came.

She'd failed as a wife.

Now she was all alone.

My child, I am with you always.

Olivia gasped as the words rushed over her. She looked around. How she wished that God was present before her now like He'd done with Abraham. The loneliness threatened to choke her.

I am with you always.

But she didn't deserve Him. She didn't deserve His grace. She didn't deserve His forgiveness.

She closed her eyes against the tears and breathed deeply. It hadn't been an audible voice. It had been within her heart. Dunking herself under the water, she let the water roll over her face and hair.

I will never leave you, nor forsake you.

The words pierced her like a knife. She came up for air and lifted her chin to the heavens. "But I am so wretched. I've failed You. I couldn't help my parents. I failed Hezekiah."

No answer came. But as her mind recalled Psalm 23—the very words she'd spoken over Hezekiah's grave—her tears lessened.

Olivia went under the water again and scrubbed at her face and hair. This was not what she had wanted. Not ever. No matter that she had made a hasty marriage, she would never have wished for Hezekiah to be. . .gone. And for her to be alone. But here she was.

A widow.

Sucking in a few more deep breaths, she tried to calm her heart and mind. The Lord was with her. Yes, she'd made mistakes and had an attitude that needed adjusting. But she was forgiven. She knew that deep down.

If she could just forgive herself.

Stepping out of the creek, Olivia sat on the bank in her underclothes. It had felt good to cry, but it also exhausted her. Weariness filled her limbs. Grief overflowed her heart.

Why had God taken her parents? Olivia had prayed so hard. . . had begged God to spare them. If they hadn't died, she wouldn't have made the decision to marry Hezekiah. If she hadn't married him, he wouldn't have gone off trying to hunt something for them to eat. He'd still be alive.

Shaking her head, she tried to dispel the condemning thoughts. She couldn't do anything to change the circumstances. The guilt would remain, but she needed to think about her survival and what she would do next.

The only logical step was to head to San Francisco, sell everything, and beg her brother for a job. Her dreams of being happily married and raising a family in a quiet little town—with a church and a school at the center—were gone. She was twenty years old and a widow. A very poor one at that.

Wrapping herself in her dressing gown, she looked down at her left hand. Because he couldn't get her a ring, Hezekiah had shaped a piece of wire to fit around her finger. It had pinched at first, but she'd gotten used to it as it molded to her finger, and she at least appreciated his effort. But it was all for naught. Tugging at the metal, she pulled it off her hand. She didn't have much to show for her hasty marriage to Hezekiah Brighton, and she didn't deserve to wear his ring no matter what it was made of.

She grabbed Buttercup's reins and headed back to the wagon—the emptiness of her stomach a harsh reminder that she had no food or money.

A soft nicker greeted her as she made it back to her campsite. Their other horse—Julius—had returned and was eating the tall grass by the rear wagon wheel.

"You came back!" Olivia raced over to the horse and patted his neck.

At least she would be able to hitch the horses up in the morning to pull the wagon, and the horses had food and water.

She even found a couple of hard biscuits that she'd forgotten about. If she was careful, that could get her through tomorrow. She could drink plenty of water to keep her stomach feeling full, and she could pray that she would make it to the town to find her brother.

Life wasn't at all as she'd hoped, but tomorrow was a new day. She would just have to take it one step at a time and pray for God to show her what to do and where to go.

CHAPTER 3

B uttercup and Julius plodded along ever so slowly as if the past days' circumstances were thick mud around their hooves, weighing them down. Olivia couldn't blame them. Hezekiah had driven them hard for weeks. They'd started off with a prance in their step this morning, but the hours and hilly terrain had worn them down. The wagon was heavy—Olivia knew that—and she didn't have the heart to urge them on any faster. She was tired. They were tired. And the closer she came to San Francisco, the more she worried about what she would say to Daniel. It'd been a long time since they'd seen each other.

Sweet memories of her childhood competed with the doubt in her mind. Daniel had always been her protector, her loving big brother. Until he left home, they'd spent hours together every day. And even though time and distance had kept them apart for years, his love and care for his family had always been apparent in his numerous letters. Shouldn't she rest in that?

Thoughts and memories of Daniel brought Mama's face to mind. Daddy had always said that Olivia looked just like her. But Olivia didn't have the wisdom and courage her mother had. Oh, how she wished Mama were here to talk to right now. Then she'd know what to do and what to say.

Blowing out her breath, she resolved to keep her emotions in check. It wasn't helpful for her to continue to dwell on things that were out of her control. She'd just have to tell Daniel the truth.

The afternoon was getting on, and a new worry settled in that she wouldn't make it to San Francisco before dark. The dirt road had wound through some pretty terrain, and she'd even seen the ocean once or twice. All she knew was that the town was at the end of the peninsula—but how far would that be?

A cloud of dust appeared on the road ahead of her. Before long, she realized it was a wagon. Not having seen another soul in some time, Olivia's heart sped up. She pulled her team to a stop and hoped the others would do the same.

The wagon grew larger as it neared her, and Olivia stood and stretched for a moment. Taking the reins back in hand, she sat down and breathed deep.

"Hello there," an older man in a suit with a proper lady beside him hailed as he brought his wagon to a stop.

These people looked like fine folk. "Good afternoon." Olivia smiled. "I was wondering if you could tell me about how far San Francisco is from here?"

The woman pursed her lips.

The man cleared his throat and frowned. "I hope you aren't headed there alone, miss. It's a wicked town." The couple both looked down their noses at her.

The words weren't encouraging, but what else was she to do? "My brother is there, and he is a fine, upstanding man. Do you know how far it is on this road?"

"Three hours at least." The man shook his head, all friendliness from his initial greeting gone.

The woman tsked at her. She lifted her shoulders and eyebrows, making her look quite severe. "I would suggest you find your brother and head out of that nasty town as fast as you can. No *God-fearing* folk would stay in such a den of iniquity." She patted the man's arm and turned her gaze straight ahead. Conversation over.

"Good day." The man's words were clipped as he flicked the reins and set his horses back into motion.

"Thank you." Olivia's soft words were lost in the rumble of their wagon.

Not entirely sure what to make of the conversation, Olivia prodded Buttercup and Julius back into motion. One thing was certain: those people didn't think much of San Francisco or of people who chose to live there.

Well, she didn't have any other choice. Daniel was the only person she had to turn to, and he was in San Francisco. At least it was only a few more hours. Prayerfully she'd make it there before dark.

The horses moved a little faster, almost as if they could feel her anticipation. After a little time had passed, Olivia saw another cloud of dust on the horizon. Not wishing to stop for another unpleasant conversation about how she shouldn't be headed to San Francisco, she decided to keep moving.

When the oncoming wagon reached her, she was glad she hadn't stopped. The disorderly behavior of the drunk men it held was not encouraging. The one driving belted out some horrid song about how he would soon be rich, while the other man tried to get her attention and made lewd comments about how she should join them.

Olivia's face filled with heat as she flicked the reins a bit harder than she intended, but she felt a sense of relief as her horses picked up their pace and took her farther away from the filthy men and their lecherous words.

Was this what she was headed into? Maybe the stern words of the couple were true after all. But what would Daniel be doing in such a place? And his letters made it sound as if his restaurant was upstanding and classy.

Another cloud appeared on the road. With another one after it.

Olivia braced herself and urged her team on faster.

Wagon after wagon passed her. All were filled with men, none of whom seemed to be of high moral character. Or *any* moral character. In all her years, she'd never heard such language or foul songs. San Francisco must be a very wicked place indeed.

Every muscle in her tensed as she reached the outskirts of the town. Men were everywhere. And the severe woman from the first wagon was right—none of them looked God-fearing. Tents filled the street as far as her eye could see, with a dilapidated shack here and there thrown in. Garbage blew around in the wind and filled the space between the tents. And the smell! Was *this* actually San Francisco?

Men who noticed her began to shout comments as she passed. Lifting her shoulders, she urged the horses on and kept her gaze straight ahead. Certainly this wasn't truly the town. Her brother wouldn't be in such a place, would he? Making her way down the street, Olivia was overwhelmed as the number of men and tents grew. Pretty soon she could hear the tinny sounds of pianos being played in fast tempos with shouts and cheers coming from the saloons.

The tents had given way to larger shacks and ramshackle buildings that burst at the seams with activity and sounds. She looked to the side for a moment and counted eight saloons before she looked the other way and saw men in a drunken brawl in front of her. One extremely large man picked up another and threw him to the ground. A whiskey barrel broke his fall and smashed to pieces beneath the smaller man. The unmistakable smell of alcohol filled the air, and Olivia tried not to breathe it in.

Booming voices and saloon music competed for everyone's ears. Filth and unwashed bodies filled the walkways and sides of the streets. If she had had anywhere else to go, she would have turned the wagon around right then and there. But she had no one else. No other choice.

Tears burned at the edges of her eyes, but she clamped her jaw tightly and sat straighter on the wagon bench. More lewd comments were thrown at her from the streets, but she refused to acknowledge them. On and on she drove, praying for help to find Daniel. The mass of people—almost entirely men—surprised her. Daniel had told them in a letter that there were only a few hundred people in the town of San Francisco, but there were thousands of people here. What had brought them all? The thought of gold?

Some larger buildings appeared ahead, and they didn't seem nearly as rickety. As she approached that section of town, the noise died down a little as well. A large mercantile sat on the left side of the street ahead. Then she spotted it. Livingston's Restaurant.

She wanted to shout with relief that she'd finally made it, but she held herself in check. As she pulled her wagon up as close as she could get to the nice wood building, which looked like a mansion compared to all the shacks she'd seen in the rest of town, several men approached. The hitching posts were filled with horses. Apparently, a lot of people were here. Her heart beat faster, and she prayed for safety. Peering into the windows of the restaurant, she could see it was indeed quite full and busy. Dozens of tables filled the space. The place was massive. How would she get Daniel's attention? What if he wasn't there? And would her wagon be safe out here? Would *she* be safe venturing in alone?

A spindly kid wiggled his way to the front of the crowd that had gathered around her wagon. All men. All grinning at her.

"Hey, miss?" the kid's voice squeaked. "Whatcha doin' here?"

She raised her eyebrows and looked at him. "I'm looking for Mr. Daniel Livingston. Do you know him?"

"'Course I do. Everyone knows him." The kid moved a step closer.

"Do you need me to fetch him? I can do that right now."

"Yes, please."

As the boy pushed his way back through the men, they in turn pushed closer to her.

"What's a pretty lady like you doing here in a place like this?"

"What's yer name?"

"I been lookin' for a pretty girl to be my wife."

"I've got gold. Dontcha want a man that can provide for ya?"

The men got braver and came closer, throwing out more and more statements and questions until they all mixed into a blur of sound. Voices rose and fell all around her as bodies pressed up against the wagon.

"That's quite enough, gentlemen!" A voice she recognized hushed the crowd. Before she knew it, Daniel climbed up onto the wagon seat next to her and took the reins.

Groans, curses, and murmurs rose from the men.

"Daniel!" She threw her arms around her brother and could contain the tears no longer.

"Move on," he said to the crowd, which was clearly unhappy that he was taking the reins. He smiled down at her. "It's good to see you, Sis." He shook his head as if in disbelief. "You're all grown up. And you look just like Mama." The emotion in his eyes about did her in.

All the stress and grief and fear she'd carried came to the surface. She grabbed a hankie just as the waterworks began. Daniel didn't say a word. He simply drove the wagon down the street, around the corner, and behind another large building. He hopped down and opened the doors to a large barn and then led the horses in. He helped her down as the tears continued to stream down her face, and went to close and bar the doors behind them.

He came back and put his hands on her elbows. "You look done in, Olivia."

She managed a nod.

"I am so sorry that you had to face the loss of our parents alone." He put an arm around her shoulders. "I've been worried sick ever since I got your letter."

"I'm all right. I'm just glad that I made it here." Wiping the tears from her cheeks, she looked around the barn as relief took up residence. At least she didn't have to share the news of their parents' passing. "This town isn't anything like what I imagined."

"It's not how it used to be. It has only become this way in the past few months."

"Why are you still here?"

Daniel walked over to a bale of hay and sat down. "Because God has me here for now. Someone has to shine a light to these people and stand up for what's right. And I don't have a wife or a family to worry about. A lot of the other men that had families left when things got out of hand."

"Does that mean I shouldn't stay? Is it safe for me to be here?" She had to admit that the way the men looked at her and spoke to her had made her nervous. Never in her life had she been around so many men at once—especially ones that didn't seem to own an ounce of decorum.

Her brother rubbed his face. "As long as you are always with me, I think you'll be fine. But I don't want you going anywhere without me or someone we trust. And some parts of town you need to stay away from at all times."

"I don't want to be a bother, Daniel. . ." What could she say? "I just don't have anywhere else to go."

He grabbed her hands. "You are not a bother at all, Olivia. You're not. So get that out of your head right now. You are my sister. My family. I've missed you so much, and I love you." Squeezing her hands, he winked at her. "Tell me, do you still use sarcasm to cover up your fear?"

The question made her laugh. "Dad must have written you about that."

He laughed along with her. "I remember your quick wit as a child, but yes, Dad wrote often of your banter. I didn't mean to put you on the spot, but I want you to feel comfortable being yourself with me. You've been through a lot, and I'm here for you. No matter what."

"Thank you, Daniel."

"If you are still willing to work at the restaurant, I could use the help, and I also think it would be safer than to leave you alone during the day. I've got strict rules in place about no brawls or fights of any kind. The customers know if they break the rules, I don't let them back in. We'll just establish additional rules about how they need to treat a lady. I've got the best food in the city and the best prices. No one wants to lose that." He stood up. "You look like you're about to wilt, so let's get you settled upstairs. I built my own living quarters above the restaurant, and there's plenty of room."

Too weary to argue, Olivia grabbed a few personal items from the wagon and followed her brother. "I've got to figure out what to do with all our things."

"Let's not worry about it tonight. You need a decent night's sleep first. We'll get up early in the morning, you can fill me in on your life, and we'll decide what to do."

Olivia nodded. Everything would be all right. She had her brother now.

The next morning, Olivia paced the length of the parlor while she told Daniel most of what had happened. While he was shocked to hear of her hurried marriage, he hadn't scolded her. And he seemed even more sympathetic to learn that she'd lost her husband as well. It made her heart ache to think of him not seeing their parents for so long—not being able to say goodbye. His grief was still fresh—she could see it in his eyes.

Reconnecting after all these years was wonderful, but she couldn't stand the thought of him hurting and grieving not only for himself but for her as well.

Daniel was still her brother and protector. Almost as if he'd never stepped out of that role even though the miles had separated them for a decade. But it seemed he took on a heavier weight now because their parents were gone.

It was understandable, and she wished she wasn't such a burden. She needed a place to live, and he'd offered her a job. Maybe as time went on, she could show him how valuable it was to have her around. They needed to get to know each other as brother and sister again.

As he left to go down to the restaurant, he leaned over and kissed her on the forehead. "I'm so glad you're here, Livvy. It'll all work out. You'll see."

Once she was alone with her thoughts, she hoped he was correct. He'd helped her bring up all her personal belongings from the wagon and told her to unpack her things. She could start at the restaurant tomorrow. He even said that she could make a lot more from her husband's gold supplies here since they were in high demand and he'd take care of that for her in a few days if that was what she wanted. He'd seemed so excited that she was here and told her she wouldn't be destitute and wouldn't be a burden. Isn't that what she wanted?

All the events of the past few months rushed in again. Daniel hadn't judged her for marrying Hezekiah so hastily, although he'd expressed his concern for her. He'd been so kind and loving, telling her over and over that he was sorry he hadn't been there for her.

It was nice to not feel so alone anymore. . .to be with family.

Guilt spread in her stomach again. What would happen when he found out that it was all her fault her husband was dead?

CHAPTER 4

One Week Later

Weary of the road and the wagon seat, Joseph couldn't wait to get back to Livingston's and eat a decent meal. He really should take a bath to wash the dirt and grime from him, but his growling stomach took precedence. Daniel wouldn't mind his appearance anyway, even though Joseph had never arrived looking as filthy as he did today. It wasn't nearly as bad as some of the other customers. At least he kept telling himself that.

As he made his way to his regular table, the past eight days drifted through his mind. He'd had too much time to think through every aspect of his life. God had done a mighty work in him and turned him around. It was an incredible thing. And even though Joseph knew that God was using him in the town of San Francisco, the trip had made him realize several things.

One had weighed him down the most. Even though he was surrounded by people and busyness at home, he was lonely. Unsure whether he was ready to share that with his friend or not, it at least made Joseph a bit more thoughtful. Before he'd always been ready to just dive into everything headfirst. Now. . .maybe the time had come for him to slow down and think it all through.

Daniel was the best friend he'd ever had, but the poor man was so busy. They both were trying their best to make a difference in their town, but it was like skinning a cat most days. An impossible task.

They only had a couple of people coming to church services right now. How were they supposed to reach more? What could they do differently? And how could they get a pastor to come out to the town that most people had dubbed the wickedest place in America?

The gangly kid. . .what was his name?—Stephen?—came to his table. "Mr. Sawyer, we have roasted chicken for the special today. But you know everything else we serve."

"Thanks, I'll have the special." Joseph leaned forward on the table. "It's Stephen, right?"

"Yes, sir. I didn't think you'd remember my name." The kid smiled at him. "I'll get your food."

"Thanks. Is Mr. Livingston here?"

"Yes, sir. I'll tell him you're looking for him."

"I appreciate it."

Joseph scanned the room and watched the customers. The men flocked to Livingston's for every meal because the food was good and the prices beat out everyone else in town. As soon as the rush of gold diggers had hit, merchants flocked to San Francisco and started selling their wares and food stuffs at nearly double and triple the normal prices almost overnight. Those who were anxious to strike it rich with gold had to pay the exorbitant fees to get what they needed. Even baths and everyday meals cost what seemed like a small fortune. Daniel had to raise prices when the cost of his supplies had gone up, but he still tried to keep everything as affordable as possible.

It was another thing that Joseph admired about his friend. Daniel still made good money for himself—even without trying to cheat his customers.

Stephen returned with a steaming hot plate and a coffee pot. "I figured you wanted coffee?"

"You know me already. I'd love some."

The kid beamed under the praise and poured the cup of coffee.

"I'll be back if you need anything."

"Thanks, Stephen."

"You're welcome, Mr. Sawyer."

The table next to him emptied, and Stephen took all the dirty dishes to the kitchen. After saying a quick prayer of thanks for his meal, Joseph dug into his dinner. He wanted to close his eyes and moan at the tastiness of the food—especially after eating his own pathetic biscuits and jerked beef the past week—but he restrained himself. He hadn't seen Daniel yet, but when he did, he'd have to compliment his friend again.

The table next to him filled up with four rowdy-looking men. Not that the rest of the customers weren't rowdy, but their conversation started to make Joseph feel like his space was being crowded too. He'd gotten used to being on the road by himself the last week and away from the noise of San Francisco.

It might be best if he just finished his food and left. He and Daniel could catch up later—maybe once the dinner rush was over and Joseph had time to get cleaned up. But then a dark-haired young woman walked up to the table of new guests with a notepad in her hand. A stern look etched on her brow, she appeared ready to do battle with her customers. "What would you gentlemen like to order today?" She kept her eyes glued to the pad of paper. "The special today is roasted chicken."

"The special for me." The one on her left tried to make eye contact and smiled. But no luck.

"Me too," the three others chimed in at the same time.

She scribbled on the pad. "All right. I'll bring out your dinners and some coffee in a bit." She began to turn.

A hand shot out to stop her. "Wait. We'd like to order pie as well."

Evading the man's hand with a step to her right, she lifted the pencil again. "What kind? We have apple, peach, or cherry."

The men all shouted their responses. She scribbled them down and walked away.

As the four men began to discuss their waitress, Joseph tuned them out and watched her. Her dark hair was neatly pulled back into a bun with tiny curls framing her face. While her expression had been quite harsh, Joseph understood that was the only way a woman could hold her own in a town of ninety-nine percent men. She'd handled herself well. Who was she? And what was she doing here? How had Daniel hired her? Women were scarce in these parts. . . . Wait a minute. Could that be his sister? Had she made the long trek already? They didn't look anything alike. . . .

Sipping his coffee, Joseph decided maybe waiting on his friend wouldn't be so bad after all, and he could ask all his questions.

The object of his thoughts returned minutes later carrying all four plates at the same time. For a second, he almost jumped up to help her but realized she didn't need his assistance. In less than half a minute, she served all the men, poured their coffee, and left.

The thought made him chuckle to himself. She was impressive.

It wasn't long before she returned with four smaller plates filled with large pieces of pie. "Sorry, gentlemen, but we are short-staffed today, so I brought your pie now." She plopped a pie plate beside three of the men's dinner plates in quick succession. When she made it to the last one—the man who'd been bold enough to try to reach out and stop her—he put a hand on her other arm. She stopped in her tracks and narrowed her eyes.

"Now, missy, the way I see it, you and me should get hitched."

She yanked her arm away. "Well, I don't see it that way. The answer is no." She set the plate of pie on the table next to the man's dinner, but as she turned, he put an arm around her waist and pulled her closer.

"Come on now. I got gold. And you're just too pretty for me to let get away."

Joseph came out of his chair.

Without warning, the young woman picked the pie plate back up and smashed it into the proposer's face. "Let's get a few things straight, sir. You will be paying for your piece of pie today along with your whole dinner and I'm quite certain a generous tip. You and your friends will be welcome back in this restaurant only if you agree to never touch me again and to mind your manners. And one more thing. I will never, *ever* marry a gold miner." She turned on her heel and walked back to the kitchen.

Joseph took his seat as the men at the other table laughed at their friend wiping pie from his face. Surprisingly, they all continued to eat, and nothing else was said about their waitress. Probably because no one wanted to be denied entrance to Livingston's Restaurant.

No matter how hard he tried, Joseph couldn't get the dark-haired waitress out of his mind. As he finished the rest of his dinner and coffee, he caught sight of her several times throughout the restaurant, but she never came back to his area again. He'd just have to ask his friend about who she was and hope he could one day meet her.

❧

The man frowned. Finding decent help in this town was getting harder and harder. It made it difficult to build his empire. His assistant, George, was slicker than a snake, but at least he knew how to keep his mouth shut and how to schmooze his way around people.

Besides George, he had a small group of loyal and well-paid employees who would do anything he requested. But the rest of his help all left for the gold fields as soon as they'd earned enough money for supplies. Stupid fools. The money wasn't going to be made in gold. The idiots who did find gold were going to spend it. The fortune to be made was in gambling, liquor, and women. But they hadn't seen it like he did.

Walking to his window that looked out onto the wharf, he knew that he'd have to change up how he did business. It wouldn't hurt to expand his enterprises either. Thousands were coming into his little town, and it probably wouldn't stop. More ships arrived every day. Plenty of people out there were waiting to be exploited. He'd have to seize the opportunity and build up his employee base. It wouldn't hurt to bring in some women as well. The demand for prostitutes grew with every passing day. He'd keep throwing money at all the good and decent things that people needed to see, and then behind the scenes, he could do the rest. No one would be the wiser.

Pacing in his office, ideas grew. His dream would be realized here in San Francisco. Money and power would be his. Although he already had plenty of money, a little more couldn't hurt. And he wanted a good deal more.

The real thing was power. Power came to the wealthiest, the ones who practically owned their cities. He intended to own this town.

It was a good thing he came here when he did, before anything had been developed. He'd seen the potential of a large city being built on this beautiful peninsula. The shipping trade was at his fingertips. Then came the gold. While he owned several mining operations himself, he really didn't care much about it. What he cared about was that gold brought people who needed supplies, entertainment, and loans. People who were desperate to make their own fortunes and would do anything to gain them.

There were other ways to get workers and loyal employees. He'd build a larger, trustworthy entourage around him who cared about the army of workers he needed. There were ways to get what he wanted.

A smile split his face as he watched a group of Chinese men leave a ship. A new thought crossed his mind. He needed workers for all his businesses. Why didn't he just steal them? He could continue to help the downtrodden and support the city council publicly, all the while using it as a screen to mask what he was up to behind the scenes. Upstanding citizen to the masses. Underground slave trader behind closed doors. The best of both worlds.

The dinner rush was finally over, but customers still came into the restaurant. Olivia walked into the kitchen and blew her hair off her forehead. While she'd been at this job a week and had learned how to deal with the customers, it was still exhausting.

"Livvy!" Daniel's voice behind her made her turn. "There's someone I'd like for you to meet. Do you have a minute?"

"Of course." She put on a smile and turned back to the door. "I've only got a few tables for now, and I've already served them their meals."

Following her brother through the restaurant, Olivia wiped her hands on her apron. Hopefully this wasn't anyone important. She was a mess.

In the corner at Daniel's favorite table stood a tall man covered in what looked to be miles of road dust. Her heart did a little skip. She'd seen that man earlier. He'd come to his feet when one of her customers grabbed her and she promptly pushed pie into his face. Hopefully, this man wouldn't bring that up.

Daniel stopped at the table and pointed his hand to the man. "Olivia, I'd like to present my friend, Joseph Sawyer. Joseph, I'd like you to meet my sister, Olivia Livingston."

The filthy man with blond hair smiled, and his eyes crinkled at the corners. "It's nice to meet you." He held out a hand in greeting.

She took his hand and shook it, hoping that her cheeks weren't turning too pink. "Actually, it's Olivia Brighton, but it's nice to meet you too."

Confusion passed over the man's expression.

Daniel leaned closer to her. "I'm sorry. I forgot." He straightened and pulled out a chair for her. "Joseph is a close friend. The closest I've got. And I wanted you two to meet each other."

Olivia allowed herself to be seated. "I can only stay a moment until my tables are finished. It's not my break yet, and I wouldn't want to get in trouble with the boss." She gave her brother a mischievous grin and then glanced at her customers to make sure they didn't need anything. Looking back at Joseph, she gave him another smile. "It's so nice to meet a friend of my brother's."

"Daniel is the best, as I'm sure you know." Joseph took his seat, and Olivia watched his eyes. There wasn't any condemnation for her handling of the situation earlier. She'd have to tell Daniel about it later that night. Not that he would scold her about it. They'd had worse things happen with their rowdy customers.

Her brother laughed as he sat down as well. "Joseph and I meet every day for lunch and discuss what we can do to make our town better."

"That's very noble of you."

"Joseph is on the city council. They threw it together after the Shades Hotel burned down in January. Everyone knows we need some organization and order, but crowds of people come in every week and the chaos is barely manageable. So we've been meeting to see what else we can do."

Olivia had known that her brother wouldn't be in such a place without a good reason. It made a lot more sense now. San Francisco was his mission field. And it looked like at least one other good man lived here—even though he might stink to high heaven and be covered in dirt.

How could a city councilman be as unkempt as the rest of the grimy men? It didn't make sense. But it'd be best if she showed her support. "I'm excited to hear about what all you've done. Is there any way I can help?"

"Well, so far we've built a church and provided clothes and meals for those who don't have anything. A lot of them were swindled as soon as they got here." Daniel shook his head. "It's sad to see how money drives these men to do all kinds of horrible things."

"So the little church we went to on Sunday is the one you built?"

"One and the same." Daniel grinned.

The building had been lovely—especially compared to the rest of the town, which appeared to be thrown together with whatever the so-called builders could grab—and Daniel had done a wonderful job leading the handful of people in a short study of the Word. "I'm impressed, you two. That was no small feat. You did a wonderful job." Olivia caught Joseph's gaze. His deep brown eyes fascinated her.

As soon as she realized her thoughts, shame filled her. What was she doing? Thinking about another man's eyes when her husband hadn't been buried quite a fortnight. She turned to look away at the rest of the restaurant and noticed one of her customers waving from across the room. Thankful to be saved by her job, she stood and looked at Daniel. "I'm sorry to cut this short, but it looks like I'm needed."

Both men had stood with her, but her brother was quick to speak. "Of course. We'll visit another time. And when you have your break later, we can eat together."

With a nod, she headed to her customers and hoped they wanted to order pie and visit a while. She needed to stay busy and keep her mind off finding *any* man's eyes fascinating.

Out of the corner of her eye, she saw her brother's friend leave. She thought she'd feel relief. Instead she found herself struggling to remove the image of Joseph Sawyer from her mind.

CHAPTER 5

When Olivia's midafternoon break finally came, she found herself famished. Grabbing a plate from the kitchen, she inhaled the aroma of the roasted chicken and headed to Daniel's table, knowing that he would meet her there if he had a chance. Most days, this was her favorite time. Diving into her new life helped her to forget about the past. Catching up with her brother helped her get to know him as an adult. He was everything she'd imagined him to be from his letters. All the doubts she'd had when she'd first driven into San Francisco were gone. She was proud of Daniel.

That didn't mean she had to like the town, but at least she understood why he was here and why he stayed. That was good enough for her. And she really had no place to judge.

The first bite of chicken practically melted in her mouth. No wonder people flocked to the restaurant. It really was the best food she'd ever eaten. Maybe one day she could learn to cook like this.

"Good afternoon." Daniel appeared just as she popped a bite of pan-fried potatoes into her mouth.

She covered her mouth with her napkin as she chewed and swallowed. Beaming him a smile, she filled her fork again. "Sorry. I didn't see you. Apparently, my attention was completely on my food."

His chuckle washed over her and warmed her heart. Having family was a wonderful thing. "I must be working you too hard. I know the food is good, but you never miss a thing around here. Some of the customers have even said that you must have eyes in the back of your head."

"You have to around here. You never know what one of those men will try." She shook her head.

"I hear there was an incident today. . . ?"

"Oh?" Knowing full well what he was getting at, she decided to play along.

"Something about another proposal and a piece of apple pie?" Daniel quirked a brow. Then his lip twitched. It was apparent he was trying to hold back his mirth.

She tried to keep a straight face but couldn't hold it. "When he ordered his pie, I don't think that was how he expected it to be served."

Their laughter was comfortable. Daniel took a sip of his coffee and turned serious. "Are you okay?"

Unsure how to answer that question honestly, Olivia thought back to the last week. Seeing how the men in this town behaved had been eye-opening. They made Hezekiah look like a saint. But it didn't take her more than thirty minutes to learn how to handle things. If the men wanted to return to Livingston's Restaurant, they would learn how to behave themselves around her. She was the only female employee there and one of a very small percentage of women in the population. "I'm fine. Truly. You know I receive at least twenty proposals a day. Those I can handle just fine. But I won't abide the men touching me, and you said I could handle things as I saw fit. The most fitting thing at the moment was for his pie plate to meet his face. If he wants to eat here again, he'll remember not to grab my arm or put his arm around me."

Daniel leaned back and crossed his arms over his chest. "You're quite amazing."

"Why thank you." She finished the last few bites on her plate and tried not to giggle when she remembered the man paying for his dinner and apologizing. He wouldn't even look her in the eye. Word had already spread that there was a woman working at the restaurant. It wouldn't take long for word to get out about how she handled men who got too forward. That was fine with her. The sooner the men learned to behave themselves, the better.

"I'm glad you finally got to meet Joseph today." Daniel's words interrupted her thoughts.

"Your friend?" She refrained from describing him as stinky and filthy even though that was her first impression. Most of the men in San Francisco smelled worse and were dirtier. But she also had to suppress the thoughts she'd had about Mr. Sawyer's eyes. While it was fine and dandy for her to live here with her brother and continue the masquerade day in and day out that she was perfectly normal, inside she knew better. She couldn't allow herself to have feelings for anyone. Not ever.

"We're really working to change things around here. And it's not easy. But I trust him with my life."

"That's wonderful." If only he would change the subject. She didn't want to have any more reasons to be interested in getting to know her brother's friend.

Daniel went on to rave about Joseph Sawyer.

And that didn't help any. But after Hezekiah, she'd had to put a wall up around her heart. Being impressed by a man wasn't going to happen anytime soon. She couldn't let it. Ever. Especially one who needed a bath. Daniel's friend obviously meant a lot to him, and that meant she would probably see him quite often. She shouldn't be so judgmental.

It probably didn't help that she received all those proposals every day. It was easy to harden her heart toward men, especially the gold miners. They only came back to town for food and entertainment.

She hated to think about it. The gambling and drinking were always raucous. Then there were the brothels. Even the thought of it made a shiver race up her spine. How could men do such a thing?

"I can see your mind is elsewhere." Daniel's words cut into her reflections.

She looked back at his eyes and grimaced. "I'm sorry. My thoughts took off in another direction."

He reached across the table and patted her hand. "No. I should be the one apologizing. I can't believe I introduced you today with the wrong last name. I'm really sorry about that."

"No need to apologize. It's silly really. It's not like anyone here knows about my marriage to Hezekiah. But I wasn't a very good wife, so the least I can do is honor my late husband with my name."

His brows lowered. "What do you mean you weren't a good wife?"

Looking out the window, she let out a long sigh. "Daniel, we've been over this. I told you what a negative person I was and that I complained in my thoughts and prayers about my husband all the time. I have to live with the fact that I was a terrible wife."

"You didn't know what kind of man he was. You'd only known him a day." Daniel's argument to defend her just wounded her more.

"That still didn't give me the right to behave like I did. Don't you get it? It's my fault my husband's dead!" She hadn't meant it to slip out that way. Over the past week, she'd told her brother about her behavior, hoping that she could build up to the point where she had to be honest about what happened. If she couldn't forgive herself, how was her brother supposed to?

"That's ridiculous, Olivia. Didn't you tell me that he shot himself in the leg? How are you responsible for that?"

With an abrupt move, she stood from her seat and picked up her plate. "I can't talk about this right now. I need to get back to work."

"Olivia—"

She held up a hand. "I need you to understand that I can't talk about this right now. Maybe not for a long time. So please. . .let it go." Turning on her heel, she headed back to the kitchen. Although her brother was a great man, he'd never understand. She was just going to have to live with what she'd done. Forever.

Early the next morning, Joseph watched the *Philadelphia* as her crew readied her to sail. Every day it seemed the number of ships coming into San Francisco grew. The city council was meeting in a few days, and he wanted to be prepared with solid information about their plight. If they were going to have any chance at making San Francisco a great city, they had to do something and soon. At least from his point of view.

Ships stacked into the harbor with no rhyme or reason. The ones trying to come into the bay fought with the ones leaving. Then there were the many ships that had been abandoned as all passengers and crew headed to the gold fields. Those ships were looted for supplies. If they sat long enough, the ships themselves were torn apart for their wood and parts to build something else. Truth be told, their wharf was just one huge rat's nest.

The actual city itself was worse. While the city and streets had been planned out, the buildings—if you could even call some of them that—had issues as well. The majority were thrown together willy-nilly with whatever people could grab. Filth and trash were all over the place. Tents crammed every nook and cranny for all the people who didn't have the funds or time to build a shanty for business or living.

Crime was prevalent everywhere, and they didn't have police

officers or firemen. But the worst area was around Pacific Street. The gang that called themselves the Hounds occupied that part of town. They were known for their thefts and beating of anyone Chilean, Mexican, or Peruvian.

Even though Joseph didn't know about the instances personally, he'd heard far too many stories to discount. Some even said the Hounds had murdered multiple people, but without any government in place, everyone's hands were tied.

This was the reason why Joseph had agreed to join the city council. To try to fix the problems. But the longer he investigated, the more he found there was to fix.

As he walked back up the hill toward town, he debated which item was the most pressing. There wasn't any way their small council could tackle all the city's needs in one meeting. They hadn't accomplished much of anything yet, but he definitely hoped he could change that. What good were they as a city council if they didn't actually *do* anything to help the city?

"Fire!" The shout from behind him made Joseph turn back toward the wharf.

The *Philadelphia* was on fire in the bay. In a matter of minutes, flames engulfed it. Joseph watched in horror as crewmen jumped from the ship—many of whom couldn't swim—to escape the blaze. Their cries for help resounded throughout the other ships. He ran back to the bay, hoping something could be done. But without organized help of any kind, it was to no avail.

Flames licked at the sails and masts as smoke billowed into the sky. The ship creaked and tilted on its side. Screams rose from the water.

Joseph ran as fast as he could toward the dock.

As the wind picked up over the water, sparks from the fire began to rain on the city. A tent caught fire, but the occupant ran out and poured a bucket of water on it. What could have happened if it had gone unnoticed? What if more sparks ignited fires across the ramshackle city?

As Joseph digested the chaos surrounding him, he realized the first order of business for their council meeting had to change. If they didn't address it, San Francisco would be doomed to burn. They weren't prepared for this, and he could only hope that he could convince the others to see the grave need they faced.

Out of breath, he reached the end of the dock and removed his shoes and coat. At the moment, he needed to help rescue the men flailing in the water. Praying that the wind would die down so no more fires would be ignited, he resisted the urge to look back at the town and instead focused on the bobbing heads in the water. With a deep breath, he dove into the bay.

CHAPTER 6

L ater that evening, after a bath and change of clothes, Joseph headed to Livingston's Restaurant with every muscle in his body aching. He'd managed to rescue three men and swim them to shore during the *Philadelphia*'s fire, while several of the other crews hauled other men onto their ships. Sadly, four men remained unaccounted for. They most likely drowned, and the thought made his stomach turn. He hadn't been fast enough to save them all, and not many other men knew how to swim.

The captain refused to tell what had started the fire and left on another ship barely two hours after the *Philadelphia*'s disaster. A few more sparks had ignited small fires around the town, but thankfully, they'd all been caught and put out in time. All of it made Joseph think long and hard about a solution, but he hadn't come up with one yet.

Prayerfully, his friend Daniel would have some good suggestions.

Walking into the restaurant, he spotted Daniel and his sister at their favorite table. He started toward them, and for a moment, he forgot about the matters of the city and watched Miss Livingston—er. . .Olivia. What had she said was her last name? Her dark brown hair was pulled back into a braid that she'd wrapped up into some sort of knot at the crown of her head. How women did such decorative things with their hair was beyond him, but he found that he really liked it, especially as several curls had loosed themselves and framed her face.

Her features were animated as she talked to her brother—something he hadn't seen when they'd first met—and it enchanted him. It helped him think on lighter topics. Something he desperately needed at the moment.

Daniel spotted him first. "Joseph! How good to see you this evening. Join us, won't you?"

He nodded at his friend and then to Olivia. Brighton! That was her name. "Good evening to you both. How are you, Miss Brighton?"

Her smile diminished a bit. "It's Mrs. . . . I'm a widow. But please, you can just call me Olivia." She took a sip out of her glass. "And I am well. Thank you for asking. I have to admit, I didn't recognize you at first."

Joseph laughed at her straightforward remark and the hint of mischief in her eyes. "If I recall when we met yesterday, I'd just returned from a long journey for your brother and was still covered in layers of dirt from the road. I assure you, had I not been half-starved, I wouldn't have been seen in public in such a manner. But as you well know, the food here trumps even the need for a bath."

Her cheeks tinged pink. "Indeed it does. I apologize—"

"No need to apologize, Miss"—he stumbled over using the wrong title—"forgive me, *Olivia*. I was a mess when we met. It should be me who is apologizing to you for being in such a state of disarray." He gave her a gallant bow and took his seat.

Her light laughter floated over the table toward him. "It's nice to hear a gentleman speak." She leaned back in her chair. "As you can imagine, I don't get a lot of civilized conversation serving tables in here."

Daniel joined in the laughter and put his elbows on the table. He quirked an eyebrow at his sister. "But you do get plenty of proposals of marriage. How many was it today?"

"Twenty-three. Not counting the young boy who couldn't have been more than fifteen. Although his was the most romantic of the lot."

Joseph felt his eyebrows shoot up. "You receive that many proposals a day?"

She nodded and tucked her chin, a wry smile on her face. "You should try being the only woman in a restaurant full of men. And I promise I don't always answer with a plate of pie to the face of my admirer."

Daniel stood up and looked at him. "Sorry, Joseph, you look starved. Let me get you some food and coffee."

Normally, he would offer to go get his own food, but Joseph wanted the time to talk to Olivia. "Thank you. I appreciate it." He smiled at his friend and turned back to Mrs. Brighton. "I didn't realize you were a widow. Daniel hadn't told me. I'm so sorry for your loss."

She looked away for a moment and spoke toward the window. "Thank you. We weren't even married two full months. That's why Daniel misspoke. It hasn't been that long. He never met Hezekiah."

Realizing he'd lost her to her memories, Joseph wished he could do something to put the smile back on her face. A change of subject was in order. "Your brother once told me a story about the two of you picking berries. . . ."

She slowly turned her head back to him with a smirk on her face. "I don't have any idea what you're talking about."

"You don't remember the berry-picking story?" Joseph winked at his friend as he approached.

"Oh, I think you do." Daniel set a plate down in front of Joseph and eyed his sister. "It involved me taking a nap and you painting my face purple with the berry juice."

She lifted her eyebrows. "I was all of six years old, and *you* were supposed to be watching me, not falling asleep in the sun. Even though Mama scrubbed my hands, they were purple for days after that."

Daniel chuckled. "My *face* was purple for days."

Joseph laughed along with the siblings. "I don't know, my friend. It sounds like you probably deserved it."

"Whose side are you on?"

He shrugged and put a large forkful of potatoes into his mouth.

"He's on the *right* side. That's what I think." Olivia smiled at him. A genuine smile that made her blue eyes shine.

Daniel pointed his coffee cup toward him. "I'll let it slide this time. But just remember that we've been friends a while now. I'm going to need you to stick up for me with Olivia around. You have no idea how difficult it is for me these days."

The pathetic look on his friend's face made Joseph's grin widen. "If you can't handle your sweet sister here, then it's no wonder you haven't settled down yet." Their long-standing jokes back and forth with each other about why the other one wasn't married had kept both of them from getting discouraged.

"Sweet? She may be sweet, but she's a spitfire and has quite the wit. I can barely keep up." Daniel narrowed his eyes. "You need to watch out for this one."

Olivia crossed her arms over her chest. "And if you two don't stop it, you both just might get your pie in your laps rather than across your face."

Joseph eyed his friend and tried to contain his humor. But he knew she was capable of it—he'd witnessed her feistiness first hand and had to admit he enjoyed it.

Daniel winked at him and took a sip of his coffee. Taking a bite of his pie, he held up a hand to his sister like he was swearing a vow. "I'll behave, I promise."

"Good. It's about time." She turned her gaze to Joseph and raised an eyebrow.

"Me too." Joseph nodded at her. The light conversation and

unwinding with friends had been soothing to his soul, but the events of today came back to his mind in a tumble of emotions and weighed him down. In that moment he saw the faces of the men in the water...crying out for help. Their cries filled his ears. He looked down at his plate and tried to make the images and sounds disappear.

"You look like you've got something on your mind. Anything I can do to help?" His friend's face turned serious.

Looking down at his food, Joseph wasn't sure how to express it without just laying it out and being honest with his friends. He took a deep breath and let it out. "The *Philadelphia* caught fire as she was leaving today. It spread so quickly that many of the crew jumped overboard to escape the blaze." He fidgeted with his coffee cup. "Most of those men couldn't swim. I tried to help. . ."

Olivia gasped and put her napkin to her lips. "Oh my. Were you able to rescue them?"

"A few. But four men are missing. They're believed to be drowned."

"I'm sorry to hear that." His friend's expression had turned grave. "It's a good thing you were there to help. I don't think too many people know how to swim."

Joseph shook his head. "I know you're right, but it's still hard to think that I could have done more. And it's more than just the sailors in the water. You should have seen the sparks raining down on the town. Several small fires started from those sparks, but thankfully people got them out quickly."

Daniel nodded. "I think we all know the disaster we would have if a large fire started in town, but people just ignore it. We've grown from a few hundred people to tens of thousands of people in just a few short months. Is there anything the city council could do? Anything we can do to help?"

Joseph leaned back in his chair and placed his napkin on the table. He swiped a hand through his hair. "I've been thinking about it all afternoon. We've got to do something, but you know the resistance I've had to deal with. The council is brand new. Everyone has their own ideas about what the most important needs are. General Riley has had to deal with the same things as the governor of the territory. The violence keeps escalating, we don't have a real government, and more and more prospectors arrive daily. He has to deal with deserters too. All because of gold."

A huff from Olivia across the table pulled his attention up. "I'm sure you've heard what *I* think of all these gold miners. The Bible clearly tells us that the love of money is the root of all evil, and we've got the proof surrounding us on a daily basis." Her tone was marked with disgust.

A twinge of guilt hit Joseph in the gut. *He* was a gold miner. Very few people knew that about him, but he'd made a vast amount of wealth with his mine. That lust for gold had been his at one time too. But thank God, he'd been rescued out of the depths of his sin. He looked at Daniel, who gave his head a tiny shake. Now was probably not the time to tell Olivia about his livelihood. Nor was it the time to argue that all gold miners weren't hideous criminals. Olivia was right to be skeptical about most of the men.

"What can we do to convince the new town council that we need plans for fire control?" Daniel tapped his fingers on the table.

"What if we were to get people to sign a petition?" Olivia perked up with her idea. "I could help get signatures. The customers here will do just about anything for me." Her mischievous smile while she wiggled her eyebrows caused the table to round in laughter.

"While I know it's true the men would do most anything for a smile from you, I don't think it will do much good since the meeting's in a couple days." His friend patted Olivia's hand. "We couldn't get nearly enough signatures for the council to take notice."

Joseph watched Olivia's features fall. While they didn't have enough time right now, the idea really had merit. He reached over and tapped the table. "But it *is* a great idea." He leaned an inch or two toward her. "If you want to get started on that, I think it will help us in the coming weeks."

She gave him a slight smile. "Only if you think it will help. I don't want to waste your time."

"It's not a waste of time, Olivia. I really think the idea is great. But I just don't know what to do at the next meeting to show them the importance. I doubt any of them were at the docks when the fire happened, so to them, it's not real. Besides the fact that we have so many other issues to deal with. Crime. Roads. Housing." With a sigh he looked back and forth between his two friends. "I think I'm just going to have to stand up to the rest of the council if they fight me on this and demand we put measures in place."

⸎

After leaving the restaurant and his friends, Joseph decided to ride outside of town to think. The noise and people of the city often overwhelmed him. And right now, he needed to clear his head of all the sights and sounds of today.

Daniel and Olivia had been encouraging and supportive, but he knew full well what he'd be facing in the council meeting. One man in particular—George Banister—seemed to object to anything that wasn't his idea. It didn't help that George's mysterious and unnamed employer was funding the council and their efforts. Why General Riley gave his approval was beyond Joseph's understanding. But this was the hand he'd been dealt, and he somehow had to figure out how to work with it. George might have the most sway right now, but what if the rest of the council sided with Joseph? If he could convince the others of the need, maybe real progress could be made.

Olivia's idea of the petition popped into his mind. If they were to garner enough signatures, certainly the council would have to listen to the requests of the people. He wasn't sure how many men they could get to sign, but the more he thought about it, the more Joseph liked the idea. And it wasn't just because he found Olivia captivating.

Joseph pulled back on the reins and slowed his horse. He'd enjoyed their banter this evening, but she was a widow and a recent one at that. Which meant she needed a friend, not another admirer. Then there was the small fact that she'd said she'd never marry a gold miner. Who was he kidding? Why was he even entertaining the thought of marriage? They'd just met. But it didn't stop his heart from pounding at the thought of her smiling at him.

He steered his horse toward one of his favorite spots: the top of a hill that overlooked the ocean. Out here with nothing but the stars shining down and the sound of waves lapping up against the rocks below, Joseph dismounted and closed his eyes.

"Lord, I don't know what to pray. You know the situation I'm in with the council. I want to be wise in my decisions and in my speech. I fear for people's lives in our city. I know You've got me here for a purpose. You've made that clear. But I struggle with the violence and ugliness that surrounds me." Olivia's face popped into his mind. A bright spot in the midst of all the darkness. For the first time in a long while, thoughts of the future didn't seem so lonely. "Thank You for bringing Olivia here safely. Please help us to keep her safe and heal her heart after the loss of her husband and parents." Joseph wanted to voice more, but God knew his heart. Right now, the best thing he could do was pray for her and be her friend. Maybe over time, he could change her mind about at least one gold miner. Him.

Chapter 7

Olivia walked up the stairs to their living quarters above the restaurant. Another long day of serving people had come to an end. The ache in her feet matched the one in her heart.

Why was it that at the day's end, grief seemed to always find her? The loss of her parents was especially difficult today, the day that would have been their wedding anniversary. Daniel hadn't said anything about it today. He'd brought it up yesterday, and when she'd refused to talk about it, the sadness in his eyes just about did her in. He expressed his concern about all the loss she'd faced recently. He worried that she'd find it difficult with not only the reminder of an anniversary that their parents wouldn't be celebrating, but the reminder that she'd never celebrate one herself.

But even after she'd told him the truth about how she'd been a horrible wife, he still didn't understand. Her heart was numb when it came to her late husband. It was almost as if their marriage hadn't even existed. How could she tell her brother that she felt cold and heartless? If she did, he'd probably think less of her. That thought was too much for her to bear. Daniel was all the family she had left, and she'd do anything for him.

Maybe it was selfish to want to keep her relationship with her brother on good footing, but it was what she had to do, because he just couldn't seem to understand the burden she carried.

Removing her apron, she walked over to the window that over-looked the barn and storehouse. A full moon was high in the sky. How had she gotten here?

The last time she'd seen her parents had been horrific. Sick and dying, they'd told her they loved her, and then she'd watched them writhe in agony. Tears stung her eyes. Then what had she done? After she'd seen her parents buried, she'd sold the farm and every-thing they owned to pay off the bank. Daddy had mortgaged their farm multiple times to keep them afloat, but it hadn't done any good. She'd still owed one hundred dollars when all was said and done. So when Hezekiah Brighton stepped into the bank and offered a solution, she'd taken it.

Regret filled her being for all the ways she'd failed as a daughter and the things she wished she'd said to Mama and Daddy more often. For selling everything too quickly. For marrying Hezekiah.

More tears spilled down her cheeks. Poor Hezekiah. He'd had big dreams. And he'd been sweet to pay her debt. He definitely didn't deserve to die. Especially not all alone.

"Olivia? Are you up here?" Daniel's voice penetrated the haze around her.

Swiping at the tears on her cheeks, she swallowed and took a deep breath. "Coming!" She met him in the center of their quarters, which they used as a parlor. "Did you need me?" She reached for her apron. "I'm sorry, I thought we were finished downstairs."

He stilled her hand. "Everything's done." His penetrating gaze made her look away. "I know today is difficult and that you don't want to talk about Mom and Dad." Taking her hand, he led her to a room he used for storage. "I've found something that I think should be yours."

As her eyes adjusted to the dim room, she noticed crates and a few trunks. Daniel bent to pick up a small trunk.

Recognizing it instantly, she covered her chest with her hands. "That was Mama's."

He nodded. "Yes. You may not remember, but when I was about twenty-two, I fell in love and was going to get married. That was when Mother gave me this box to pass down to future generations."

Olivia stared at the box and shook her head. "I have memories of this box in their bedroom from when I was little. When they died, I looked all over the place for it without success. I thought I'd lost it." The reality of her brother's words sunk in, and she looked from the box to him. "Wait. What happened? Why didn't you marry?"

"Madeleine and her family were killed in a storm."

A sob caught in her throat. How had she never known this? "Oh, Daniel. I didn't know. I'm so sorry."

His smile was forced as he patted her arm. "It was a long time ago." Wiping the dust from the top of the trunk, he pulled her forward. "I think you should have this. Women are much more sentimental than men anyway."

Tugging her hand free of his, she shook her head and backed away. "No, Daniel. I can't take that. Mama wanted it to be passed down to future generations, and I'm not ever going to marry again."

His brows lowered. "Why would you say such a thing? You're only twenty."

"I don't expect you to understand right now, Daniel. It's much more complicated than I wish to explain."

With a sigh, he wiped a hand down his face. "Listen, we don't have to talk about this right now. But you need to at least look in the box, all right? It's stuff that's been passed down from the women in our family. Women who have faced loss and unknown futures just like you."

Instantly regretting her harsh words, she reached out to her brother. He'd just shared about his own horrific loss, and she'd lashed out at him. "I'm sorry, Daniel."

"I'm sorry too." He handed her the trunk and walked out of the storage room.

She followed him out, the small trunk in her arms feeling like the weight of the world.

He stopped and turned to face her. "Look, I know you don't want to talk about any of this, and I'll accede to your wishes for now. It's been a rough few months for you. We're both beat, so why don't we get some rest, and I'll see you in the morning?"

She bit her lip and nodded, a single tear escaping her eyes. Daniel had been so gracious to her, and she hadn't really done anything for him. Perhaps she could make it up to him tomorrow.

As she walked over to her room, she looked down at the box. She could almost hear her mother's voice. . . .

"My sweet Olivia, it's important to remember the hardships of those who have gone before us and to see how they persevered and survived." Mama had lovingly caressed the hand-carved trunk.

"But what's in the box, Mama?"

"Memories of our family."

"Your memories? Daddy's memories?"

"No, my child. Long before your daddy was born. Long before I was born."

Her eyes widened. "That's a long time ago."

Mama's laughter drifted over her like a warm blanket. "Yes, it was. And this goes back to your great-grandmother and five generations before her. It's my history. And it's yours."

Her mother's words from all those years ago brought more tears to her eyes. At the time, Olivia had just been a little girl. Maybe six or seven years old. The box had always fascinated her as a child, but she hadn't understood the meaning of it. Now here she stood with the very object of her childhood wonder in her arms.

As she set the small trunk down on her bed, she took a deep breath. She lit the lamp beside the bed and changed into her nightgown. The day had not been her best, and she knew sleep was a long way from her mind. Maybe it would be nice to see what was in the box after all.

With shaking hands, she lifted the lid. A small lap quilt sat on the top with a note pinned to it: *Made by Grandmother Livingston 1816 on the occasion of Horatio and Caroline's wedding.*

Olivia lifted it out and set it on the bed. The beautiful piece was made from white fabric with blue embroidery on each quilt square. As she looked closer, she realized it was letters. Spelling out Livingston. She didn't remember any Grandmother Livingston, but Horatio and Caroline were her parents. Her mother must have thought this precious indeed to keep it in the trunk like this. Mama had often said that the work of their hands was to be used, otherwise it was wasteful.

Turning back to the trunk, she pulled out two tiny sets of white baby clothes. Another yellowed note pinned to each. She felt a smile slip into place as she read the words. They were the first outfits that Daniel and Olivia wore to church.

When she'd set them aside on top of the quilt, Olivia found stacks of letters tied with ribbons and several leather-bound books in the bottom of the trunk. Examining the stacks, she found two bundles that were letters from Daddy to Mama and from Mama to Daddy. Another bundle was from other relatives over many years. And the last was Daniel's letters that he wrote to them after he left home.

She replaced the letters in the trunk and pulled out the books. The one on top was the newest of the bunch, and when she opened it up, she realized it was her mother's journal. Closing the book and clasping it to her chest, Olivia closed her eyes against the tears.

Perhaps one day she'd be able to read her mother's words, but it probably wouldn't be for a long time. She set it aside and pulled out the next book. The inside cover read: *Faith Lytton Jackson Weber*. As she thumbed through the yellowed pages, she saw dates from 1755 all the way to 1789. This must have been her great-grandmother!

She set the book on top of her mother's and reached for the last book. The simple leather cover was cracked with age. Lifting it with careful hands, Olivia wondered about the lives represented in the pages before her. Could this be what her mother had referenced all those years ago? Five generations before her great-grandmother?

The string tying the book closed was newer than the book. Perhaps the original had crumbled with age. As she untied it, a little twinge of excitement filled her heart. To think of generations before her. . .penning their words for future generations—like her—to read. The realization was almost overwhelming.

Opening the book, she found the pages were a darker yellow, and the ink had faded over time. Olivia brought the book close to the lamp so she could decipher the words.

22 July 1620

It is with great trepidation that I begin a log of this journey across the ocean to the New World. In the span of a few short weeks—just this past month—everything I knew changed. My life will never be as it once was, and I am still finding the courage to swallow that truth. Courage has never been a strong trait of mine, and Dorothy, my lifelong friend—dear Dorothy—gave me this beautiful book to record my thoughts. . .and quite possibly to find my courage. She is convinced it resides within me somewhere. While I think that it is quite hidden. My beloved friend has always been the one with courage and the sense of adventure. Not me. But my prayer to our heavenly

Father above has been constant for courage. I'm quite afraid, you see.

Afraid of change, of what may be ahead, of the unknown. . .

My heart grieves for the loss of Mother. It has been a year since she passed from this world into eternal glory, and I feel it every day. But it is not just the physical loss of her presence. I feel I have lost my connection to her since we left Holland. I can no longer visit her grave and share my deepest thoughts. She was the only one who understood me completely. My trips to the cemetery to visit with her were healing, and now I do not know what to do with my feelings.

That is why Dorothy bought me this precious book. I have never owned anything so luxurious as paper—that which its simple purpose is for me to record my thoughts and feelings. Dorothy knows me well. I will cherish this journal and make the best use of it that I can.

So now I must pray for courage once again. The journey has only just begun, and my heart is heavy with anxious thoughts and doubts.

Our two ships, the Speedwell and Mayflower, will voyage across the vast ocean together and prayerfully reach the Virginia Territory, where our patent lies, in time for us to build shelter before winter sets in around us. But our ship began to leak today, and the ship master was none too pleased. We've been reassured that all will be well and repaired before we leave England, but it made many of us worry nonetheless. It does not bode well for the expedition ahead to begin on such a sour note. Again, Dorothy encouraged me to look at the positive and find my courage. So that is what I must do.

For mother's memory, for Father, and for precious little David. He relies on me.

I will not let them down.

Lord God, please do not allow me to fail. My prayer is for courage.

I can do this. With Your help.

~Mary Elizabeth Chapman, aboard the Speedwell

Olivia reread the entry carefully. Dated 1620. More than two hundred years ago, her relative had started this journal. Stories of the *Mayflower* were shared with them when they were schoolchildren. It had been a horrible journey, and so many people had died. Olivia found herself fascinated and continued to read.

Hours later, as the lamp began to sputter, she wiped tears from her face and carefully closed the precious book. So much heartache and loss embraced in hope and joy.

At the beginning of the journal, Olivia had felt exactly like Mary Elizabeth. Afraid and in need of courage. Grief stricken and alone. But by the end. . .her ancestor had grown in strength. In love. And in faith.

Olivia wanted to feel that way. Reading the journal had felt inspiring. But then the guilt had crept back in. She didn't deserve another chance. Why was God giving her one?

Her faith was weak. Everything felt like it had crumbled beneath her. Yet her circumstances weren't nearly as grim as Mary Elizabeth's. And while she had a lot to feel guilty about and to make up for, she could at least do some good in her new town, couldn't she? Could that make up for all the heartache she'd caused?

With new determination, Olivia swiped at the tears on her face again. She hadn't been living life here. Not really. Instead, every day it was like she put on a costume and played a role. Taking men's food orders, listening to their marriage proposals and dreams of finding gold, and waiting on them. . .all day, every day.

Falling into bed exhausted every night.

But each time Daniel wanted to *really* talk, she shut him down because she was afraid to be real. Afraid that if he found out the truth, he would hate her. It was easier to be the no-nonsense waitress in the restaurant.

Maybe she just needed to pray for courage like Mary Elizabeth. That she would be brave enough to step out of her comfort zone. Maybe then she could feel alive again.

CHAPTER 8

O ne of those sparks could have set the entire city of San Francisco on fire. The time to act is now." Joseph had been laying out the case for the need of a fire-fighting enterprise to the council for the past ten minutes. What appalled him the most was that many of the members seemed surprised to even hear of the blaze in the first place. Didn't they read the paper?

"Gentlemen, gentlemen. . ." George Banister took his time getting to his feet, a smug smile on his round face. "We all know that fire safety is an issue. But Joseph, you just told us that the fires started by sparks from the *Philadelphia* were extinguished by the good folks of our town. If everyone continues to be vigilant and do their part, I don't see a need for us to waste precious funds on a fire-fighting endeavor when we have so many other substantial needs before us."

Joseph raised his brows. "And what *substantial* needs could be more important than the safety and lives of everyone in this city?" He hated to sound so defensive, but George had become the bane of his existence. The man shifted the conversation at every turn and always dodged the question at hand, tabling any discussion that didn't fit his own agenda. And of course, everything was on behalf of his "esteemed employer," the man who refused to come to any meetings but touted himself as the richest man in San Francisco and the man who just so happened to fund the council in the first place. It made

Joseph angrier the longer he thought about it. He should write a letter to General Riley and get his advice on the matter.

"And the roads need to be widened for the significant growth in population that has occurred. We can't have people getting trampled in the streets." George continued listing everything he deemed more important than fire safety. "Then we have the issue of the filth and trash in the city, which could cause disease and death. And shouldn't we consider the fact that if our buildings were built in a better manner, we wouldn't need to worry about fires coming through and burning down tents and shacks? And what of the crime in this city? We must address the fact that we will be needing some form of police in the very near future."

Discussion rounded the table at that point. Only two other men seemed to be concerned about the threat of fire in the city, while the others all joined into discussion with George about what they should implement next. Each time one of the other men brought the topic back to the table, it was quickly tossed aside for the next meeting. Joseph watched in shock over the next hour as a vote was taken in favor of widening the existing streets and further planning into expansion of other roads around the city.

George started to close out the meeting when Joseph took that opportunity to stand once again. "Gentlemen—"

"I believe we've heard your opinion, Mr. Sawyer, but the vote has been taken and you will kindly hold all of your remarks for our next meeting. This meeting is adjourned until our next session." George Banister tapped his gloves on the table and then promptly left the room.

Shock rolled over Joseph as he watched several of the other council members leave without another thought to their city going up in flames. Had they not heard a word of what he said?

Silas Abernathy walked up to Joseph. "I'm glad to see you trying to help with this, Sawyer, but I don't know what we can do to get everyone else on board."

Joseph looked around the room for a moment and then back at Silas. "As much as everyone on this council wants to see California become a state and many want to be elected government officials, I say we bring the voice of the people to the council. That's what a democracy does."

"What do you have in mind?"

"A very smart friend of mine had an idea, and I think we should put it into action."

"I'm all ears."

Joseph made his way home and realized he would be late for his weekly meeting with Dewei. He hoped the man would have good news from the mine. His foreman was a Chinese man whose work ethic surpassed anything Joseph had ever seen. It was no wonder his name meant *highly principled*. And Joseph trusted him with his life.

"Good evening, Mr. Sawyer." Dewei greeted him at the door in practiced English.

"Good evening to you, Dewei. How are you tonight?"

"Very good." The man bowed.

"I'm sorry for my tardiness. The council meeting went late."

"Understand." Dewei sat at the table and opened his ledger. He was a man of few words and never wasted time. "The mine doing very good. Workers doubled profit this week."

Joseph raised his brows. "That's great news. Let's give them all a bonus for their hard work."

"Very good." The man nodded and scribbled in the ledger. "No one quit. They like having good boss."

It made Joseph smile. The men who worked for him didn't know his name but continued to work for him because it was steady pay with bonuses every time the profit increased. Dewei had taught him that taking care of the hard workers was essential.

Dewei closed the ledger. "Request I have for you, Mr. Sawyer."

Joseph nodded at him. "Of course. What can I do?"

"I have brothers coming soon. They look for work."

"If they are anything like you, you know I will hire them. Especially if the profits continue to rise, I will need more workers."

Dewei nodded continuously. "Gold is plentiful. More profit. More workers make even more profit."

"You let me know when they arrive, and I will gladly hire them and arrange housing for them."

"Thank you, Mr. Sawyer, sir." Dewei stood and bowed.

"You're welcome." Joseph stood and bowed as well. "Thank you for all you do."

"Very good." The man bowed again, took his ledger, and left the house.

Joseph watched his foreman walk away. The man amazed him at every turn. When he'd first met him, Dewei didn't know any English, but he had been a quick study. Once the man set his mind to something, he accomplished it. And he was honest about everything, a trait that was hard to find in *any* man, much less an employee. There was no doubt in Joseph's mind that his profits would continue to grow under Dewei's supervision as long as the mine had gold.

Now if he could just be as successful at convincing the council to take fire control seriously. He walked to his bedroom and removed his coat and necktie. Loosening his high collar, he let out a long breath. Tomorrow he would talk to Olivia about her petition idea. She'd seemed a bit defeated the other night when Daniel had said it wouldn't help much for this month's meeting. But the more thought he'd put into it, the more he realized she'd landed on a brilliant idea.

If they could get hundreds, possibly even a thousand or more signatures, the city council would have to take the wishes of the people into consideration.

For a moment, he felt a bit guilty. Was he trying to get the council to revisit this issue because it was truly that important or because he wanted to beat George at whatever game he played? Joseph sat on the edge of his bed and pondered the question. As much as he disliked George Banister, he knew that preparing the city for a disaster such as fire was of utmost importance.

But another great need had been brought up by George in the meeting as well. The need for police. Crime had skyrocketed. Maybe the way to get everyone's attention was to work for both. Perhaps then they could see some real change in their city.

"You just keep doing what you're doing, George." The man looked at his employee.

"I don't know who this Sawyer fellow is, but I feel like he's going to be a problem." His assistant lifted his chin and played with his collar.

"Everyone knows that you're in charge of the council for now. As soon as California becomes a state, everyone will be clamoring for a position in the government. Our job is to make sure that I have the men in place who will do the best for *me* when that time comes. Let Sawyer have an opinion, but make sure you let him know who's in control." He walked behind his desk and sat down. "If that's too much for you to handle, I'm sure I can find a replacement." Sometimes he really detested George.

Banister stiffened and walked closer to the desk. "No, that's not necessary. I can handle it, I assure you."

"That's what I was hoping you'd say." Dipping his pen in the inkwell, he went back to his ledger. "I didn't give you this position for you to whine and complain about everything that happens. Hold off on voting for police and fire safety for as long as is reasonable; that way we can smuggle in the rest of our workers this summer without too many people looking over our shoulders. Then handle the issues with grace and compassion so that the people of the community know how much you care for their well-being. No one will be the wiser. Too many people are coming into the city every day, creating too much chaos for anyone to take notice of you stalling. You know your job; now go do it." He looked up over the rim of his glasses.

"Yes, sir." George straightened his coat. "It's a privilege to work for you."

He let a smile form on his lips. "I'm glad to hear you say that. Keep up the good work, and there will be something extra for you this month."

The man simpered and oozed his appreciation on the way out of the office.

Loyalty could be bought after all.

CHAPTER 9

The morning had gone better than any she'd had so far. Perhaps it was the congeniality of the customers or the lack of quite as many troublemakers. The fact that Olivia had gotten a lot less sleep because she stayed up too late finishing Mary Elizabeth's journal had her worried that she'd be grumpy with people all day. But surprisingly, she'd felt boosted by reading her ancestor's thoughts about loss, grief, change, and insurmountable trials. It made her eager to read the one belonging to her great-grandmother.

Carrying plates to Daniel's table, she saw Joseph joining him for a late lunch. It was a good thing she had two plates in her hands. Never mind that one was hers.

Joseph stood up when he saw her approach. "How are you today, Olivia?" His smile made dimples in his cheeks appear. Had she noticed that before? Or just his fascinating eyes?

"I'm quite well, thank you." She set a plate in front of Daniel and one in front of Joseph.

"No, I'm not going to take your plate." Joseph put it back in front of her and pulled out a chair for her as he flagged down one of the other waiters. "Daniel told me you were joining him for lunch."

Words left her as she eyed her brother. She'd just assumed she would go back for another plate. It wasn't any big deal. But the gentleman beside her took care of things before she even had a chance to say anything.

Daniel gave her a little smile. "You have to allow us to treat you like a lady, Olivia. Just because most of the men in San Francisco don't have any manners doesn't mean that there still aren't a few gentlemen left." He flicked his napkin into his lap. "I used to eat lunch with Joseph every day before he left to take my supplies to Sacramento, and as you've noticed, we've been so busy that you and I have had to move our lunch later and later so that we can take a break. I told Joseph about that so we could all eat together. Is that all right with you?"

"Of course." How could she deny her brother the conversation with his friend that he'd obviously enjoyed for a long time before she ever came along. And it wouldn't hurt for her to have another friend in the city. She gave Joseph a smile and picked up her napkin just as another waiter brought out a plate for him.

She waited until Daniel had said the blessing before she picked up her fork. "Would you mind walking me to the mercantile later? Before the supper rush?"

Her brother chewed the bite he had in his mouth and made a grimace. "I don't think there's any way I can get away today. A new shipment just arrived this morning, and I haven't had a chance to even look at it. It's the new stoves for the kitchen, and my cook has been giving me the eye all morning, waiting for me to get them set up and installed. With the number of people we feed every day increasing, I might just have to order two more." He looked over to his friend. "Would you be available to accompany her? I advised her not to go anywhere in the city on her own."

Joseph nodded. "I heartily agree. This is no place for a woman to be alone." He turned his attention to her. "I'd be happy to walk you over there. What time would you like to go?"

She'd watched the men volley their thoughts back and forth but wasn't about to put anyone else out. "Don't worry about it. I'm sure you are much too busy, and I can wait for another day."

"Nonsense. I'd be honored to be your companion to the mercantile." There were those dimples again.

Daniel reached over and put his hand on top of hers. "Livvy, I'm sorry that I can't go with you, but Joseph will take good care of you and make sure you're safe."

While she was hesitant to accept, it seemed rude not to. "Thank you." All the time she'd been in San Francisco the past month, she'd gone up and down the stairs from the restaurant to their living quarters and had walked with her brother down the block to the church. That was it. It wasn't like she was feeling adventurous and wanted to see the city—she saw plenty of the city's citizens and wasn't all that impressed. But it would be nice to visit the more reputable stores and get to know her way around.

Daniel pointed his fork at her before scooping up another huge bite. "I forgot to tell you that I asked Joseph to take care of selling your extra supplies."

She raised her eyebrows and looked at Joseph. "Thank you for handling that. I'm sure that was quite a chore."

"Not one bit. It was my pleasure. I have an envelope for you, so perhaps when we go to the mercantile, I can also take you to the bank."

"Oh, that isn't necessary. I don't have a bank account."

"But this is quite a sum. I don't think you want to keep it hidden away. It would be safer at the bank." Every time he smiled, she got distracted by his dimples. "I can assist you in opening an account if you need it."

A little thrill of excitement bubbled up inside her. She'd never had an account at a bank. "Did you truly get that substantial of an amount from those few supplies?"

Joseph leaned over and whispered into her ear. "Two hundred fifty dollars."

She gasped and put her hand over her mouth. Looking at Daniel, she saw his big grin. "You knew?"

"He told me this morning." He tilted his coffee cup up and swallowed the rest of its contents. Wiping his mouth with his napkin, he held up a finger. "I told you those supplies would go for a pretty penny here. It makes me feel better knowing that you have some money of your own. I'm sure paying off Dad's mortgages left you little to deal with."

If he only knew the truth. "Wait...you knew about the mortgages?"

Daniel nodded. "Yes, that's why I was so worried about you having to sell the farm on your own. Mom and Dad didn't have a lot because they gave most of it away to help people."

A fresh wave of grief hit her. That was true. They had always given away most everything they had.

"I'm sorry we didn't really get to talk about anything, but I need to get back to the kitchen and those stoves." Her brother stood and leaned down to kiss her on the cheek. "I'll let the others know that you'll be back in time for the supper crowd." And with that he was gone.

Olivia looked down at her plate that she'd barely touched. Did she really have two hundred fifty dollars? The thought was too much to believe. And she still had the wagon and her horses. All of a sudden, she felt quite rich.

"I can see you're a bit overwhelmed." Joseph's voice interrupted her thoughts.

Glancing up at him, she gave a brief nod. "I am, but I appreciate your offer to help me today. Thank you."

He finished his food. "I'm hoping we can become good friends, Olivia. Your brother is the closest thing I've ever had to family, and I would do anything for him."

She tilted her head and watched his face. Something in how he said that statement made her think that he'd been through a lot of heartache in his life. Not knowing how to respond, she took a bite of her food.

He leaned back in his chair and crossed his ankle over his knee. "I've been thinking a lot about the idea that you had. The one for the petition?"

She'd forgotten completely about that. "Oh?"

"Would you help me put one together? I think you were right— you could garner a lot of signatures just by talking to people here at the restaurant. As many men that come through these doors every day, I think we could have plenty of signatures by the next council meeting."

"Of course I'll help." Something inside warmed at the knowledge that he liked her idea. "I can get started right away. What do we want on the petition?"

His brow furrowed as he thought. "I think we need to address the concerns about crime, violence, and safety. Not only do we need fire safety measures in place, but we need police to clean up the town. Things have gotten way out of hand."

Olivia didn't have any trouble cleaning her plate while discussing with Joseph how they would handle their petition. It felt good to be working toward helping their city rather than spending time in grief, worry, and skepticism, as she had for the past few months. She found that he was really easy to talk to. No wonder Daniel thought so highly of him.

When she was finished, he stood and offered his arm. "Shall we get to our errands?"

With a light laugh, she removed her apron and took his arm. "I don't know if buying a new bonnet is an errand worthy in a man's opinion, but I must admit I'm excited about going to the bank. You'll have to teach me how all of this works because this is all brand new to me."

He held the door open for her as she exited. "Well good, we will just have to help each other because bonnet buying is a new adventure to me as well."

She couldn't help the smile that broke out over her face. It wasn't just Joseph Sawyer's eyes that intrigued her, and she couldn't wait to spend more time with him. Even though her mind told her she shouldn't.

The rest of the afternoon passed in a blur as he took her to the bank just down the street from Livingston's. She deposited all but ten dollars into an account that had her very own name on it. The thought was thrilling. Placing the remaining money into the pocket of her dress, she felt strange to be carrying around that much cash. Never had she had more than a few coins. But with Joseph accompanying her, she felt a bit safer.

At the mercantile, she walked up and down the rows of goods, amazed that she could afford to purchase a special item or two if she chose. It made her smile as she touched a pair of gloves that were softer than anything she'd ever experienced. Glancing up, she noticed Joseph watching her. The soft light in his eyes made a blush rise up her neck. Had he observed her fascination? The last thing she wanted was to embarrass herself in front of a man of means—at least Joseph appeared that way—by showing him that she was a novice around beautiful things.

Moving back toward the front of the shop, Olivia decided it was best to focus on what she came to purchase—a serviceable bonnet. As she perused the small assortment, she couldn't believe the prices. No wonder they'd gotten so much money for Hezekiah's supplies—everything seemed to be doubled or even tripled in price.

A beautiful deep blue bonnet caught her eye. The entire hat was covered in velvet and had lighter blue silk flowers sewn around the wide brim. It was lovely. But as soon as she saw the price tag, she walked away and settled for a much simpler and *cheaper* cotton bonnet.

Joseph had stayed within a few steps of her in the store but had given her space as she'd looked around. While she appreciated his consideration, she realized she missed the easy conversation they'd had at the bank and on the walk over.

After she made her purchase, he met her at the door and offered his arm once again. "Would you like to see any other shops on this street before we head back?"

"That would be nice." She fell into step beside him. His tall frame made her feel safe and secure.

"I'm sorry. I don't mean to pry, but those were your husband's things I sold?"

"Yes. He had the notion to come to San Francisco and find gold." She tried to keep the sarcasm from her voice, but it didn't work.

He was silent for a moment. "I can imagine it's difficult for you with him gone."

She hesitated before she answered. It seemed like such an intimate thing to share, but he was her friend and she desperately needed a friend. "I didn't know him very well, and we were only married a few weeks. I don't quite know what I feel, especially since I'd just lost my parents. I guess I just feel a bit lost." Why had she told him that last part? She certainly didn't need him thinking that she was searching for a man to fill a role in her life.

"I'm so sorry for all the loss you've had to endure."

"Thank you." She needed to get the topic of conversation onto something safer. "I just realized that I don't know what you do, Mr. Sawyer. It appears that you do quite well for yourself. I know you helped my brother out with a load of supplies and that you are on the city council, but do you have any other occupation?"

"I. . .uh. . ." He cleared his throat. Then he looked down at her with a sad sort of a smile and stopped walking.

Whatever could be so shocking that he couldn't say it out loud? "I didn't mean to embarrass you or make you uncomfortable."

"My apologies. It's best to just be honest. But you see I already know what you think of my occupation, and I'm hesitant to tell you because I don't want you to think poorly of me."

She released his arm and faced him. The fact that he cared about her opinion impressed her, but it didn't stop her heart from skipping a little faster. "Now you really have my curiosity piqued, Mr. Sawyer. But I can tell you that I know too much about you already to think poorly of you."

"I'm glad you can say that, but I understand if you change your mind." He looked away for a brief moment and then turned back to look into her eyes. His gaze serious. "Because. . .I own a gold mine."

CHAPTER 10

Y ou're a gold miner?" As her eyebrows shot up, Olivia couldn't keep the shock from her voice. Of all the things in the world, she'd never expected to hear Joseph Sawyer tell her that he did the very thing she despised most. And it wasn't just because Hezekiah had gone off and gotten himself gold fever. No. But the evidence of what that profession established was all around her in this crime-infested, ramshackle city. Day after day she'd witnessed one gold miner after another.

He looked out to the street and then back to her. "Well, not anymore. . . That is, I mean. . .I *own* the mine but don't do any of the mining myself these days. I have men who work for me."

"I see." The look in his brown eyes—almost as if he begged for her approval—made her feel like a hypocrite. Didn't she just tell him that she knew too much about him to think poorly of him? But how could she justify that in her mind? Turning forward, she started walking again. What was she supposed to do with this news? "Your business must be doing very well for you to hire employees. I haven't been here long but know enough for that to be true."

He kept his stride in sync with hers. "It is. I must say that the Lord has really blessed me."

A volcano of emotions warred within her. Could his success truly be a blessing from the Lord? Here was a man who was her brother's closest friend. He seemed honorable and a gentleman—especially when she compared him to every other man she'd met in this sin-filled city—yet she wanted to dislike him because of his occupation. In her defense, that occupation had turned countless men into a bunch of money-crazed idiots.

Shaking her head of the judgmental thoughts, she remembered the little white church he'd built. Didn't it make a difference that a man with such a depraved line of work did something noble and good with his money? Besides Daniel, Joseph was the only friend she had.

"Olivia, I'm sorry. I know you despise it. I was just hoping that we could still be friends. I couldn't be dishonest with you about this."

She stopped and turned to face him again. "I appreciate your honesty." And she did. That meant more than he would ever know, because the majority of men were less than truthful, another thing she witnessed day in and day out. But his revelation bothered her just the same.

"Friends?" He offered her his arm again.

Oh, what did it matter? If Daniel trusted the man, she had no reason to doubt him. She slipped her hand into the crook of his arm and smiled. "Friends."

In amiable silence, he led her down the street and back to the restaurant, the one building she knew. Of course, it was also her home. Could she really call this place home? Never in a million years would she choose this town as a place to live. It wasn't anything like what she'd dreamed and hoped for, but here she was.

It had been so pleasant to get out for a bit. And if she were being honest with herself, it had been nice to be accompanied by Joseph. Even his revelation didn't seem to affect her in the way she expected. Just because the man owned a gold mine didn't mean he was heinous.

Her thoughts flew back to the journals. Maybe she could learn a thing or two more from her ancestors. Mary Elizabeth had overcome her fear and hesitation when it came to so many things, especially the people with whom they'd traveled to the New World. Why, she'd even married one of the Strangers—something that, as a Separatist, she thought she'd never do. The thought brought a smile to Olivia's face. After reading that first journal, her heart didn't feel nearly as heavy or depressed. So maybe she was a widow and would remain alone the rest of her life, but couldn't she at least make the best of it and stop all these judgmental thoughts when a man as good as Joseph had proven himself trustworthy?

He opened the front door of the dining room for her.

Allowing her smile to grow, she gazed into his eyes. Such nice eyes. "Thank you for a lovely afternoon and for all of your help."

"I am glad to be of assistance." He gave a slight bow.

"Even if the assistance has to do with bonnets?"

His deep chuckle washed over her and made her feel warm. "Yes. Although I believe I proved *not* to be very helpful in that department."

"Maybe with practice you'll get better at it. I know for certain that I wouldn't have understood a thing at the bank today without your help. So please, accept my deepest thanks."

"You are most welcome. Perhaps we can do it again sometime. . . the outing, that is." The smile he shot her made her stomach do a little flip. What was wrong with her? First his eyes, then the dimples, and now his smile.

"I'll look forward to seeing you at lunch tomorrow, Joseph." She offered her hand.

His brows lifted a bit as he glanced down at her hand, but then he clasped it and shook it. "I'll see you then."

Joseph made his way back to the wharf to check on all the men he'd rescued. He easily found out that not only had everyone recovered, they'd taken other jobs—one even went off to look for gold. He wished he'd known that sooner. He would have offered to hire the man himself. But with Dewei's brothers coming, it was probably for the best. Of course, his mine could probably use at least five more able-bodied workers, but that was if he wanted to find all the gold as fast as they could. At least at this point, he knew that he'd be able to keep his men employed for a while.

As he strolled down Market Street, he shoved his hands into his pockets. He hadn't given a lot of thought to what he would do *after* the mine. Truth be told, he really hadn't thought about anything other than gold mining. Once he'd gotten his life straight, he'd given all the credit to God and thought the blessing of the mine was his to bear.

Seeing the look on Olivia's face had made his heart sink. It didn't take a genius to know that she loathed gold miners. Then there was the statement she'd made that she would never marry a gold miner. So where did that leave him, especially since he hadn't been able to get the pretty widow off his mind? It was not something he wanted to admit to Daniel anytime soon, but his friend was astute. Before long, Joseph was sure that the restaurant owner would figure it out.

Joseph was smitten.

The woman had overcome a lot of hardship and obstacles in the last few months, including making it all the way to the city by herself. That told him a lot about her character. But if he was completely honest, he had to admit he'd admired her as soon as she'd given that customer his pie. In the face. It made him chuckle just to think of it.

Olivia Brighton wasn't a dainty flower—even though she was as pretty as one—and he liked that. Most men seemed to want women who were sweet and docile, but Joseph had come to realize he wanted a woman he could also respect. Granted, he hadn't met more than ten women in this city, but Olivia was different.

Today when they were at the bank, her genuine interest in learning about financial and banking matters made him proud. As they'd perused the mercantile, he'd silently watched her blue eyes light up at a bonnet that clearly struck her fancy, but practicality had won out for the widow even though she had the money to pay for the much more expensive hat.

Perhaps if he'd known her longer, he would have purchased that blue bonnet for her straightaway, but that wasn't the case. Besides, he was determined to get to know her better over the coming weeks.

Thoughts of her continued to fill his mind until Joseph shook his head. It couldn't be healthy for him to continue to daydream about his friend's sister. Then there was the problem of his still owning the mine. He couldn't imagine ever gaining Olivia's favor if he continued. But what would he do? Was mining for gold for the rest of his life what the good Lord had for him? Or could he build a business like Daniel had? Perhaps he could still do a lot of good in this city that way. He thought he'd never want to raise a family here. Or would he? That was a thought that hadn't crossed his mind too often, because he'd never had someone that interested him like Olivia.

Turning around at the dock once again, he headed back to town. He had more than enough work to keep him busy. It was just as well. These thoughts weren't getting him anywhere. Perhaps it would be good to have a discussion over prayer with Daniel about the mine and whether he should keep it. Joseph still felt new at his faith and wanted to do the right thing. The last thing he wanted to tell his friend, though, was that his thoughts were motivated by a woman. And not just any woman. . .his friend's sister.

As he started back up the hill, a familiar figure caught his attention. The man looked both ways and darted between two buildings. If he wasn't mistaken, it was George Banister. Now what was that man up to?

Out of instinct, Joseph followed the man's tracks. Was he being presumptuous? Assuming the worst? While it was true that George irritated Joseph, it still didn't mean that the man was up to no good. For Pete's sake, the man was on the city council with him, and they'd all sworn an oath to protect and do what was best for their city. But that didn't stop the feeling in his gut that something wasn't right.

After winding in between tents and shacks, Joseph thought he'd lost the man. He scanned the area around him and didn't see George. But the farther he pushed into this section of town, the worse the feeling got in the pit of his stomach. Sounds of crying reached his ears. Trying to locate the source, he had to pull a handkerchief out of his pocket to cover his nose because the air was quite rank. As the crying grew, the smell intensified. It seemed to surround him at every turn. Filth and decay encircled him. Heaviness at the mess in his city pressed down into his chest.

The cries grew in volume and turned to the sounds of sobs and howling. Had he heard someone cry for help? Or was it just the stark misery around him that made him conjure up that word?

Standing in the middle of the street, he wished he could find the source of the wailing. What bothered him most was that it wasn't just one voice—it seemed to be multiple voices. Had someone died? Could that be the reason for the sad sounds?

Joseph closed his eyes and tried to sense the direction of the clamor. The more he listened, the more his gut told him that, yes, he was correct. That was the sound of multiple people crying.

A bump from a solid form almost knocked him over. "Good

gracious, Sawyer! What on earth are you doing in this part of town?" George's voice penetrated his thoughts.

Joseph's eyes flew open. "Why, I was following the sound of crying. I could ask you the same question, Banister." Raising an eyebrow, he wished he could intimidate the man to tell the truth, but he doubted that would ever happen. George was slippery at every turn.

"Well, as you know, my employer is extremely generous and has a heart for the downtrodden. I bring meals down here for the poor wretched souls as often as I can."

"Down here." Joseph pointed to the ground. "On Pacific Street?"

"Of course. The Hounds know me and wouldn't dare instigate any fights with my employer." George put an arm around Joseph's shoulders. "But I wouldn't put them past messing with a dandy like you, Sawyer. I suggest you leave while it is still daylight. I would hate to see some ill fate befall a fellow city councilman."

George pushed Joseph's shoulders, trying to get rid of him. Of that Joseph was sure. But why? It certainly wasn't for his safety. Joseph couldn't figure out any other good options, however. "What about the crying? Don't you hear it?"

"Oh, there's a lot of sickness going around in this area right now. That's why I brought so many supplies." The man looked down at his hands. "But I'm all finished now, and it's best to leave before we catch the death ourselves." George put a hand to Joseph's back and started walking away. "It was good to see you, Sawyer, but it's quite unsafe for you here."

Why the push to go? And what had the man been up to? Deciding it was best to leave this part of town for now, he nodded at George. "Well, keep up the good work. Perhaps at our next council meeting, you can tell us all about this extra charity work that you perform. Maybe we can all pitch in and help."

"Of course, of course!" The smile on the man's face was anything but genuine.

Joseph let it slide for the moment. As he walked away, he decided that there had to be another way to find out what George Banister and his employer were really up to. And he aimed to find out as soon as he could.

Chapter 11

July 1849

Life settled into a good routine for Olivia. Her days were filled with working at the restaurant, a late lunch with Daniel and Joseph as they discussed what they could do to help their city, and then more hours serving the customers their meals. Whenever she could, she spent a few minutes convincing every customer they had to sign their petition for the city council.

The only difference came on Sundays, when they closed the restaurant for the morning hours and went to church. Oh, there'd been lots of complaints about no breakfast on Sunday mornings, but she'd made sure to tell all the men that they'd do better to be in church than in the restaurant for breakfast anyway. Not that the complaints stopped, but every once in a while one of the men would show up at church. And getting any of the ne'er-do-wells in church was a good thing.

As she climbed the stairs to her home, she realized that the constant schedule had kept her from thinking about Mama, Daddy, and Hezekiah too much. Hard to believe that her parents had been gone more than three months now. While her heart ached, it didn't feel like an open wound anymore.

Every night, she opened the small box of keepsakes and held her mother's journal up against her chest. Even though she longed to read the words and see her mother's script once again, Olivia could never keep the tears at bay. So she'd read through Mary Elizabeth's journal two more times, savoring each entry and picturing herself among the passengers on the *Mayflower*. It gave her a lot of encouragement to read her ancestor's words from when she'd been so young. It seemed that Mary Elizabeth lacked courage or even the desire to try anything like adventure. . .yet she'd gone anyway. She'd prayed for bravery and peace the whole way. Even in the midst of facing so much loss, a quiet strength had seeped onto the pages of the precious journal. And for that, Olivia was so very grateful.

If she could just get past her own mistakes, she'd love to be that kind of woman and pass down to generations the kind of faith and love that she'd witnessed through Mary Elizabeth's words.

Shaking her head, she picked up the journal that belonged to Faith Lytton Jackson Weber, another woman in her family who'd faced great loss. Not only did she lose her parents as a young child, but then she lost her first husband, whom she'd only been married to for a week. In the tumult of war, Faith had fought for the freedom of their country and had even been a spy!

Olivia marveled at Faith's feisty personality and willingness to do whatever it took to do what was right. Faith had been a widow for a long time. Many years. That spoke to Olivia's heart. If her ancestor could weather the storms of life, then so could she. Couldn't she?

Opening the leather book to the page where she'd left off, Olivia tried to put herself into Faith's shoes. They were big shoes to fill and honorable ones too. Would anyone ever say that about *her*? Tears pricked her eyes. No. She couldn't pass anything down because her dream of a family was gone. She didn't deserve a husband and family after her behavior toward Hezekiah.

"Livvy? You up here?" Daniel's voice brought her head up.

"I'm here." Taking a shaky breath, she returned the book and swiped at her cheeks. No sense getting Daniel all worried about her. He'd already done so much for her.

He leaned up against the doorjamb and crossed his arms over his chest. "I realized tonight that I haven't given you a single day off. You must be beat."

She waved him off. "I don't see you ever taking a day off. You were good enough to give me the job and a place to live. I'm happy with that."

He looked at her for a long moment. "Something's bothering you. What is it?"

"Nothing. I'm simply tired."

"No. It's more than that. . . . Did someone say anything ugly to you today?"

She laughed. Every day at least one man said something that she deemed vulgar, but she'd learned to deal with that the first day she started working in the restaurant. Not much bothered her anymore. Unless, of course, if one of the men touched her. Then it was always a bit unpredictable how she would handle the man. "That's like asking if the sun rose in the east this morning."

Daniel shook his head and laughed with her. "Why don't you come join me in the sitting room." He turned and went into the other room, leaving her little choice but to follow.

"I'm fine, Daniel. Really."

He sat down and undid the tie at his neck. "I know. I can see that. But what I really want to address is a subject that I've left for too long."

Dread filled her stomach. She perched on the edge of the settee and felt her spine stiffen. This was it. What if he'd thought about it and decided she was indeed responsible for her husband's death? What was she supposed to do then? She thought of the money in the bank. Perhaps that plus her earnings from the past month would help her to travel somewhere far from here and start over. But then she would probably never see her brother again. A new sick feeling formed in her gut.

"Olivia?" Her brother had leaned forward and placed his elbows on his knees. Had he said something? He looked quite concerned.

"I'm sorry. You were saying?" She took a long, deep breath and tried to prepare herself for whatever was to come.

"I'm worried about you. That's all." He looked down at his hands and then back to her face. "Ever since you said that you would never marry again, it's been bothering me. Now please don't get me wrong. It's not like I want you to leave—you are welcome here for as long as you need—but you're so young. I don't think you should discount the fact that you may very well fall in love one day."

As soon as she realized what he was about, the door inside her slammed shut on all her worry and buried it back down. In its place, a bit of anger welled up. "I told you that I would rather not speak on this subject."

He held up his hands. "I know, I know. But I'm your older brother. And your last living relative. It's my duty to provide for you and to protect you—but that also means protecting you from yourself. I know Hezekiah's death is fresh, but it's not your duty to be a widow for the rest of your life. And you shouldn't avoid talking to me about it."

Emotions she couldn't even explain pushed her to her feet. "I confessed to you about what I did, Daniel. And I know you were none too pleased. On top of that, I told you that I wasn't a very good wife—and look at what happened! Hezekiah is dead. And I'm to blame—"

"Oh good grief, Livvy, you are most definitely not to blame. I'll have none of that talk because it's not true! And yes, while I might have been disappointed that you up and married someone you'd only known a day, I still understood why you had to do what you did. You weren't even with him when he died, so how on earth could it be your fault?"

A sob invaded her throat and made her choke. Then the tears came gushing out with a vengeance. "Because…don't you see? I complained about not having any food. But not just that. I'd given him quite a piece of my mind about spending the last of our funds on all his silly gold-digging supplies when we didn't even have a decent meal to make it to the next day. Hezekiah wasn't a hunter, but he went out because his wife had nagged him to go."

"And so it's *your* fault that he shot himself in the leg?" Daniel stood, walked to her, and placed his hands on her shoulders. "No. It's not. No one would blame you for his death. It was an accident."

She shook her head as the tears kept coming.

"God isn't blaming you either, so you need to get that thought out of your mind right now. I can see it in your eyes."

"But don't you see what a burden this is to bear? I made a bad choice by marrying so hastily and putting my faith in a man rather than God—but God still allowed me to try and be a good and decent wife. Yet every day I whined and complained about my husband. About what he did. About his lack in so many areas. About driving around in circles and him never finding a job. Don't you see? I was *never* grateful for what I had, and so God took it all away."

"That's not how God works, Livvy." The look on her brother's face turned into a grimace. "Grief, if God took away my chances because I hadn't been honorable or hadn't obeyed or had complained about something, then I'd be dead already! We all would because we're all sinners in the need of His grace. Jesus paid the price—for *all* of our debts including our complaining—on the cross. I know deep down you believe that. God can still use you exactly how you are—mistakes and all—and you are allowed to have a happy future." He took her hands. "Just because you haven't been perfect doesn't mean that you have to live out your life in penance for the rest of your days."

Everything in her seemed to drain out through her limbs. She sat in the chair behind her and let out a long sigh. "In my heart I want to believe that what you've said is true, but why do I still feel so ashamed for my actions? I confessed it to God many times, and after Hezekiah died, I felt His presence and that He would never leave me. But it still overwhelms me at the oddest moments every day. Especially when I'm stern with one of the customers. Or perhaps a bit too sarcastic. I was a *horrible* wife. That's why I shouldn't ever think of remarrying."

Daniel shook his head and blew his breath out through his teeth. "It sounds to me like you are having a hard time forgiving yourself, Olivia. But I still think there's more to the story."

Her heart sped up. She never wanted him to know how wretched she really was.

His brows drew down, and he patted her knee. "Look. I can tell that you're upset. I won't push anymore tonight. But please, Livvy. . . know that you can trust me with anything. I'll love you no matter what."

Biting her lip between her teeth, she could only manage a nod as another tear slipped down her cheek.

"And please promise me that you'll be praying about this? Give it some good thought?"

Another nod.

"Good. Now let's talk about happier matters. I saw the sheets of paper you had filled up with signatures for our petition. You seem to be quite persuasive with our customers." He stepped back and smiled.

Taking a deep breath, she buried the guilt and the topic. "Probably because I hold their food hostage until they listen." It felt normal to fall back into their sibling banter. Normal was safe and a place where she could ignore everything she'd buried.

Daniel's laughter filled the room. "There's no harm in that if we want to see change."

They spent the next half hour in pleasant conversation about the antics of the men who frequented the restaurant, and Olivia felt her dread melt away. She'd never be able to get Daniel to understand why she carried around her guilt—and she hoped to never have to tell him.

Things were best this way.

CHAPTER 12

The day of the next city council meeting arrived, and Joseph looked forward to being able to bring more needs to the attention of the other council members. He'd been making a list with Daniel and Olivia over their lunches each day, and it struck him that it would take months—possibly even years—to gain the headway needed to make San Francisco great.

As he stood in front of the mirror and retied his cravat into a knot, he rehearsed what he hoped George would allow him to say. "Gentleman, it's time we stopped stalling at every turn and put the needs of our city first—"

Knock-knock-knock!

The urgent sound from the front door made him jump. Who could be coming by tonight?

Joseph ran to the door and opened it. Dewei stood on the porch with his hands clasped in front of him, his face portraying what his calm stature did not. Complete and utter distress.

"Dewei. Please, come in. What is troubling you?"

"Mr. Sawyer, sir, I no wish to interrupt but have urgent request."

"Of course. What's happened?"

The man who never seemed to show any emotion had a tear glistening in his eye. "My brothers. They were to arrive and no show. So I look for them. They held in chains in brothel on Pacific Street."

"In chains? In a brothel? Which one? Whoever would do this to them?" Joseph had heard rumors about slaves in the city, but he hadn't seen it with his own eyes. Could this be true?

"I not know. I sneak in window to see them. Brothers say that some man chained their feet and hands and force to do laundry and clean. Say that until debt paid, they stay."

"What sort of debt could they owe that would warrant them to be chained up for slave labor?" It couldn't be real, could it?

"Brothers owe no one. Pay for trip before come." Dewei stepped closer. "It is no clean. No food. I need help, Mr. Sawyer. Please."

Joseph put his hands on his hips and paced the room. San Francisco was filled with some evil people. Pacific Street was the worst—and the territory that belonged to that horrible gang. How on earth was he supposed to help free men in that area when they didn't even have a sheriff? Could he go to the council? The idea made him shake his head. Perhaps the governor would be a better choice. "Dewei, please know that I will do everything in my power to help free your brothers. I don't know how long it will take, but I won't stop until they are safe."

Dewei's face showed his relief, and he bowed. "Very good. Thank you, sir." The proud Chinese man walked away, his steps straight and purposeful. Joseph watched him for a moment and then closed the door. He'd never had a better worker than Dewei. He trusted him with his livelihood and would trust the man with his life as well. The news felt like a blow to the gut.

Checking the clock on the mantel, Joseph decided that he had enough time to draft a letter to the governor of the territory before heading to the council meeting. The matter was too urgent to wait.

After detailing the plight to General Riley, Joseph offered to do whatever he could to help, even if he needed to start funding some sort of police himself. Something had to be done, and although he had expressed the pressing need, he doubted any action from the governor could begin to address the true depths of the problem. A great evil seemed to dwell beneath the surface of San Francisco, and looking at their city at face value didn't show much good. But the idea that so much more—an even deeper level of evil—was hidden from view scared him.

The clock chimed, and he realized he'd better get to the meeting. Perhaps tonight he'd have a chance to at least mention the possibility of what he'd heard. Good men served on the council. Joseph just didn't trust George Banister, which could be a problem since he was the head.

His horse's legs ate up the distance quickly. Tying him at the post, Joseph took a deep breath and went over in his mind what he'd hoped to share before Dewei brought the disturbing news. But as he entered the building, he heard voices. It sounded like the men were already discussing items on the agenda.

He walked into the room. The men appeared to have been settled in for a while. How could that be? He was still fifteen minutes early. "Gentlemen." He tried not to look too stern. "What are we discussing? Has the meeting come to order already?"

George gave him a slimy smile. "My apologies, Mr. Sawyer, I sent messages to all the council to meet an hour earlier."

"I received no such message." Joseph frowned.

"Again, my apologies, but we are well under way. Please take your seat." Without waiting for a response, George just went on with what he was saying.

Joseph took a minute to listen and realized that the man was discussing bringing on an alcalde—a mayor—for their city. Apparently, several men had been nominated already, and they would vote in early August. So much discussion took place around him, that it took him a while to process it all. While he agreed that establishing a mayor and some sort of government for their city was much needed, it seemed odd to him that George would start this meeting early—without him—and then barrel ahead with such a task so quickly. They had moved at a snail's pace ever since the council had been put together in January. Now it was July. Was the city really prepared to vote this quickly? Joseph would just have to investigate each man on his own, because at this point, he wouldn't put anything past George. Something about the man didn't sit right with him.

Glancing around the room at each council member, Joseph was appreciative that many men really wanted to do right by their town. But could he trust all of them? Or were some of them in George's proverbial pocket?

As the clock struck the hour, George held up his hands to halt the discussion. "Gentlemen, we've accomplished all we can for the evening. Let's meet again on the first of August, and we will finalize details for the upcoming election. We know that we all have an obligation as elected officials of this city to do the very best that we can to improve things here. Thank you for your time. This meeting is adjourned."

Joseph felt a bit stunned that everything had happened so quickly and without him. Everyone stood, and chatter erupted again around the room. What was George's game? Perhaps it was a bit pessimistic of him to think such a thing, but he couldn't negate the niggling thoughts at the back of his mind. He watched each of the men and wondered if there was anyone in this room he could truly trust like he trusted Daniel. Realizing that he wasn't entirely sure anymore, he decided to head back home. Tomorrow he'd have to discuss it all with his friend.

His gut told him that an alcalde was a good idea. Maybe a police force and fire protectors would be next. Wasn't that what they wanted?

His mind returned to Dewei's visit and the horrors he'd described. Maybe Joseph should do something more. As a new thought grew, he wondered if he was sincerely willing to do what he'd conveyed to Dewei—to do everything within his power to help and not to stop until they were safe. The weight of his promise pressed into his chest. Letting out all the air in his lungs, he pondered that question. It could mean a great sacrifice on his part. Perhaps even his life.

Olivia sat on her bed, leaned up against the wall, and pulled the covers up under her arms. Opening Faith's journal, she felt a deep sense of humility wash over her. The past few days she'd spent more time reading her Bible than she had in a long time, all thanks to inspiration from her ancestor.

She'd wasted so much time in the past few months, not only using the excuse of her grief but in her complaining and dissatisfaction. Instead of giving it all over to God—like she should have in the first place—she'd tried to manage on her own. Oh, she'd prayed and asked for help more times than she could recall, but it didn't change the fact that she hadn't turned completely to the One who wanted to help carry her burdens. Instead, she'd prayed for help but kept tight hold of the reins of her life.

Looking down at the journal in her hands, she shook her head. God had definitely used Mary Elizabeth and Faith to open her eyes. But could she actually forgive herself for all the mistakes she'd made? It didn't seem possible. Deep down in her heart, she knew the truth of God. She *knew* that she was forgiven by Him. She *knew* that she should be thinking forward rather than dwelling in the past and wallowing in all her failures. So why was it so difficult for her to live that?

Faith Weber must have been such an amazing and godly woman

who trusted God through being a spy, being married, having children, and surviving the war for their great country's independence. Everything she'd read so far in the journal had dumbfounded Olivia. How did one woman remain so steadfast, strong, and positive? It was true that her family had always teased Olivia about her pessimism and sarcasm, but she now saw how she'd allowed those bits of her personality to take over and become negative traits. She'd really let it go the wrong way.

Only through reading the journal had she thought more about her need to grow. Until Mama and Daddy had died, she'd relied on them for their spiritual guidance and direction. She'd loved the Lord and come to know Him at an early age but hadn't taken on the responsibility of her own relationship with God. Faith's words had helped her to see it and reminded her of so many things her parents had taught her over the years.

One thing was abundantly clear about her great-grandmother: the woman studied God's Word on her own and wrote down her thoughts and life applications in the journal. Olivia would be forever grateful for it. How many times had she read Faith's notes and then looked up the scripture for herself. The passage that Olivia had read about yesterday was from 2 Timothy. She'd memorized the verse that struck her heart the most: "For God hath not given us the spirit of fear; but of power, and of love, and of a sound mind."

Faith had shared that passage in her journal when she'd been going through a frightening time. The war was raging all around them, and she feared for her life and the lives of her children as her husband, Matthew, fought alongside George Washington. As fear threatened to overtake her, she'd spoken the words of that verse aloud so that she and her children would remember.

Olivia hoped and prayed that reciting that same verse would help her too. Snuggling under the covers, she read the next entry.

October 17, 1781

I must admit that this war has become tiresome to me. Perhaps because I am tired from the birth of our third blessed child, and I fear for the health and safety of our family not only here at the farm, but as Matthew and George fight for our independence. As discouragement and fear have threatened to overtake me, I have been thinking of all my inadequacies and shortcomings. There are numerous ways in which I have failed miserably, which gives birth to the questions: Am I enough? Why am I here? Do I have the strength to continue on? What if I fail again?

But this morning, as I was having our scripture study time with the staff, we started the book of 2 Peter. So many things struck me as we started reading that it brought me to tears. I want to record all my thoughts here so I do not forget the insights I have learned.

"Simon Peter, a servant and an apostle of Jesus Christ, to them that have obtained like precious faith with us through the righteousness of God and our Saviour Jesus Christ."

Even the greeting brought tears to my eyes. Why? Because I am of this precious faith. It's not through anything I have done but completely through God's righteousness. I realized how much I had come to rely on my own self yet again.

"Grace and peace be multiplied unto you through the knowledge of God, and of Jesus our Lord, according as his divine power hath given unto us all things that pertain unto life and godliness, through the knowledge of him that hath called us to glory and virtue:

"Whereby are given unto us exceeding great and precious promises: that by these ye might be partakers of the divine nature, having escaped the corruption that is in the world through lust."

Oh, the promises that I have! Why haven't I been clinging

to them—because by them I'm a partaker of the divine nature!
My way of escape is clear through Him. The encouragement that
has thrilled my heart today, I can only wish that it seeps onto this
page and I am reminded of it again and again.

"And beside this, giving all diligence, add to your faith vir-
tue; and to virtue knowledge; and to knowledge temperance; and
to temperance patience; and to patience godliness; and to godliness
brotherly kindness; and to brotherly kindness charity.

"For if these things be in you, and abound, they make you
that ye shall neither be barren nor unfruitful in the knowledge of
our Lord Jesus Christ."

I am not inadequate. All of these have been added to me
through my faith in Jesus Christ. They are within me. They
abound in me. Which means I will be fruitful.

I guess it all comes back to the fact that I have been relying
on my own strength yet again. No wonder I am so utterly tired.
But this I know—He is within me. And He will perfect in me
the work that He has for me to do. Oh Lord, help me to look for-
ward to You—for You are at the finish line waiting for me. Do
not let the distractions of this world bring me down, for I know
this is not my home. My home is with You for all eternity. What-
ever you have for me, my family, my household, Lord please give
me the strength to endure and to continue to be fruitful for You.

Tears filled Olivia's eyes as she read Faith's passionate words.
How many times had she thought that she would never measure up?
That she too was inadequate? But after reading the journal day after
day, she now felt challenged to do better. God had a plan for her. He
was with her. The feeling she'd had at the creek the day that Hezekiah
died flooded her being. God would never leave her.

While her future was still quite unclear, she knew she needed to do her best. At her new job. Even serving those oft times vulgar and unruly characters, she needed to fight for her city. Yes, this was her city. Her home. Whether she liked the town and the people in it or not, she was here. It was time for her to stand up for what was right and do things differently. Prayerfully, tomorrow could be the new birth of Olivia Brighton.

CHAPTER 13

Y ou believe he might be up to something?" Daniel forked a piece of chicken into his mouth.

Joseph took a deep breath and nodded. As much as he hated to say anything against someone, he had to trust his instincts. He leaned forward and put his elbows on the table. "After seeing him in that very part of town, I have to admit, I do." He shook his head. "If I'm wrong, though, there could be grave consequences for any accusations, so I'd like to be sure. But how can I do that? And then there's the issue of the meeting last night. Something just doesn't set right."

Daniel nodded. "I agree that Banister is an interesting character. He's good at convincing people to see things his way, but I wonder if it's all just a facade. No one really knows this mysterious employer other than the fact that he's extremely wealthy and provides for all kinds of things in the city. No one wants to buck him for fear that he'll stop funding needs in town."

"Why do you think he doesn't want anyone to know who he is?"

"Because he—at least as much as Banister has said—wants to remain anonymous. He's afraid that if people know that it's him, he will get bombarded on the street by beggars and can't be a 'common man.'"

Joseph leaned back and shrugged. "I guess if I were to give him the benefit of the doubt, I would believe that line of thought. It's the very reason I don't disclose anything about my own mine, but the fact that George is his right-hand man makes me distrust this man. George loves the spotlight. He also loves to be in charge. It seems if he actually worked for a man that wanted to remain anonymous, wouldn't he be more like his employer?"

Daniel wiped his mouth with his napkin and pointed at him. "I'll agree with you on that. In fact, those are some of the very thoughts I've had on the matter. Would a man hire and trust a man such as George if he were as good and honorable and humble as he would like to be portrayed? Or is he a wolf in sheep's clothing? I don't know. But it's best that we keep our eyes and ears open." He placed his napkin back in his lap and looked around the restaurant. "I wonder where Olivia has gotten off to? I know she said to eat without her, but I thought she'd join us by now."

"I hope she comes soon." Joseph took a deep breath and gave his friend a sideways smile. "I don't want to come across as too forward, but I have appreciated getting to know your sister over the past weeks."

A smirk crossed his friend's face. "I was hoping you two might enjoy each other's company. What more could I ask for than for my best friend and sister to get along?" The smile slipped from his face, and he turned serious. "But I must warn you that she has gone through a lot this past year. She's got it in her head that she can never marry again. I've tried talking to her about it, but it may take some time to heal these wounds."

The comment made Joseph furrow his brows. While secretly he'd been admiring Olivia and hoped to get to know her better, he hadn't thought that a woman as young, bright, and beautiful as she was would ever consider remaining a widow for the rest of her days. Then there was the fact that he knew how she felt about gold mining. Once he'd admitted to her about his profession, they had gotten on just fine.

He'd hoped that she would see him as Joseph and not by his occupation. At the time, he thought that would be his biggest obstacle. With a deep sigh, he looked at his friend. "Well, I'm willing to wait and be her friend for as long as it takes. Besides, there's still so little that we know of each other."

Daniel gave him a slight smile, but it didn't reach his eyes. "Give her time. I know she admires and respects you, so that's a good start. I'll be praying for you."

"Praying for what?" The object of their conversation appeared at the table holding a thick stack of paper. Olivia's smile was bigger than Joseph had ever seen it.

He stood from his chair. "I'm so glad you could join us. Please, allow me." He pulled out the chair for her.

Daniel cleared his throat. "I was just telling Joseph that I'd be praying about a personal matter." He waved one of the other servers over. "So, my dear sister, what kept you so long?"

Her face lit up even more brightly. "I was counting the signatures that I've gotten so far on the petition."

"And?" Joseph couldn't help but catch her enthusiasm. He gave her a big smile.

"So far I have 2,122." She plopped the stack of papers in front of them.

"That's amazing, Livvy!" Daniel leaned over and kissed her on the cheek.

"Thank you. . .and thank you for purchasing the paper. I know it was costly." She turned to look at Joseph. "I'd like to keep gathering them if that's all right."

"Of course that's all right. I'm thrilled." He couldn't help it, but he reached out and covered her hand that lay atop the papers. Their eyes connected for a brief moment that gave him hope. He lifted his hand and went back to his dinner, praying that she couldn't see straight through him. More than anything, he wanted to give her time to grieve, to heal, and to know him. And to change her mind about remaining a widow.

Olivia cleared her throat. "That brings me to my next question for both of you." She folded her hands on the table in front of her. "I've been reading a journal from one of our ancestors, and it's challenged me to do more. If change is going to happen, it has to start with us."

"Which one have you read?" Daniel's face lit up with approval.

Olivia looked a little sheepish. "I started with Mary Elizabeth, who came over on the *Mayflower*. I have to admit that I've read it several times. I've been reading Faith's—our great-grandmother's—the past few days."

"Livvy, I'm so glad this has been encouraging for you. I've been praying that box would be a blessing." The brotherly look he gave his sister made Joseph wish he had family.

"It has been. Thank you." She looked back and forth between them. "Well, it's given me an idea. Why don't we start a Bible study in the afternoons? Right here in the restaurant. We have about an hour of downtime when there aren't many customers. We could do it then. Invite other employees and customers."

Joseph saw the passion in her eyes and loved it. If only he could keep it there. "I think it's a great idea. Might make it easier for people who have questions but are afraid to go to church."

"That's a good point," Daniel agreed.

She looked at her brother. "Well. . .what do you think? Can we try it?"

He paused and looked to be weighing his options. "I think we should at least give it a try and see what happens. I think Joseph's point is a good one—it might make it easier for us to reach people, and I definitely don't mind giving up an hour of time. There may be times when things get a little crazier here, but I've got good workers, so we can always figure it out. Which one of us were you thinking would lead it?"

Olivia looked first at Joseph and then back to her brother. "I was hoping that the two of you would do it together. Or switch off, whatever works the best for you."

Joseph couldn't help but smile. He glanced at his friend. "I'm game if you are. It's not exactly like we've found a pastor for our church yet, and who knows, maybe this will help us reach people with the Gospel. We might be able to get a pastor out here if we have an actual flock for him to shepherd." Laughter rounded the table, and he felt excitement at the new possibility.

A young man brought Olivia her plate of hearty beef stew, and she talked to Daniel about how the kitchen staff adored the new stoves. Joseph watched on in pleasure. Even though he didn't have any family left, he felt like part of the family here, and that made him burst with pride. He and Daniel had worked side by side for a good while, but something about Olivia's presence seemed to make him feel complete. Her enthusiasm for the new Bible study was contagious.

Besides, it would give him the excuse to spend more time with Olivia. He'd always felt drawn to her, but now there was something that captivated him even more. It was impressive really. Here she was a widow in a less-than-ideal place, but she now seemed determined to make the best of things despite living in a town she hated. It reminded him of what had drawn him to God—Daniel had that same passion for God and doing what was right.

Maybe Olivia was beginning to heal from her wounds.

Whatever it took, Joseph was willing to wait and to take his time getting to know the fascinating Olivia Brighton.

"I'm afraid we're running out of room, sir." George's whining was getting on his nerves.

Of course they were running out of room—he'd just brought in two hundred more slave workers. "That's why I'm building two more buildings. They're not anything fancy—definitely not anything to draw attention—but enough to keep business booming." The man reached up and made sure his neck collar was still stiff and straight. Lifting his chin, he looked down a bit at the arrogant Mr. Banister. "Please remember that your work for me does not include trying to tell me what to do."

His employee, who was rarely silent, sputtered for a moment before he found his words. "My apologies. In my defense, it is my place to keep you apprised of the situation."

"And you've done that adequately enough. But your real job is to keep our cover in place and my identity a secret. As much as I know it was important that an alcalde be elected, I'm trusting that you will continue to do your job on the council to keep all attention off my. . . less than savory business dealings. When I feel the time is right, I'll let people know who I am and do all the charitable things that will keep my nose clean. But until then, you will be my spokesman." He buttoned his waistcoat. "There's another ship arriving in a couple of weeks. This time, there will be a load of children."

Banister's eyebrows rose, but he remained silent.

So maybe George had learned a bit of wisdom after all. "I can see the question in your eyes. Let's just say that I have some clients that prefer their needs be met by some *younger* workers." He turned to look into the mirror and straightened his striped ascot. "What else is going on in our quaint little town that I need to be aware of?"

George let out a sigh. "Joseph Sawyer and Daniel Livingston have started a Bible study at Livingston's Restaurant in the afternoons." He chuckled. "I can't see that they have much of an attendance, but if it keeps their attention over on that side of town, then that's better for us."

"Do you see any problems arising with any of the other council members?" When he'd instructed George to put all this into play, he'd hoped that people would elect slightly more shady characters. But alas, a number of moral and upright men had been chosen.

"While there are several do-gooders on the council, I've managed to keep them all in line with our plans for now. I think bringing on the alcalde will be good for us. They'll think that we're getting a handle on crime and forming some governance, and we'll continue to be able to keep our eyes on things."

"Good. I'll continue to fund whatever you need to show that we also want the best for our city. You just make sure that no one is the wiser about our other business dealings. Understood?"

"Of course, sir." George stood and left the room.

Even though Banister was his right hand, he would keep many things from his employee at this time. Or perhaps forever. It was best that way.

If all went according to plan, by this time next year, the most powerful man in the country would be the man staring back at him in the mirror.

CHAPTER 14

Olivia's days melted into one another, and for the most part, she had to admit that she loved her new home. The city wasn't much to speak of. Neither were the people—who were mainly male, smelly, and foul-mouthed. But in the midst of all the things she'd thought were despicable, she found herself enjoying life for the first time in a long time.

Work in the restaurant was taxing as day in and day out she was on her feet, taking orders, delivering food, fighting off the advances and marriage proposals of more men than she could count. But something in her heart had changed in the time that she'd been here. She'd finished the other two journals a number of times, always hoping to glean more from her ancestors' examples. The only journal left was her mother's, and she still couldn't bring herself to read it. At least not yet.

As she tied her apron around her waist and descended the stairs from their living quarters to the bustling restaurant, Olivia pushed aside the guilt that every once in a while still liked to rear its ugly head. Deep down, she knew she was forgiven—but if she read Mama's precious words, Olivia was afraid it would bring it all back to the surface.

She longed to move forward, and Daniel was pushing her pretty hard to continue to pray about her future. A few weeks ago, she wouldn't have thought he could ever change her mind, but ever so slowly, she began to yearn for another chance at love and maybe even marriage. The wisdom from her older brother was always ensconced in love. After all their years apart and after losing Mama and Daddy, it was wonderful to have him in her life and with her every day.

When she'd first made it to San Francisco, the thought of staying in this horrid place was repulsive. After being here a couple of months, spending time with Daniel, and reading the journals, she found herself wanting to stay and take on the challenge. Truth be told, she couldn't think of being anywhere else.

It didn't help that a certain blond-haired friend had started to wriggle his way into her thoughts. Joseph came every day for their late lunch together and then would stay for the Bible study. The first few days it had just been the three of them gathered in the dining room of the restaurant with their Bibles open. Gradually, a few staff members braved the group. Now, each day they had five or six present. It made Olivia a bit giddy to think about, and not just because today was Joseph's day to teach.

The thought made a blush rise to her cheeks as she set out to adjust tables on the dining-room floor. Best to focus on work rather than Mr. Sawyer's fascinating qualities. But as much as she tried not to think of him, he kept coming to mind. What did that mean? She'd never had this happen before.

Shaking her head, Olivia focused on the tables. Many of the red-and-white-checkered tablecloths were askew. She'd raced upstairs to change after the breakfast rush because she'd spilled an entire bowl of gravy when one of the men got too frisky. She must've been in too big of a hurry to notice the tables earlier.

Those poor boys who worked here. They were fabulous workers but didn't understand why it was important for the tablecloths to lie evenly on each table. Maybe it was just a difference between men and women. Every day, she straightened tablecloths, napkins, and silverware. Daniel had started asking for her opinion on decorating the restaurant, which thrilled her because he said that he'd noticed a difference since she'd arrived. She placed her hands on her hips and looked around.

Curtains should be the first thing. Daniel always kept the windows clean, but it sure would spruce up the place to have matching curtains on all the windows.

That's another thing Daniel had done well—the building was built sturdy and strong, not like most of the ramshackle businesses in the town. He'd also made sure there was plenty of light. With six massive windows down each side of the dining room and twelve glorious windows across the front, it really gave the eating establishment a welcoming, bright, and cheery appeal. The glass alone must have cost Daniel a small fortune. Of course, it didn't matter to most of the customers what the place looked like. All they really cared about was the food and whether they could get a table. It was the best food in town. No competition there. That's why they were packed for hours around each meal. But to Olivia, the thought and planning of this large restaurant was a testament to the quality of the establishment and integrity of its owner.

A smile filled her face. She couldn't help but be proud of her brother and his accomplishments. He'd done things above and beyond, and it kept the customers coming back. She allowed a little chuckle. It also kept them behaving themselves—with the exception of a few here and there who quickly learned their lesson—because no one wanted to lose the privilege of eating at Livingston's Restaurant.

After the last table was straightened, she stood and gazed at the room again. The lunch crowd would be upon them soon. Then they'd have their own lunch and Bible study. Her heart picked up its pace at the thought. What was wrong with her?

Charlie—an old, crusty man who made it to the restaurant every single day—strode through the front door. He gave her a toothless smile as he approached her. "These are for you, Mrs. Brighton." He thrust a handful of wildflowers at her.

The gesture made her give him a wide smile. "Why, thank you, Charlie. Where would you like to sit today?"

"Makes no difference to me, as long as you are my waitress."

She shook her head at him. "I think I can manage that, but you have to promise to behave yourself."

He straightened his shoulders and held up his right hand. "You have my word."

Olivia laughed and pointed to a table. "You go on over while I put these in water. I'll be back to take your order."

"Yes, ma'am." The older man winked and hobbled off.

She made her way into the kitchen and found a simple glass bottle that she filled with water for the flowers. An idea struck her as she arranged them in her makeshift vase.

"Livvy, I was hoping I'd find you in here." Daniel's voice made her turn.

"Just the person I wanted to see!" She giggled and raised her eyebrows. "I just had a great idea. What if I get one or two of the boys to pick flowers for me every morning? We could put one flower in a small vase on each table. It would freshen things up a bit."

Her brother crossed him arms over his chest. "Won't that be a lot of work for you? We just added more tables, and it's close to fifty now."

While she knew they had a lot of tables, she hadn't thought about the actual number. Striding back into the large dining room, she bit her lip and looked around. "I think it would be worth it. Of course, we'd have to order enough vases. And it would only be for the spring and summer months, when we have flowers. In the winter, I'll have to come up with something else. . .but you *did* say that you wanted my help decorating the place." Tapping her chin with her finger, she glanced around again. "We also need curtains, but I can do those easily myself in the evenings if you'll purchase the fabric. What do you think?"

His laugh filled the open room. "I think they're great ideas. As we clean up the city, hopefully we'll gain more families and married couples. That would certainly be a good way to draw the women in." He leaned in and kissed her on the cheek. "Let's do it. But where will you find the flowers?"

"I think I can help with that." Joseph's voice washed over her, and she turned to see him walking toward them. His brown suit tailored to the height of the day's fashion accentuated his broad shoulders, and his eyes drew her into their depths. "I know of two fields that are full of wildflowers right now. Perhaps I could show the boys who will be picking them and could even offer my assistance."

Still caught up in his eyes, she made herself blink several times and then looked away from him to her brother. Gracious, what had come over her? "That would be wonderful. Thank you."

Joseph turned to Daniel. "I know I'm quite early for lunch, but I had a few things that I really needed to discuss with you. Would you have a minute?"

Thankful for the chance to escape, Olivia headed back to the kitchen. Somehow she needed to collect herself during the lunch rush before she sat down to lunch with the men. Which shouldn't be difficult because she was always so busy. Why was today any different?

She checked the list of lunch offerings one more time before serving their customers. It was important that she knew all the details just in case anyone had a question. With a deep breath, she looked around the kitchen before heading out to the dining room, where hopefully Daniel had taken Joseph off to a corner somewhere so she would be able to concentrate. She pinched the bridge of her nose. Already, he'd come back to mind. Focus. That's what she needed.

Taking another deep breath, she fixated on the room around her. The smells made her mouth water. Fried pork chops sizzled in cast-iron skillets on the stoves. A barrel of pickles was open as another worker pulled them out and sliced them. The spicy scent of cinnamon filled the air—was it baked apples or apple pie? She couldn't tell. The massive cast-iron stoves were covered in several other pots that steamed and bubbled. The cooks worked together in the rhythm of experience. Daniel had hired the best for everything, which made her smile again. This was her world. It made her feel like her perspective was back in place.

Pushing through the swinging door into the dining room, Olivia lifted her shoulders and headed to Charlie's table.

After two and a half hours of scurrying back and forth from the kitchen to the dining room and back again, Olivia finally brought a plate to the table to join her brother and Joseph. Both men stood as she approached, and her stomach grumbled loudly. "I'm sorry for making you wait." Even though she smiled at them, she was too tired and hungry to worry about it or anything else. She needed food. After Daniel prayed for their meal, she dug in without saying a word. The breaded pork chop almost melted in her mouth; it was so tender and juicy. Then the mashed potatoes and gravy! The meal was like heaven. It wasn't until half her food was gone that she realized the men had been conversing without her. When she lifted her eyes to them, they went silent.

Mirth sparkled in her brother's eyes. "I take it the food is satisfactory?"

Putting her napkin to her lips, she attempted to hide her smile. "Yes, quite. And yours?"

"Wonderful as usual." Daniel chuckled. "Please. . .don't let us keep you from eating. You've definitely earned it."

She couldn't help but laugh with him. "My apologies, gentlemen. I guess I didn't realize how hungry I was. I didn't mean to neglect your conversation." Glancing at Joseph, she liked the merriment in his eyes. And his dimples.

There her thoughts went again. What was going on with her? It was better when she was too busy to think about the handsome—yes, she admitted it, *very* handsome—Joseph Sawyer.

"It's all right." The smile he gave her lifted her heart a notch. It was so nice to have him as a friend. God had been good to place her here, even in the midst of all the ugliness. Perhaps her second chance had come.

CHAPTER 15

The first of August was upon them, and Olivia settled into a chair at the table for their daily Bible study. Letting her mind drift for a few moments, she looked around the large, almost-empty dining room, picturing faces and names. She felt quite comfortable among their regulars now, a fact that made her grin. Oh, she didn't trust the majority of them as far as she could throw them, and she would never venture out of the building to go shopping or visiting by herself, but inside the restaurant, she knew how to handle things, and the customers all knew she wouldn't put up with any shenanigans.

That didn't stop them from proposing left and right. No matter how many times she refused the same men, they continued to try. They probably hoped that one day they would wear her down. She shook her head. The tenacity of some of them often made her giggle. They were—for the most part—dishonest and dirty. But when push came to shove, she was pretty sure that most of those men would help in time of need if she asked it of them.

Proving that fact was the petition. She'd been shocked that so many men didn't simply sign it because she asked. They actually expressed the desire to see changes in their town. It had gone better than she'd ever anticipated. With almost seven thousand signatures, she felt quite proud of herself for taking on the monumental project. Hopefully, Joseph could convince the city council that protection and safety mattered to the people.

She watched Joseph as he led their little Bible study. Seven people had joined them today—three of them young boys who couldn't be older than twelve. It gave her a little thrill to see them watching and listening with such intent.

Lord, please work in these young boys' lives. I don't know their situations, but You do. Show us how we can help them.

Her heart clenched at the thought that they might be living on the streets, but as Daniel had told her last night, they would continue to take it one step at a time. They couldn't change the whole city overnight, and they certainly couldn't rescue everyone either. She'd learned so much through their studies the past few weeks that her heart overflowed with excitement every day. It didn't matter how many people came—they *were* making a difference.

Joseph's excitement over the passage of scripture made her look back down at her Bible. "Isn't it amazing to think that the God of the universe—the Creator of everything—loves us so much that He sacrificed His only Son to pay the debt that we owed?"

One of their young visitors raised his hand.

"Go ahead, Tommy. Do you have a question?" Joseph's tone was kind and friendly.

"So yer sayin' that I woulda had to die like that?"

"Yes, Tommy. We all owed that debt for our sin. You have sinned, I have sinned, Mr. Daniel has sinned, and Mrs. Brighton has sinned. The Bible tells us that 'For *all* have sinned, and come short of the glory of God.' And 'For the wages of sin is death; but the gift of God is eternal life through Jesus Christ our Lord.' That means every single one of us deserved death for our sin, but God paid the price— the penalty—for us so that we can all have His gift, which is eternal life with Him."

The young boy's brow furrowed, and he chewed on his lip. He

looked at the other two boys next to him, who seemed to wait for what he would say next. Was he the leader of this little troop?

"Could I maybe talk to ya about this private like? Ya know, man to man?"

Olivia tried to keep the smile from her face and watched Joseph for his response.

He nodded and looked at the rest of the group. "Why don't we dismiss in prayer?"

As his words poured over Olivia, she sent up a little prayer of her own for the hearts of these children. Who knows what horrors they'd faced or how they lived, but she would be forever thankful that they'd had the chance to hear the truth today.

After a hearty "amen," the boys followed Joseph to a corner table, where he sat down with them.

"That was pretty wonderful, wasn't it?" Daniel put an arm around her shoulder.

"Yes, it was."

"Joseph is gifted as a teacher, don't you think?"

"Yes, he is." Watching the little group in the corner made her heart swell.

Daniel chuckled. "So I take it that you might like Mr. Sawyer just a little bit?"

"Of course I like him, Daniel, he's our friend."

"But you admire him. I can see it on your face."

She turned to her brother and looked into his gaze. "What are you implying?"

The twinkle in his eye signaled his merriment, but his tone wasn't teasing. "Well, I was hoping that perhaps you've come to care for him."

His statement took her off guard. Olivia swallowed. "I. . .I don't know what to say." Words seemed stuck in her throat. No matter how much she had tried to deny it the past few weeks, Joseph Sawyer had invaded her thoughts—and her heart—a lot of the time.

"It's all right, Livvy. Take your time. There's no rush, and Joseph isn't going anywhere."

She covered her mouth for a brief moment as a thought flitted across her mind. Lowering her hand an inch, she leaned closer to her brother and whispered, "You don't think he suspects anything, do you?"

Daniel tucked his hands into his pockets. "No. He admires you a great deal and respects you as a friend. I think I only noticed it because I've seen the change in you the past few weeks. It's been so good to see you healing and breaking through the grief and walls you had built up around you. You're my Livvy again."

While his words encouraged her, she also felt a flood of embarrassment. If her brother noticed her admiration of Joseph, had anyone else? All the doubt she'd had resurfaced. It was too soon. She shouldn't even be thinking of another man. Shouldn't be thinking of remarrying. It was all a big mistake.

"Did I say something wrong?" Daniel lowered his brow.

Olivia shook her head and patted his arm. "No. I'm fine. But I think I'll slip out the side door for a bit of fresh air."

"I don't know if that's the best idea—"

She held up a hand to cut him off. "Give me a minute, all right?" The words came out harsher than she intended, but prayerfully Daniel would forgive her.

Customers were already heading into the restaurant for the dinner hour, and she needed a moment to regroup and think. She walked across the dining room floor, weaving through tables and people, her voluminous skirt swishing back and forth. Even though she didn't want to admit it, yes, she'd begun to care for Joseph. Now what did she do with this?

Anxious thoughts riddled her mind, and her heart picked up its pace. Daniel had said it was all right for her to take her time. Time. That's what she needed more of. Time to understand her feelings. Time to finish grieving. Time to get to know Joseph Sawyer. No one was pushing her into anything. There was no rush. Dread and guilt began to fill her. No. She shouldn't even entertain the thoughts. Couldn't.

Oh God, help me. Please. Daniel's been right—every time I feel like I can move forward, all the negative thoughts and feelings come flooding in. Why can't I forgive myself?

Fighting off the sting of tears, she opened the side door into the alley, the stench of garbage filling her nose. Fresh air. Ha! What was she thinking? But the blast to her senses helped her to get a handle on her emotions.

Muffled thumps came from behind the door followed by, "No! Stop!" The cry was weak. Olivia stepped into the alley and closed the door to see who was in trouble on the other side. A large man was beating a young boy with his fists. She should have called for help from one of the men inside, but as the door clicked shut, she realized her mistake a second too late. She definitely shouldn't be out here alone. Prickles of fear shot up her spine. Before she could think it through, she yelled at the man, "Stop it, this instant!"

The man held the boy by the collar and turned his angry face to her. "Ain't none of yer business, woman!" He spat at her feet.

"Let the boy go." She put her hands on her hips and straightened her spine. Oh, how she was tired of bullies.

The man leaned his large and smelly frame toward her. "What are ya gonna do about it, little lady?"

Blinking several times, Olivia realized she had no idea. There weren't any police to call. She'd come out here alone. The man was twice her size. What had she been thinking?

God, help me.

She looked down at the boy. His face was covered in blood, and she couldn't even tell if he was conscious anymore. "Let him go."

The man sneered. He dropped the boy to the ground in a crumpled heap and stepped closer to her. "You need to keep yer pretty little nose outta things that don't concern ya." His beefy hand shot out and grabbed her arm and squeezed. He closed the distance between them until she could smell his rancid breath. "Maybe I'll just take you instead." He grabbed her other arm and picked her up off her feet.

Kicking her legs with everything she was worth, Olivia screamed at the top of her lungs.

"Who's gonna come help ya? The sheriff?" The man leaned his head back and guffawed.

She kept yelling and screaming, "Help! Hel—"

One of his hands had released her arm but now wrapped around her throat. "No need for none of that now." The wicked smile on the man's face made her shudder.

Gasping for air, Olivia's mind traveled over her life. This could very well be the end. Was she ready? Had she wasted her life? God had clearly given her a second chance after Hezekiah's death. Had she wasted that as well? Whether or not she'd saved the boy a few moments ago, he would be in danger as soon as this nasty man finished her. What had she done? Spots began to dance in front of her eyes. If only she could do things over again, she'd live her life without fear, without hesitation. *God forgive me. Save the boy. . .please.*

Slam!

"Put her down! *Now!*" a deep voice bellowed from the side door.

Her captor released his grip, and she tumbled to the ground. When she looked up, she saw Joseph's face, red and full of anger. She'd never seen him look so fierce.

The hulking man stood for a minute and then sprinted down the alley.

Joseph came to her, a crowd of customers behind him, watching. "Are you all right?"

She put a hand to her throat and rubbed at it. No wonder the man had taken off. Too many men were ready to fight him. After a few deep breaths, she nodded. "I think so." Jerking her head to where the boy lay, she gasped when she saw he was still there. "He's not. . . dead. . .is he?"

Joseph helped her to her feet and walked her over to the boy. He knelt down and picked the child up in his arms. "I think he's still breathing. We need to get him help."

"Is there a doctor?"

He nodded. "Just a few blocks down. Can you walk?"

"Of course. I'm going with you."

Daniel appeared at her side. "Are you sure you're all right?" His concern touched her.

"I'm fine, but I don't know about this child." Her voice cracked on the last word.

"Go on. I'll make sure that everything is covered in here." Her brother squeezed her shoulder as she followed Joseph.

She grabbed Joseph's arm to stop him for a moment and turned back to her brother. "Is it all right if I bring him home with me if there's nowhere else for him to go?"

"I was going to suggest the same thing." He pulled several coins out of his pocket. "Give this to the doctor, and if that's not enough to cover it, tell him I will pay the bill."

"Thank you." Her heart overflowed with emotion. God had given her a wonderful brother who cared so much for other people. She turned on her heel and placed her hand on the boy's head as she looked back to Joseph. "And thank you for rescuing me."

He gave her a brief nod, his face serious. "I would never want anything to happen to you." He shifted the load in his arms. "Let's get this boy to the doctor. I'm afraid it looks pretty serious."

Joseph ran a hand down his face as they watched the doctor patch up the child, who was nothing but skin and bones. There was no doubt in any of their minds that the boy was starving. Where were his parents? What had happened to him? And why was that man beating him in the alley?

The rage that had overtaken Joseph when he realized Olivia was in trouble had blinded him to the man's appearance. He'd gotten a look at him yet couldn't know for certain if he would recognize the man. Surely Olivia could, but he never wanted her in the presence of her attacker again.

Dr. Morgan turned to them. "Do you know the boy's name?"

Olivia shook her head. "No."

"I've done all I can for him now. We'll have to wait and see what happens when he wakes up. It's a good thing you found him when you did." The man shook his head and wiped his hands on a towel.

She sniffed and wiped at a tear on her cheek. "Should I take him home and care for him there?"

The doctor shook his head. "No. I don't think he should be moved for a while. But you are welcome to visit him here."

Joseph looked around the small shack of a building while Olivia peppered the doctor with questions. The need for doctors and medical care—possibly even a hospital—was desperate in their town, especially with all the mining accidents, the dirt and filth, and people coming into port from all over the world. Outbreaks always spread like wildfire in the overpopulated tents and shacks. This was something else he needed to address with the city council.

The council! They were meeting tonight. Pulling his pocket watch out, he opened the cover. He barely had an hour before they started, but he couldn't leave Olivia.

"Joseph? Are you all right?" Her sweet voice cut through his thoughts as she laid a hand on his arm.

"Yes. Quite. I'm sorry, my mind was elsewhere."

She turned back to the doctor and handed him the coins Daniel had given her. "We will take care of any additional costs you incur for his care."

The man nodded and walked to a back room.

"Dr. Morgan has told us to go on home tonight. I'll come back early before breakfast in the morning and then again at my lunch break and then again after dinner."

"Do you need someone to escort you?" He offered his arm as they left the doctor's.

"Oh, would you? I know that would help Daniel a lot since I will be leaving him shorthanded for a bit, and he never wanted me to go anywhere alone—which right now, I don't ever *want* to go anywhere alone." She reached for her throat.

"How are *you* feeling? How badly did he hurt you?"

She shook her head and dropped her hand from her neck. "I'll probably be bruised, but I think I'm fine. It's a good thing you came bursting through the door when you did. . . ." The hanging sentence made them both go silent.

Joseph didn't want to think about what could have happened to Olivia had he not heard her scream. The potential outcomes were too hideous, but it didn't stop them from running through his mind.

Steering Olivia around a pile of horse droppings in the street, Joseph knew he needed to get their minds onto something else, but he didn't want to sound callous taking attention away from the injured boy. "I'm sorry about what happened, Olivia."

She nodded. "I am too. It was foolish of me to go out into the alley to begin with, but I can't say that I'm sorry for what I did. I don't think the child would have lived if someone hadn't stopped that. . . that. . .monster." He felt her shudder as she gripped his arm.

"It makes it more urgent for me"—he looked down at her, but her face was covered by her bonnet—"to see what other changes can be made through the city council, because they need to happen soon."

Her small hand patted his arm again. "I'm thankful you're on the council, Joseph. We need more good men like you in charge of this town."

"Well, soon we'll have an alcalde—a mayor and judge. Prayerfully, the men will vote in the right man for the job."

"I hope you're right." Her voice sounded weary.

As they approached the restaurant, Joseph knew that she was in no shape to finish waiting on the evening's customers. "I think perhaps it's best if you go straight to bed and rest. You've had a traumatic day. Would you like me to talk to Daniel?"

"Would you?" Her relief was palpable. "All of a sudden, I feel drained of all energy."

"Let me walk you to the back and up the stairs. You have your key?"

"I do." Her voice was almost a whisper as she pulled the brass key out.

Joseph led her up the steps to the living quarters while worry built in his gut. She'd slowed considerably and leaned on him more with each step. Something was wrong. When they reached the landing, he stopped and turned toward her. But before he could ask if she was all right, her hand slipped from his arm, and she collapsed.

CHAPTER 16

After using Olivia's key to open the door to the living quarters, Joseph carried her to the parlor and laid her on the settee. He patted her face. "Olivia?"

She moaned but didn't open her eyes.

"Olivia? Please, can you hear me?"

No response.

Not wanting to be inappropriate, he knew he shouldn't stay with her alone, but how could he leave her to go get help? He removed her bonnet and laid a hand on her forehead. A dark, silken curl fell over her cheek. Lifting it and pushing it away from her face, he hoped that it was simply exhaustion from the trauma of the day. As he glanced down at her neck, he saw the skin had a purplish hue in the shape of a man's hand.

Anger burned in him again as he thought of that man squeezing her throat so tight. Taking a deep breath, he prayed for forgiveness and stood. Nothing good could come from him seeking vengeance. Right now, he had to think about Olivia's health. He touched her cheek one last time and then turned to the door. He raced back down the stairs to the restaurant. As usual, it was packed with customers. The cacophony of loud chatter, silverware clanking on plates, and the bustle of people filled his ears, while the rich scents of beef, pork, and chocolate cake assaulted his senses. He stopped beside a table and scanned the room. Where was Daniel?

Taking another sweeping glance of the room, he realized he might need to check in the kitchen. As he headed toward the swinging door, Joseph stopped abruptly when he saw his friend exit. "Daniel!"

The man's brow furrowed when he spotted Joseph. "What's wrong?" He set the plates in his arms down at a table.

"It's Olivia. She collapsed." Without another word, he raced back to the stairs, knowing that Daniel would follow.

When they reached the parlor, Daniel ran over to his sister. "Livvy?"

She moaned again, but this time she opened her eyes. She blinked several times and squinted at her brother and then at Joseph. "What happened?"

"You collapsed on the stairs. We'd been walking back from the doctor's, and you stated that you felt drained." Joseph moved closer with slow steps. "I noticed you had to lean on me the longer we walked, and it began to worry me."

She sat up and put a hand to her neck. "I'm just tired."

"Livvy, are you sure? Your neck is all bruised." Her brother's concern was evident in his tone. "And I don't think I've ever known you to collapse from simply being tired."

A small smile lifted her lips. "I really do feel fine." She lifted a hand to halt her brother's response. "Well, as fine as can be expected. Really. Yes, my neck is a bit sore and bruised. I think I'm simply worn out from the horror of the event and worry over the boy. Let me go to bed, and tomorrow I'll be right as rain."

"I'm not so sure about that. You had us really worried—"

"All right, big brother. I know. I'm sorry. But truly, I'm exhausted and haven't been getting enough sleep lately. I feel confident that if I just get some rest, I'll be back to normal tomorrow."

"I'm going to go fetch the doctor." Daniel jumped up. "I don't want to take any chances."

"No. Please. He needs to focus on the boy." She stood up and smoothed her skirt. "There are so many factors that led to this. I'm overly tired. I've been working a lot. There's been a lot of things I've had to deal with from the past few months. I moved to a brand-new place. And yes, I was attacked"—she held up a hand to keep them from interrupting—"but before you two go flying off the handle, let me get some rest. I'm pretty certain that I'll be fine, and if I'm not, I will be the first to ask you to go get the doctor." Her voice had gained strength as she spoke, and the tone she'd delivered the last of her speech brooked no argument.

Joseph looked at his friend, and they shared a knowing glance. Best not to antagonize the lady any further this evening.

She turned to Joseph. "Thank you, again. For everything." With another smile, she put a hand on his arm and gave it a slight pat. It warmed him, and he longed to put his arms around her and hold her forever. She walked to her room. When she reached the door, she called back, "I'm fine. Both of you wipe those worried looks off your faces. I just need a glass of water and some sleep."

Daniel turned to him once she closed the door and let out a long sigh. "Well, she looked steady enough on her feet just now. Do you think she's hiding anything from us?"

Analyzing the situation and all he'd seen tonight, Joseph didn't have a clue. "I have no idea, although she seems much better now than she was just a little bit ago. Not that my opinion holds much sway. Tomorrow will prove to have the answer no matter what I presume."

Daniel shook his head with a wry chuckle that almost sounded like a moan at the end. "You're right, I know. It's been an interesting day, hasn't it?"

"Not quite the word I would use, my friend, but yes." Joseph pulled out his watch again. "And it's not over. I'm supposed to be meeting with the city council right now. I better go. Please send me a message if anything happens with Olivia or the boy?"

"Of course." His friend gripped his shoulder. "Thank you. I guess I should get her some water."

Joseph let himself out and went to get his horse. As much as he didn't trust George Banister and wanted to be at the council meeting, he didn't want to leave Olivia. He knew there was nothing he could do for her, but after the circus of a day, he longed to make sure she recovered and didn't have any more spells. Perhaps that was overstepping his bounds, and perhaps it was even impertinent of him to think, but he couldn't deny his growing feelings for the lovely widow.

By the time Joseph reached the meeting, George was once again wrapping things up. The man's chin lifted when he spotted Joseph. "Mr. Sawyer, this is not the best etiquette on your behalf to show up late. Again."

The scolding made Joseph's anger from earlier simmer back to the surface. "There was an unfortunate incident of a child being beaten in the street. The attacker went after a woman when she confronted him."

A twitch in George's expression raised the hairs on Joseph's neck.

Several gasps were heard from a few of the other council members.

He lifted his hands to quiet the murmuring that started but kept his gaze on Banister. "All is well, gentlemen, but I had to see to the child's needs and get him to a physician. My apologies for being tardy."

"Quite all right."

"Is the child faring well?"

"What about the woman?"

"This is why we need police."

The men all talked over one another.

George cleared his throat quite loudly. "How very noble of you, Mr. Sawyer." He didn't look impressed. "Quiet now, please, gentlemen.

Let's all remember the election this coming week and the support that we need to raise for our new alcalde. Meeting adjourned."

Joseph watched George slip out of the room while the other men surrounded him and asked questions about the attack outside the restaurant. His instincts were on high alert again. Something in the man's demeanor had changed when he mentioned a child being beaten. Certainly Banister couldn't have anything to do with it, could he?

As he refocused on the men around him, he told them of the event and then asked them questions of his own about the meeting. Everyone seemed excited about electing their new official with hopes that they would be able to really start cleaning up their city now. But as they all left, Joseph couldn't help being suspicious of George. Maybe it would be a good idea to try to follow the man again. His instincts had never let him down before.

On the ride home, he tried to think of how he would track George's movements during the week without being caught. He wasn't even sure where to find him. Or was he? The last time, Joseph had seen the man in an unsavory part of town. Perhaps he should go back there and check it out. If he changed his clothing and smudged dirt on his face, he could look the part. It wasn't so long ago that he'd looked like one of the ruffians himself.

The thoughts followed him all the way home. When he arrived, Dewei stood outside the front door, and a sense of foreboding came over him.

"Dewei," Joseph said, and dismounted. "Has there been trouble? An accident at the mine?"

"No, sir. Mine is shipshape." The man removed his straw hat and held it in his hands. "My brothers. It is bad."

A twinge of guilt filled Joseph. While he'd looked into Dewei's claims, he hadn't done as much as he could have. "Please, tell me." He ushered the man inside.

"Only one meal a day. They kept in chains day and night with no way to make clean. Brothers skinny. No good."

"Were you able to sneak in the window again and speak to them?"

Dewei gave an affirmative nod as his face grew more serious. "But no more. Window locked and chained. Brothers moved with others."

"Moved? Others? Moved to where? How many others are there?"

"Many. Full buildings."

"Buildings? More than one?" He couldn't keep the shock from his voice. The weight of his promise dropped into his stomach like a rock. Why hadn't he done more?

Dewei's lips formed a thin line, and he lifted his chin. "Many. Yes."

Joseph's gut churned at the thought. "Have their captors said anything about the debt they owe? Why they are still being held?"

"No. Only told must work for many months to pay debt."

By that time, if the conditions were as grave as Dewei described, there wasn't much chance for survival.

First Dewei's brothers and then the boy today. Were they connected? Now to learn that there were *buildings* of people being held as slaves? It was almost too much to think of and reminded him of Sodom and Gomorrah in the Bible. San Francisco wasn't exactly known as a good city, so if it was this bad where everyone could see it, the evil that was hidden must be much worse than he could have ever imagined.

"I made you a promise, Dewei. And I intend to keep it."

CHAPTER 17

The morning had rushed by for Olivia. After a much-needed night of extra sleep, she felt quite peppy today, even with all the busyness and events of yesterday. The only thing that bothered her was that her young charge at Dr. Morgan's hadn't awakened yet. This seemed to trouble the doctor as well, but he wouldn't say anything more, just told her to return and keep talking to the boy. She determined to take some cookies from the kitchen on her visit this evening. Duncan—their main cook and a very large man to boot—had a soft spot for her, so when she'd asked for cookies or small cakes, he'd only asked what kind she'd like.

Glancing around the dining room, her thoughts returned to the day before. It seemed like an eternity had passed since then. Daniel's observance of her feelings for Joseph had triggered a tidal wave of emotions, emotions that had sent her back into her guilt and then rushing into the alley for escape. Thoughts of the attack made her wince and put a hand to her throat, but she closed her eyes and reminded herself that God had been there in the midst of it all and in her time of need had provided a rescuer. If she was honest, she almost felt like God had sent her for that little boy, not just to save him but for what needed to happen in her own heart.

She'd awakened early that morning and spent a good deal of time on her knees. Much of what she'd been feeling had revolved around her own fear, and she knew that God had not given her a spirit of fear. When she'd thought it was over, she'd wished to do things differently. Now she had her chance.

A few men entered the dining room, waved at her, and took seats at a table. Olivia refocused on the work of the day. Daniel had hired two extra young men to help with serving and told her before breakfast that when Joseph came to escort her to the doc's, they would change up their schedule. Both her brother and Joseph would accompany her to see the boy at the end of the lunch rush. Then they would all eat together quickly and continue with their Bible study. It made her heart swell that both men had gone to such lengths to help her through this time.

So now she needed to put her best foot forward, take care of the customers, and get through this shift. Determination and resolve to take this additional chance to live her life to the fullest made her smile. How many people could she encourage today? She walked toward a man his friends called Toothless. "What would you like to order today? The special is beef stew."

His smile—which had given him his nickname—beamed up at her. "Special for me, young lady."

"Coming right up."

Before she knew it, the end of the lunch rush arrived, and Joseph appeared at her side. "Daniel is making sure everything is covered, and he had to run an errand, so he said to meet him out front." His smile boosted her spirits a notch higher. And those dimples. It should be a crime what one look from him could do to her heart.

Removing her apron, Olivia walked to the back to hang it up. The guilt she'd anticipated after thinking such thoughts about Joseph didn't come, which made the weight on her shoulders feel lighter. Hanging the apron's strings over a hook, she thanked God for what He was doing in her life.

When her hands were free, she reached up to check her hair. Not that it mattered—men would stare at her no matter what she wore or looked like simply because she was one of the few women in town. But she cared a bit more about how she presented herself whenever Joseph was around. The thought made her shake her head. Vanity was not something she wanted to claim as a trait. The thought of him looking at her with appreciation, however, made the fluttering in her stomach grow. She found Joseph waiting for her at the door, and she took his offered arm.

Leading her out of the restaurant, he patted her hand. "How has your morning been?" He was a good head taller than she was, and she found it endearing how he dipped his head to look at her when they spoke.

"Very busy, but that's usual." Trying to keep the conversation normal took all her concentration.

Daniel strode over to them from across the street. He gave her a wide grin and wiggled his eyebrows at her. "I hear you've enlisted Duncan's help to make cookies for the young lad."

She couldn't help the smile that filled her face. "Yes, yes, I did. And I'm quite proud of the fact. Duncan was so enthused that he decided to make three different kinds to see what would entice the boy once he awoke."

Both men chuckled. Daniel began walking on the other side of her so she was safely ensconced between the two. He leaned forward and looked to Joseph. "You mentioned earlier that you wanted to talk to us about some serious things?"

She felt Joseph stiffen as she held his arm.

"Yes, I'm afraid I have some grave news about unsavory and questionable practices that are going on in our town. My foreman has seen them with his own eyes, and I must say I am quite disturbed." He slowed their pace and then stopped for a moment and tipped his head toward her. "I don't wish to discuss anything in front of you that would make you uncomfortable."

"I'm made of some pretty stern stuff, so I think I can handle hearing about it." But what if it was something horribly grotesque? Would she be able to stomach it? "Perhaps if it becomes too much for me, I'll let you know."

"Certainly." Joseph started walking, and their little troupe headed toward the doctor's again. "My foreman is a Chinese man. Incredible worker. Very smart. Handles all the business affairs with the utmost stewardship. Anyway, his brothers were coming here to gain employment as well. Only they didn't arrive when they were supposed to, and Dewei went hunting for them."

"Did he find them? Are they all right?" Daniel's voice was laced with concern.

Joseph took a deep breath. "He did. But no, they're not all right. Someone is holding them in chains, forcing them to work in the brothels cleaning and doing laundry, until their 'debt' is paid. But that's where it gets even more complicated. They don't owe any debt. They paid for their passage up front." He let out his breath in a long, heavy sigh. "There's a lot more to the story, but what concerns me the most is that it's not just Dewei's brothers. He said there are literally buildings full of chained-up slaves in our city."

"Oh gracious, no! That can't be happening, can it?" She jerked her head to look at her brother. But the sad look on his face told her more than she wanted to know. "I can't believe this. . .I mean I know this city is wretched, but. . ." Tears stung her eyes. How could God allow such evil? It didn't make sense to her.

"I'm sorry to be the bearer of such bad news, but Dewei is getting more concerned by the day, and I don't blame him. For a while, he'd been able to sneak in through a window in one of the buildings, but now there are locks and chains there as well. And they've been moved.

Dewei doesn't know where. My fear is that there are more people being held than we can possibly know. If we were to find them in one location, by the time we were able to come back with assistance, they could be moved, and we wouldn't know where to find them or how to help them. If they're only being fed one meager meal a day and kept locked up like that, there's a chance we could have a lot of deaths on our hands as well."

Her brother had listened in silence to the information Joseph gave them. Olivia turned to him again to see what he was thinking of all this. "Daniel?"

He continued to take slow steps with his hands interlocked behind him. Obviously, the news had struck him hard. "It's completely distressing that people are being held captive, but I must say that the first thoughts that came to my mind were, 'How many more are coming? How are they being brought here? And how can we stop this atrocity before people are killed?'"

Daniel's words struck a chord in her. She hadn't thought about those details. Her stomach twisted as it all had a chance to sink in. "The fact is, we don't know if anyone has lost their life already because of all this." The thought made her swallow hard. "Lord, help us. . . ."

They reached Dr. Morgan's, and Joseph turned to look at her and Daniel. "I've promised to do all I can to help. I simply wanted you both to know so that you could be praying, and if you have any wisdom to share, I'd love to hear it. This is new territory for me, but I have to do something. And not just as a city councilman but as a Christian—and as a human being. I don't see how we can allow this to go on. The gangs, gambling, and brothels are bad enough. But when innocent people are basically stolen or kidnapped—however you want to say it—and treated in such a way, I wonder if this world is even worse than I thought."

Daniel sighed. "The depravity of man is indeed severe." He tapped his boot on the step. "I think another of our concerns should be about the gambling houses and brothels. We've talked about cleaning up this town for so long, but with someone bringing in slaves—however they are doing it—we need to be cautious." He paused and took a long, deep breath. "They could very well be stealing women and children to"—he cleared his throat—"work in those establishments. And not just for cleaning and laundry."

Olivia covered her gasp with her hand.

"I'm sorry to be so disgusting, Livvy, but I had to say it. We can't venture into this with our eyes half-closed." He turned to Joseph. "All these captive people could be feeding the industries that are visible. And as much as we thought those businesses were bad, this makes it that much worse. It's a good thing the vote is coming up."

"Yes, in a few days."

"Do you think we can convince the new alcalde that we need police?"

"It's first on the agenda."

"Good." Daniel stepped up to the doctor's door. "We're in this with you, Joseph. And we will be praying daily about it." He looked back to her. "Let's go see how the young fellow is doing, shall we?" Opening the door for her, he gave her a small smile as she walked past him.

Her brother knew that this news was bothering her, and he was obviously trying to get her thoughts elsewhere. As much as she wanted to focus on the poor boy she'd rescued yesterday, she also realized that she wouldn't be able to get this sort of thing out of her mind. She had a soft heart, and she always felt the need to stand up for those who couldn't stand for themselves.

Dr. Morgan greeted them in the room where the boy was tucked into a clean bed. "He woke up just a few minutes ago, but I haven't been able to get him to speak. I'm glad you're here." He looked straight at her. "I was hoping maybe you'd have better luck."

Pushing the other feelings aside, Olivia pasted on a big smile and walked forward. The poor little guy's face was one giant bruise. It broke her heart. "Hello there. How are you feeling today?"

Dark brown eyes stared at her, but the boy didn't respond.

"My name is Olivia. Can you tell me yours?"

The boy looked down at the blanket and started plucking at the threads.

"That's all right. I'd still like to be your friend. I'm sorry I wasn't able to help you sooner yesterday. Do you know who it was that did this to you?" Her voice rose as she asked the question, because the more she thought about it, the more she wanted to see that man punished for what he'd done.

The boy looked back up at her and shook his head.

Olivia laid a hand on his small one. "Don't you worry about it. We are here to help you. Do you have any family?"

The blanket captured his attention again.

"Well, I'd like to introduce you to *my* family." She turned pleading eyes to Daniel and Joseph. Never had she dealt with a child who wouldn't speak to her. And he looked so small and scared. "This is my brother, Daniel." She pulled her brother forward and then turned to her other side. "And this is my good friend, Joseph."

"We're glad to see you awake." Joseph beamed a smile at the child.

Daniel rested a hand on the bed. "We've been praying for you."

The little guy looked at each of them but continued to be silent.

Olivia shot a glance at the doctor, but he just shrugged his shoulders. Turning back to the boy, she thought about trying a different tactic. "I'm going to bring you cookies later today. Do you like cookies?"

For the first time, a bit of light sparked in the child's eyes.

It was all the encouragement she needed. "Well good, I'm having the cook at the restaurant bake us three different kinds so we can find which one is your favorite." She tried to keep her voice light and a smile on her face.

The lad licked his lips and winced. Would he even be able to eat? The poor fellow, she'd never seen a grown man this beat up, and it broke her heart into little shards that threatened to slice up the last of her emotions. It made her relive the moment—something she never wanted to do again—and she put a hand to her throat where the bruises were an all too vivid reminder of the man's hand shutting off her airway.

"Don't worry. I'm sure they will be soft, and I'll even cut them into small pieces so you'll be able to enjoy them."

For a moment, she thought for sure a slight smile had lifted one side of his lips.

The doctor came forward and helped the boy take a sip of water. He turned to her. "If you are prepared to take care of him, I think I'd allow him to go home with you this evening if that is acceptable, Mrs. Brighton?"

"Yes, of course." She smiled back at the boy. "Is that all right with you? I'll still bring you cookies; we'll just get to take them home with us."

He blinked at her and gave an almost invisible nod.

The door *whooshed* open behind them, and they all turned to see who it was.

A stout man who appeared a few years older than Daniel was dressed in the height of fashion in a dark blue tailored suit. Removing his hat, he gave her a slight bow.

"Banister. What are you doing here?" The scowl on Joseph's face made her think this man wasn't a friend.

"I'm here to collect this young lad."

"You are?" Dr. Morgan looked surprised.

"Yes, it has come to my attention that my employer knows the lad's family. I will gladly pay his bill and have transportation provided for him."

"Who are you?" The doctor put words to the same question Olivia was ready to shout.

"George Banister." He bowed again. "At your service. I'm the head of the city council of this fine city."

"And you know the boy? What's his name?" Daniel was the one to pipe up.

The slick man in front of her tilted his head. "Well. . .I. . .that is, like I said, my employer knows the boy's family. I'm just here to escort him home."

"But you can't—" Every reason that she'd thought of in the last few seconds was whisked out of her mind. She didn't trust this man— whether it was because of Joseph's cool response to him or her own instincts, it didn't matter—and she had no desire to see him take the child away. "That is to say, I was there when this boy was attacked. I was planning on taking him home with me."

Mr. Banister stepped closer. "I admire your heart and desire to take care of those less fortunate than you, Miss. . ."

"*Mrs.* Brighton." She lifted her chin.

"Mrs. Brighton. My apologies. But I'm sure his family is missing him greatly. Thank you very much for taking such good care of him."

"Banister, how do you know that this is the right child?" Joseph had stiffened and stepped forward to confront the man.

It didn't seem to affect the well-groomed Mr. Banister. He stepped closer as well. "As I said, my employer sent me to pick up the child. He has vast resources. He knows the family and knows this is their child. I wouldn't think that you would want to stand in the way of reuniting a family, Sawyer."

"But I was going to bring him cookies." The excuse sounded sad even to her own ears. It made her turn back around and look at the boy. A single tear slipped down his cheek. What did it mean? Was he sad to miss the cookies? Or happy to be reunited with his family?

She leaned down close to him and spoke in a hushed tone. "Do you know this man?"

The child didn't respond.

Her heart broke a little more. What could she do?

She lowered her voice even more. "I'll always be your friend. I'm at Livingston's Restaurant if you ever need me." She squeezed his hand and straightened up.

The doctor sighed. "Well, I guess I'll let Mr. Banister get him home."

"Thank you." The man pulled several coins out of his jacket pocket. "And thank you for all you've done for the boy."

Olivia couldn't take it. She rushed out the door and didn't stop until she was across the street, Joseph and Daniel close on her heels. Breathing heavily, she let the tears release from her eyes. Why was she so upset? Shouldn't she be glad that the boy had a family?

"Are you all right, Livvy?" Daniel laid a hand on her shoulder.

"I don't know." She pulled a handkerchief from her pocket and wiped at her eyes. When she looked up, she turned to Joseph. "You know that man?"

"Unfortunately, yes." His eyes remained on Dr. Morgan's door.

"Did we do the right thing?" The thought choked her. How could she let that boy go into a stranger's care, although she realized that she was just as much a stranger.

"I. . .I'm sorry. I need to go." Without another word, Joseph ran back toward the restaurant.

It was so unlike him. Her heart picked up speed. Was the boy in danger? Olivia looked at her brother. "What do you think is going on?"

"I'm not sure, Livvy." He watched his friend with a serious look on his face. "I'm sure he was going back to get his horse. And after that, perhaps he is looking into Mr. Banister and the child." He wrapped an arm around her shoulders and turned her back to the restaurant. "But it's best to let Joseph handle this. He knows what he's doing."

In her heart, she knew that Daniel was trying to keep her calm, but her mind screamed that Joseph and the boy were in danger, and there was nothing she could do about it.

CHAPTER 18

"Did the next shipment arrive?" The man looked at one of his other employees—Randy Jones—who he'd put in charge under George.

"Yes, sir. All the packages were delivered." The man had proved his worth over the last few months.

While George Banister was the face of the upstanding, wealthy assistant and his right-hand man, Randy was more of a hands-on, do-the-dirty-work assistant. And that was good, especially if they needed someone to take the fall. Of course, he wouldn't tell Randy that.

"As to the problems we were having with our Orient products, they've been moved, and the locations are secure." Jones straightened his jacket, looking quite confident.

"Good, good." With the election happening as they spoke, it was of utmost importance to keep things out of the prying eyes of any do-gooder citizens. "Did you also cover all the windows for now? I don't want any other mishaps like before."

"I did. Heavy curtains are hung, and the windows are all locked with chains. We shouldn't have any issues, but we are outgrowing the space once again."

"In light of how much business we are doing, it doesn't surprise me. I'll just have to get creative with our storage."

"There's also the discussion of food. I wouldn't want to bring suspicious eyes around because of the quantity."

The man was astute, which was good. "I've already instructed George to work with different suppliers. He changes things around quite regularly."

Randy shifted his weight and nodded. "Well, sir, if you don't need me for anything else, I'll get back to work."

"Very well." He returned to his seat behind the large mahogany desk. Everything was falling into place nicely. He'd kept his name unknown while building a vast empire. Let the citizens of San Francisco believe he was just humble and wanted his privacy. That made him even more of an enigma to the curious. But word had spread for many months of the great benefactor who'd helped fund and establish a city council, a wealthy man who had donated food and clothing to the poor, and a businessman who wanted to see their city become the greatest port in all of America. While the majority of people in town wanted to do whatever they pleased without anyone telling them what they could and couldn't do, many outspoken residents wanted to see change. If California were to become a state and a real government were to be brought in, he needed to have all his chess pieces in place.

There was nothing wrong with his giving people the picture they wanted to see while underneath it all he continued to grow the trade that had made him even wealthier. Dirty money could fund all the good things he planned to do, and no one would be the wiser even after he made his identity known at the opportune time, of course.

It was all about power. And he planned to have it.

Joseph hid in the crowd of spectators; he was dressed in raggedy garments with dirt and mud smudged all over his face. When the announcement had been made that John Geary had been elected the alcalde, his heart cheered along with the crowd. John was a good man. President Polk had sent him to San Francisco earlier this year to be the postmaster. Maybe now they could create some real change in their town.

Searching through the crowd, Joseph kept an eye out for George. The more he'd thought about it, the more he suspected the man. But of what he wasn't sure. Something in his gut just told him that the man wasn't the upstanding citizen that he portrayed. If only Joseph could prove it.

The clapping around him continued as John Geary took to the stage. Joseph continued to move through the people while listening to their newly elected official. The alcalde spoke with passion about the needs of San Francisco. "At this time we are without a dollar in the public treasury, and it is to be feared the city is greatly in debt. You have neither an office for your magistrate nor any other public edifice. You are without a single police officer or watchman and have not the means of confining a prisoner for an hour. Neither have you a place to shelter while living, sick and unfortunate strangers who may be cast upon our shores, or to bury them when dead. . . ."

From what Joseph knew of the man, he was impressed. And Geary didn't seem to be mincing words. The man was bringing up many of the things they'd talked about in the city council but hadn't been able to bring to fruition yet.

Geary continued, "Public improvements are unknown in San Francisco. In short, you are without a single requisite necessary for the promotion of prosperity, for the protection of property, or for the maintenance of order."

More applause ensued, and Joseph took part. It seemed like this was just the man they needed. But even as relief spread through him, he spotted George Banister's familiar figure—heading *away* from the gathering.

The alcalde's next words caught Joseph's attention. Geary wanted the city council to help him select a captain of police. These words encouraged Joseph but made him wonder if Geary was prepared to handle George Banister. Or did they already know one another? The thought wasn't a pleasant one as Joseph continued to follow George.

As he rounded the corner, he tried to stay hidden. Banister was a block or so ahead of him. Hopefully, the man wouldn't notice he was being followed, but Joseph was new at this. How could he keep the man from knowing he was there? His only hope was that if George turned around, he wouldn't recognize Joseph in his disguise.

As he wound his way into the heart of the worst part of the city, Joseph's gut filled with dread. Why would George be headed this way, especially when he was the head of the city council and should by all intents and purposes be in attendance at the gathering at the public square. But that was probably why the man had slipped away. Attention was on the election.

It didn't help Joseph feel any better that this was exactly where he'd run into George before. There wasn't any chance that Banister could be delivering meals to the poor and needy today, because the man didn't have anything with him. So what was he up to?

The long light of summer kept the streets lit for now, but Joseph knew that it wouldn't be too long before the sun set. While it might be easier to sneak around in the dark, it was also a lot more dangerous.

George stopped at a building on Pacific Street and looked around him. Joseph leaned back behind the corner of a shack and hoped he hadn't been seen. When he peeked back around the corner, George was pulling something out of his pocket. Light glinted off something metallic. A key. Banister opened the door, took another quick glance around, and then entered the building.

Just in case Banister checked outside again, Joseph decided to count to twenty before he got any closer. When he was done, he blew out a breath and tried to get across the street without being noticed. The building that George entered wasn't a shack, but it wasn't exactly a well-built mansion either. The structure had a number of windows, but they all had their curtains drawn. There was nothing to see, and it was eerily quiet as well. The last time he'd ventured into this part of town, there had been a lot of noise. . .and wailing. Joseph would never forget the wailing.

Joseph narrowed his eyes and tried to think of what he should do next. This wasn't like anything he'd done before. Should he wait for George to come back out? Should he look around the building?

"What are ya doin'?" A scratchy voice from behind him made him jump.

"Nothing." *Lord, forgive me for lying.* "Just looking for food." Joseph eyed the man. He wasn't dressed in rags, but his hulking frame wasn't exactly clean either.

"You new around here?"

Joseph nodded, afraid to answer too much and have to lie again and again.

"This ain't the safest place especially after dark. I suggest you head back toward the public square. Someone might find pity on ya over there." The man shoved his shoulder. "No one likes a snoop." The look on his face said he meant business.

Did he suspect that Joseph was watching George? No. That couldn't be, could it? The veiled threat in the man's eyes wasn't a joke. Joseph had better play the part. He put on his best look of fear and nodded. If he took off running, would he convince the man that he wasn't a threat?

Putting his feet into motion, Joseph trotted away, keeping his shoulders hunched. Several blocks from Pacific Street, he finally slowed and then stopped. He put his hands on his hips to catch his breath and paced in a small circle in the quiet street. All the pieces of this crazy puzzle were not fitting together if they indeed were related. And just because his instinct said it was true didn't make it so. The fact of the matter was that people were being held in slave labor, people who had been kidnapped, lied to, mistreated, and who knew how much worse. The weight of Dewei's testimony seemed to grow heavier each day.

In his heart, Joseph wanted to do what was needed to fix it and to clean up this city. He couldn't do it alone, though—he was just one man. He had to ask himself, How? How could they possibly find a solution? Would it take time to establish a police force? The thought of people chained up as slaves made his stomach turn. Were those the people who had been wailing? How much time did they have before it was too late?

The face of the young boy Olivia had rescued came to mind. He hadn't spoken a word, and Joseph thought it was perhaps because the child was afraid. But of what? Or of whom? The man who'd beaten him? Or the man who'd come to take him "home"?

Too many unanswered questions rushed around in his brain. With a deep breath, he straightened his shoulders and walked back to Livingston's Restaurant. It would still be open, and he needed to talk to Daniel. . .tonight.

When he was about a block away, Joseph realized what he was wearing. Daniel wouldn't mind—and prayerfully, Olivia wouldn't either—but he didn't want to be seen associating with his friends when he was disguised. If someone recognized him and put two and two together, he could put Daniel and Olivia at risk, and he wasn't willing to risk that.

Pushing himself back into a trot, Joseph ran home to get cleaned up. Daniel wouldn't mind the late hour even if Joseph showed up after closing. When he reached his front door, a note was tacked to it. Joseph looked around and then yanked it down. He unfolded the paper and read: *Watch your back, Sawyer.*

CHAPTER 19

The evening rush was over, and relief flooded Olivia. It seemed that every day they served more customers than they had the day before. Where were all these people coming from?

News of the newly elected alcalde had spread throughout the dining room as the evening progressed. When she'd run into Daniel and told him, he'd smiled. Postmaster John Geary's reputation was good, so it seemed like they'd gotten an honorable man for the job. Maybe things could start changing.

She hoped they would begin with cleaning up the streets. After the incident in the alley, her senses had been on high alert. For one thing, she never wanted to see a child beaten like that ever again. And it would take a long time to rid herself of the feeling of a grimy hand choking her. That was something that shouldn't happen to anyone ever, and she would do her best to make sure that it never did. She wasn't sure how, but her passion had been stirred. Daniel and Joseph were doing so much to help their town, and she wanted to help as well. Never did she want to feel the regret and longing she'd felt as that man squeezed out her very breath. No more fear. No more guilt. No more second-guessing. It was freeing to let go of those shackles.

She removed her apron and headed up the stairs to their living quarters. When she'd first come here, she'd carried such guilt about Hezekiah's death. The short six weeks of her marriage had been filled with her dissatisfaction and complaining. To be honest, she had been a mess in so many ways. But now? Even living in probably the most crime-infested town she could ever imagine, she was. . .content. Happy even. Filled with excitement about what she could do to help spread the Gospel, to help the less fortunate, and to live each day with joy. The change in her was real, and she hoped it never went away.

Daniel had played a large part in that. Having her brother close to encourage and love her had helped heal her heart. Then there was the special box from Mama. The journals had been to her like a lifeline to a drowning and weary soul. And she'd finally decided it was time to read her mother's journal. Since she'd learned and gained so much from the other women, she longed to read her mother's words and hoped that the sting of her absence would ease with time.

She flopped onto her back on her bed and let her back muscles relax and sink into the feather mattress, a luxury her brother had purchased for her. Her thoughts tumbled around with gratitude for all that had changed in her life since coming to San Francisco.

Then there was Joseph. Olivia had never known anyone like him. True, he was handsome, but Hezekiah had been good-looking as well. Looks didn't make a man. It was Joseph's substance and heart that really made her think. During their Bible study times and chats over lunch each day, she'd gotten to see what really made the man tick. He'd been quick to share that he hadn't led a good life before finding the Lord. His past didn't bother Olivia—honesty was the best policy in her book—but every once in a while, she'd remember that the man owned a gold mine, and she'd have her doubts again. Every time she doubted, though, she realized that he never actually talked about his business. He never talked to all the men about how exciting it was to find gold. He didn't carry around nuggets to brag to everyone. It was almost like he didn't own a prosperous gold mine at all.

Last, the horrific attack had taught her so much. She longed for a future, and deep down, she hoped it included a certain blond-haired, brown-eyed gentleman.

She sat up and started to unhook her boots. The enigma that was Joseph Sawyer fascinated her, even though he was a gold miner. She'd also vehemently declared to her brother that she would never marry again, yet her heart had changed. A giggle escaped her throat. Why had her thoughts gone to marriage all of a sudden? Goodness!

Joseph was a great man and her friend, but did he care for her in that way?

"Livvy?" Daniel's voice came from the hall. His footsteps grew louder as he neared.

"I'm here. Just rubbing the day's steps out of my feet."

He peeked around the doorway. "Did you get some dinner?"

She nodded and gave him a smile. "I did, thank you."

"May I come in?" He lifted his eyebrows and wiggled them.

One of the things she'd asked for when she moved in was privacy, and he'd promised to never enter her room without her permission. "Of course." It made her chuckle. While she'd always felt close to her older brother, they hadn't seen one another in years before she came. Now she couldn't imagine being without him. He was her best friend.

"I'm thinking of expanding." He sat on the chair by her desk and let out a long breath.

Every muscle that had just started to relax tightened up in full attention. "Really? What does that mean?"

"I think I could build another restaurant and have it just as busy as this one. Plenty of people are looking for work, and we never run out of mouths to feed." He shrugged. "Word is that San Francisco will double in size again in just a few months. Ships are on the way that are full of hundreds—possibly even thousands—of people. More ships arrive each day, and more leave ports around the world headed for our bay."

"Is this something you think you can handle?" Hundreds of thoughts filled her mind and vied for attention. Her days were overwhelming enough. The thought of another restaurant filled with customers was a bit too much for her mind to take in.

"I do, as long as I can find trustworthy staff, which I think I can. It will take a while to build it anyway. During that time, I can hire the cooks and someone to manage the other location. I'll just have to split my time between the two dining rooms, which means I'll need a manager for this"—he pointed to the floor—"restaurant." The look he gave her was probing, questioning.

He didn't think. . .? No. She had no idea how to manage a restaurant. Olivia bit her lip and shook her head back and forth.

"I can raise your pay and give you all the training you will need. You already know the business—there are just some things I'll need to teach you about keeping the books and managing the schedules. I'll be here to help with that. I can't be in two places at once, and the manager needs to be present. I can only oversee both."

"I don't know. . . ." She was already worn out enough just taking orders and delivering food. "Wouldn't being a manager mean more work than I have now?"

"Well. . .possibly. But you won't have to continue what you're doing *and* be the manager. We'll hire someone to take your place, and then you just do what I do all day long. A lot of it is jumping in to help in the busiest times; a lot of it is delegating."

Biting her lip, she thought about it. The title of manager was quite appealing.

Daniel patted her knee. "It *will* be more responsibility, but I know you're up for the task."

His confidence in her made her heart soar. When he'd first mentioned it, she didn't think there was any way. But now. . . The idea had grown on her and fast. She smirked. "Does that mean I can actually have a day off?"

His laughter filled the room. "Yes. I will make sure you get a day off."

"And you said a raise?"

"Yes, and a raise." He stuck out his hand as if they were making a bargain. "What do you say?"

"I'll give it a try." Taking his hand, she shook it vigorously. The exhaustion she'd felt earlier was now replaced by a thrill of exhilaration. Something new and exciting and quite impressive for a woman her age, or a woman of any age for that matter. And if she ended up remaining a single widow for the rest of her years, she'd need a good way to support herself. She could never allow herself to live off her brother. What if he got married and had a family?

"Livvy," Daniel said as he leaned in and hugged her. "Thank you. I'm so glad you came here. And not just so you can help me run my businesses." His look turned a bit sheepish. "But because I didn't realize how much I missed having family around. I didn't realize how lonely I'd become."

"I'm the one who should be thanking you." Where would she be right now if she didn't have her brother?

"Nonsense. We're family." He tweaked her nose like he used to when she was a little girl. "And by the way, I've been remiss in not telling you how great the restaurant looks with the flowers on the tables. Even a few of our crustiest customers have commented on the decorating."

"I'm glad. I'll start working on the curtains soon, now that the fabric is in. What do you think about—"

Knock, knock!

The pounding made Olivia jump and put a hand over her heart. The kitchen staff were still cleaning up, so Daniel hadn't locked all the doors of the restaurant yet. Anyone could come up the stairs and knock on their residence door.

Daniel frowned. "I wonder who that could be." He went over to the door, unlocked it, but only opened it a crack. "Joseph! Come in."

Hearing his name made Olivia instinctively put a hand to her hair.

Joseph removed his hat and walked in, bowing to her, a grim expression on his face. "I'm sorry for the late visit, but I need to talk."

"Of course." Her brother ushered their friend to the parlor.

Olivia followed close behind.

"What's on your mind?" Daniel sat down and braced his elbows on his knees.

Watching Joseph's face, Olivia ached with the emotion she saw there.

Their friend and guest looked to the flame in the hurricane lantern and stared for several moments. "I disguised myself and followed George Banister today. He went to Pacific Street again, but he wasn't carrying supplies or food of any kind. The building he went to has thick drapes drawn at every window. George had a key and went inside." Joseph swiped a hand down his face. "I tried to get closer, but a man confronted me and said no one liked a snoop, so I ran for several blocks to make him think he'd scared me off."

"Did you see anything else?" The words out of her brother's mouth were clipped—like he was holding in his anger.

"It was quiet. Too quiet. But I know it's the same place where I heard all that wailing before. Like people in pain and miserable. I decided to go home and get cleaned up before I came here because I didn't want anyone to see the filthy man that was snooping around Pacific Street coming to see *you*. I wouldn't be able to live with myself if I put you in any danger." With that he'd turned and looked at her.

The emphasis of his statement made Olivia scared. What kind of people were they dealing with?

"There's more. When I returned home, there was a note tacked to my door, telling me to watch my back."

Daniel scowled. "What do you think that's about?"

"I don't want to rush to any conclusions. I have been a bit pushy with George at a few of the council meetings. And my mine is very successful—it could just be someone in competition. I don't know. I don't think anyone saw me today other than the man who confronted me. And no one followed me—I know that for a fact."

Olivia wasn't sure what to make of all this information. Her heart pounded, and she felt a fierce protectiveness for Joseph as well as a healthy amount of fear. Who would threaten him? And was he in real danger, or was someone simply trying to scare him?

Joseph leaned forward. "There's more. Governor Riley replied to my letter. He said that if we are ever going to gain moral ground in our territory, the common man has to step up and help. I think he's correct.

"Then Dewei came to see me with news that burdened me further. He's heard that there are indeed children being stolen and forced into slave labor here. I don't know where they're coming from, but Dewei overheard a man talking about another shipment coming in soon. There's no sign of them or where they might be hidden, and that concerns me. But we already knew that San Francisco holds many dark secrets. There's been talk of the Hounds getting more territorial and violent. People are afraid to stick their noses where they don't belong, and so evil acts face no resistance."

He sighed. "I can't tell you how difficult it was to watch a man like Dewei, who's normally so stoic and unemotional on the verge of breaking down with tears in his eyes." Joseph just shook his head. "I promised to help his family, and I can see how much he's hurting for them, but now I feel tortured knowing that a lot more people are involved than we thought. Dewei said that the Chinese workers he knows in town have all been talking of the rumors of the underground slave trade, but no one seems to know anything about it or have any details."

Olivia looked to her brother. He sat there, his brow furrowed as he clenched and unclenched his hands. She licked her lips and took a deep breath. "What should we do?"

When Daniel lifted his head, his features were hardened. "First we pray."

They all agreed.

"And second? We do everything in our power to stop this atrocity from happening in our city."

"How exactly are we going to do that?" Olivia wished she could read minds at that moment, because both Daniel and Joseph wore serious expressions that almost scared her.

Joseph placed his hands on his thighs and stood. "We need a spy."

Chapter 20

No number of mud puddles or piles of manure in the streets could slow Joseph down from getting to Livingston's Restaurant. The rain had finally let up, but the streets would be a mess for some time.

When he opened the door to the dining room, he removed his hat and flicked moisture from his suitcoat. He couldn't wait to share his news with Daniel and Olivia. Pulling his pocket watch out, he glanced at the time. So, he was a bit early. That was all right. He just needed to get their attention as soon as possible. But as he looked around, he realized the place was packed as usual nowadays. It used to be that Joseph could always just go to their usual table, but not anymore. Daniel's idea of opening another restaurant was a good one, and it was much needed.

Olivia spotted him first, and her smile beamed across the room to him. Her dark hair shimmered, and she wore a dress that had become his favorite on her. It was blue and brought out the color in her eyes.

Not that he should be spending all his time thinking about the lovely Mrs. Brighton, but Joseph found himself thinking about her more often than not. Even when his thoughts drifted to all the horrible things happening in their city, he couldn't help but think of her and her safety, of her sweet heart and how she pledged to help them in any way she could. And, of course, lately he'd been thinking a lot about their future. Not that there was much chance of that—she'd made it clear she would never marry a gold miner. Then there was Daniel's mention of her imperative statement that she wouldn't marry again. But maybe God could change her mind?

"Good to see you, Sawyer." Daniel clasped his shoulder. "I'm pretty busy at the moment, but I'll find you a place to sit as soon as I can."

Feeling a bit sheepish that his friend had snuck up on him while he'd been watching Olivia, Joseph nodded. "It's not a problem, but I have news to share."

Daniel leaned in closer. "Good or bad?"

"This is good. Encouraging in fact. I'd like to share it with you and Olivia as soon you have a moment."

His friend nodded. "I'll see what I can do."

After about a half hour passed, Daniel sent Joseph to a table, but it took another half hour before the lunch rush had died down and they were all seated together.

"What's this news?" Daniel didn't waste any time.

Joseph looked to Olivia and loved the eagerness he saw on her face. Her blue eyes were focused on him, and for a moment, he forgot what he was going to say. A kick under the table brought his attention back around to the information he had been waiting to share. He shot a look to his friend, who obviously found the whole situation funny. "I came to tell you that the council has selected Malachi Fallon to be San Francisco's first captain of police."

Olivia clapped her hands. "That is wonderful news! We'll finally have law officials to help straighten things out."

"This is good news, indeed." His friend nodded.

"But that's not all." Joseph took a sip of his coffee. "Fallon has appointed a deputy captain, three sergeants, and thirty officers to comprise our first police department."

"He's a man of action, that's for certain. I'm glad he didn't waste any time." Daniel dug into the food in front of him.

When Joseph looked back to Olivia, he noticed the puzzled look on her face. "What are you thinking, Olivia?"

She bit her lip—something he noticed she often did when she was thinking hard on a subject. "I was just wondering where they were going to have an office? And do they have housing for all those men? We all know that more tents are going up every day. There's not enough room for all the people that are already here."

Her heart for people made Joseph adore her even more. "The schoolhouse on Portsmouth Square will be used as their office since all the students headed off to the gold fields, and I guess it will be a place for them to stay temporarily. But plans are already in motion to expand."

"Perhaps we could bring the men meals?" She looked to her brother. "Shouldn't we do our part to help the law in our town?"

Daniel chewed for several moments, and Joseph could tell he was thinking through all the options. "I think that's a great idea," he finally said. "We could do that once a day."

"That's a lot of food, but with the small budget the city has right now, that would be a wonderful help and much appreciated by the men, I'm sure." The council would be grateful for this news as well.

"Have you had any trouble or resistance from Mr. Banister?" Olivia's words were soft.

"Not a bit." Joseph could hardly believe it himself. George had been the bane of his existence. But now? The man was *almost* congenial. "In fact, he said that his employer is donating funds to help the budget for the police captain."

"What do you think the man is up to?" His friend's question echoed one that Joseph asked himself numerous times a day.

"That's what I can't seem to figure out. He's slick and good at getting people to see his side, no matter what side that is. Now he's a hero to the other council members for helping to get Fallon selected so that we finally have law enforcement."

"But you still suspect him, don't you? Especially after what you've seen?" Olivia watched him carefully.

"Definitely. I don't trust the man. There's some hidden agenda that none of us knows anything about."

"I haven't liked him since I met him." She lifted her chin. "I didn't like how he took the boy the way he did either. How do we prove that he's up to no good?"

"That's the tricky part." Daniel looked at his sister. "At this point, we only know that things aren't adding up. Joseph has seen him in a few situations that didn't make sense. Since he seems to have an extremely wealthy employer—a man who appears to do no wrong and has an unlimited amount of resources—we need to find out if it's George acting on his own or if the criminal activity goes much higher."

"But now that we have actual police, I believe that we can make headway," Joseph assured her, and reached across the table to pat her hand for a brief second. It had been killing him to see the worry and dismay in her eyes. If only he had the right to console her. "We still don't know what George is doing. And we have no idea if this is linked to the people being held as slaves or what Dewei has heard of as a slave trade. But I fear if we don't stop this soon, it might escalate beyond even the police's control. The city is growing every day."

Even though his news had been good news to share, the conversation had quickly turned to the serious nature of what was at stake. Perhaps he needed to change the subject. "Speaking of growing. . ." He turned to Daniel. "Have you thought more about building another restaurant?"

His friend wiped his mouth with his napkin. "Indeed. In fact, I've already got a crew working on the new building."

"Already? However did you manage it?"

"By offering to pay top dollar." Daniel laughed.

It made him turn his attention back to Olivia. "He tells me that you're going to manage this restaurant once the new one is built?"

Her face turned pink. "Yes. If I can learn everything. It's a daunting task, that's for sure."

"I have complete faith that you'll do a wonderful job." There was so much more that he wanted to say, but he'd have to wait to share his heart with her. For now, he'd have to be content to be her friend.

"So do I." Daniel grinned from ear to ear at his sister. "Now"—he turned back to Joseph—"what passage are we studying today?"

Only one of the boys from the restaurant stayed for study that afternoon, but it didn't bother Joseph. Every day, they would make an impact, even if it was just continuing to be a light in their dark place. Everything took time, especially earning trust and growing relationships.

It played out all too real in so many areas of his life. The church they'd built. The Bible study. The city council. And. . .Olivia. That relationship was the hardest to wait for, particularly since he spent time with her every day. He often wondered if she suspected that he'd come to admire her. But she never treated him any differently.

Daniel, on the other hand, had become quite a pest about it. Oh, his friend had a good heart and liked to tease him, but Joseph wasn't sure about the timing. Had Olivia even told her brother about her aversion to men who worked in gold mining?

As soon as they ended in prayer, Daniel headed to the kitchen with the boy. Joseph thought about his options and decided it wouldn't hurt to ask her for a walk. She sat at the table with her Bible in front of her, scribbling furiously in a small book.

"Olivia?"

"Hm?" She continued writing and then looked up at him.

"I was wondering if you'd like to go for a walk? Get some fresh air?"

She laid her pencil down and blinked at him. "But it's raining outside."

He looked out the window. For some reason, he hadn't noticed that the rain had come back with a vengeance. "Ah, yes." Disappointment filled him. "Perhaps another time?"

"I need to run an errand tomorrow." Her smile lit up her face. "Would you escort me then?"

"It would be my pleasure."

She closed her book and her Bible and then laid her hands in her lap. "Would you like to sit and visit for a few minutes?"

"I'd love to." As his heart picked up its tempo, he calmly pulled a chair out and sat facing her. "What are you working on in your book, there?"

She blushed. "It's my notes of everything I'm learning and of course the things that I need to study more." Ducking her head for a moment, she picked at something on her skirt before looking back up into his eyes. "I'm sad to admit that I feel lacking when it comes to knowledge of the scriptures."

"I feel lacking every day in that area. It's a good thing we have a lifetime to study the Good Book."

She nodded and bit her lip. "Joseph." Her voice softened. "I wanted to thank you."

"For what?"

"You've taught me a lot about the Bible, and I appreciate that more than you know."

How could that be? She'd been a follower of Christ for much longer than he had. "I want to say praise be to God for that. And truly, I want to praise Him. But I find it hard to believe that I've had anything profound to say to teach you."

The expression on her face threatened to melt his heart. Tears pooled at the corners of her eyes. "Don't discount what God is doing in and through you, Joseph Sawyer." It was her turn to reach out and touch his hand. It sent a jolt of warmth up his arm. "I've learned a lot. And I've needed it. So thank you."

He had no response that was adequate to give her. All he managed was a slight nod. He'd wanted to be used by God ever since he'd been rescued out of his own sin and the Good Lord had turned his life around. But he'd never been in a position to really make a difference. At least he hadn't thought so. Olivia's words touched a deep place within him. With her gracious, loving way, she spoke her heart and encouraged him, and he began to realize that everything Daniel had told him was true.

God wanted him to be willing. It didn't matter where he started. He didn't have to get all cleaned up with his life in order and perfect before the Good Lord would use him. No. He simply needed to offer himself up as a sacrifice—willing and able—for God to do *His* work through him. He closed his eyes for a moment and sent a quick prayer heavenward. What an awesome privilege to be a child of God. When he opened his eyes, Olivia was staring at him.

"I'm looking forward to our outing tomorrow." Her smile seemed a bit shy, and it made her look even prettier.

"Me too."

"I promise not to take you bonnet shopping again." Standing, she grabbed her things. "Until tomorrow." She walked away.

"Until tomorrow. . ."

It took him a moment to recover because the reality of his feelings had taken hold in his heart and refused to let go. He was going to have to pray a lot for God to help him be patient, because he was already falling in love with Mrs. Olivia Brighton.

CHAPTER 21

Dragging her brother by the arm, Olivia hiked up the stairs to their home.

"What is going on?" Daniel wasn't used to being ordered around by his little sister and had said as much when she'd grabbed him in the dining room. At least he'd laughed about it.

When they were safely inside and she'd closed the door, Olivia paced the floor in the parlor. "I need your advice."

He straightened and crossed his arms over his chest. "Of course. Whatever you need."

"It's about Joseph." Watching him closely, Olivia was a bit surprised to see a corner of Daniel's mouth lift. What was that all about? It almost seemed like he was ready to laugh. She gave him a scowl.

"What about him?" His face went back to all serious.

"Well..." She sighed a long, drawn-out sigh that meant she wasn't sure how to proceed. Oh, bother. Best to just get it over with. "I asked him to escort me on an errand today."

"Very wise decision. You know I don't want you ever going anywhere alone."

"I know." She wanted to roll her eyes and tell him she wasn't five years old anymore, but she bit her tongue. "But I'm wondering if I should..." She couldn't say it.

"Should what?" Her brother narrowed his eyes and pushed his

chin out. "Buy another bonnet? Mail a letter? What could be so serious that you need my advice?"

Exasperating man. She placed her hands on her hips. "I know that Joseph is your friend."

"The best."

"Yes, I know." She gave him a look that she hoped conveyed to him that he should be quiet and let her get it out.

He grinned and didn't say a word.

"And I've been so amazed at how hardworking he is, how much he sacrifices to help with Bible study, church, the council, plus taking care of his own employees. His heart to help those who are less fortunate—and those that have been taken advantage of—is a blessing to me."

He raised his eyebrows but didn't say anything.

With a huff, she flung her hands out in front of her. "I just think that maybe you were right."

"Oh?" One eyebrow spiked while a smile spread across his face.

"Yes, I know. You've been worried about me. And I even appreciated all the lectures." She held up a hand. "Well, for the most part, because they made me think and pray and grow. So I have to admit that I've been thinking about Joseph a lot. About how he's the kind of man that I'd always hoped I would marry, but it makes me nervous to even think about that. He's my friend. We spend a lot of time together, and I don't want to lose that on top of the fact that I don't know if I'm ready to fall in love. But my heart seems to pick up its pace whenever he is around. And I admit that I really *like* it when he is around." The words had spilled out before she could do anything about it.

Daniel put a hand to his chest. "I'm crushed. Am I not good enough for you anymore?"

All the tension she was feeling drained as she began to laugh at his dramatics. "You know I love when you're around too. But I get to see you *all* the time. And you're my brother. It's different."

"I know." He stepped over to the settee and sat down. "I'm sorry for teasing you, but you looked so distraught that I just had to break the strain before that vein in your neck exploded."

Self-conscious, she put a hand to her throat then saw the mirth in his eyes. "You are rotten." Laughter bubbled up again. "But I love you." She sat next to him and relaxed. "I guess I have never experienced anything like this, and I need my big brother's advice. It scares me and thrills me all at the same time."

He took her hand. "Why don't we pray about it together, all right? You know that I think that Joseph is the best man around. I trust him with my life. But you've had a lot of emotional upheaval the past few months. It won't hurt for you to take your time and truly get to know him. Give him a chance to show you the man that he is. And pray. A lot."

"I can do that." Sweet peace settled over her again as Daniel prayed for her. Just like it had at the creek the day Hezekiah died. Once again, she was reminded that God was with her. She wasn't alone and didn't have to walk this journey by herself. Not only that, but Daniel was there too. "Thank you."

After they prayed together for several minutes, Olivia's heart felt refreshed. No longer did she feel like she was carrying a huge weight. She checked the time on the clock and hoped that the next few hours would pass quickly.

After Bible study, Olivia excused herself and raced up the stairs to get her bonnet and reticule. Joseph was waiting for her downstairs, and it made her heart flutter to think of him. The only time she'd ever had feelings like this was when she was fifteen and a young, unmarried missionary had traveled through their area to speak with her parents. She'd fancied herself in love with the man as soon as she'd heard all his exciting stories about traveling and telling people about Jesus. She'd even written him a letter the night before he left, hoping that perhaps he felt the same toward her. But when he'd left early without even saying goodbye to her, she burned the letter and promised to never be a silly, lovesick girl ever again.

Practicality had won out the rest of the time. There weren't many young men her age around, and she spent most of her time on the farm with her mother. But when Mama and Daddy died, she'd met Hezekiah at the bank, and he'd offered to rescue her. It hadn't been a whirlwind romance. It had been a marriage of convenience. Oh, Hezekiah said that he loved her and told her how beautiful she was. But she'd never felt any heart flutterings for him even though he was very handsome. To be honest, most of the time, she was aggravated with him no matter how she tried not to let it show.

As she walked down to the dining room, she had to admit that Joseph stirred something in her. Was this what the beginnings of love felt like? She wasn't sure.

"You look lovely as always, Olivia." He tipped his top hat and offered his arm.

With a smile, she tucked her hand into the crook of his arm. "Thank you." Hopefully, her cheeks weren't turning too pink. "I appreciate you escorting me today. I don't leave the restaurant much, and you know how protective Daniel is, especially after the horrible day in the alley. I don't even want to walk outside the building by myself."

He patted her hand. "Which is wise, considering how danger-ous things can be here. And there are not very many women as you well know, so you are quite a fascination. Maybe once we get more upstanding married men to move into the area with their wives and children, things will be different and hopefully safer. I know it will take time, but I'm already seeing a bit of difference since the alcalde was elected and we have a police chief."

They walked in a slow, steady pace down the street. Olivia turned her face toward him. "Do you think that families will move here? I mean, I hope they do—there's just so many men coming in seeking their fortunes in gold. It doesn't seem like much of a place to raise a family."

"You're correct. It's not. But I am encouraged that we need businesses to supply for all these people coming in. Restaurants, bath houses, laundries, and stores for supplies."

"Haven't you seen how many men have come just to throw up a shack to start these businesses and then because their items are in demand, they get greedy and drive the prices to outlandish numbers?"

"That is true. Nevertheless, look at your brother. He took the time and money to build a decent building. He serves excellent food. And he doesn't hike up his prices like the others. His business is thriving and overflowing. It's men like Daniel—who I know wants a family of his own one day—that I'm hoping we'll garner more of in the future."

She thought about it. "I hope you're correct. I was shocked to find out that there were so many men in this city and not even a school operating."

"All the students—and the teacher—took off hunting for gold as soon as word spread. Now there aren't any children who are around to be taught."

That was why the schoolhouse was being used as the police office now. Were the rumors factual, though? Were children being sold into slavery? Her heart sank as she thought about the little boy she'd tried to rescue. "Do you think that what your foreman heard is true?"

He sighed and took several steps before he responded. "I hope not with everything in me. But I'm afraid it could be. I've been praying that if it is, we will be able to find them and help."

"I'll pray that too." Heaviness filled her heart. *Lord, help us.* "I apologize for taking our conversation in such a disheartening direction."

He patted her hand again and gave it a tiny squeeze. "It's quite all right, Olivia. I love your heart for people."

The praise made her smile. "I just wish I could do something more to help."

"You are. You're praying, you're helping us with the Bible study, your idea of meals for the police captain and his men was brilliant. . ." He stopped walking and turned to face her. Their arms still intertwined, he was quite close. "And you stopped that man from killing the boy. That was one of the bravest things I've ever known anyone to do."

Staring into his brown eyes, she felt lost in the emotion she saw there. What was it? Whatever it was, it pulled her in, and she didn't want to stop it. "I don't think I'm very brave, but thank you."

"You're welcome." He licked his lips and took a deep breath. "You are a fascinating woman, Mrs. Olivia Brighton." With a smile, he turned forward again and led her down the street.

The compliment made her feel things she hadn't felt before. Deep down, she knew she'd begun to care deeply for Joseph; and if God was giving her a second chance at love—possibly even marriage and a family—it overwhelmed her with emotions and questions. She'd failed Him miserably the first time. Could she really do better? She shook her head. All the negative thoughts were things she needed to rid her mind of—that's one of the things she'd been working on after reading Faith's journal. She just wasn't sure how to accomplish it day in and day out.

"You look deep in thought. I hope I haven't offended you." Joseph's voice broke through her thoughts.

"No. You haven't offended me." How much should she tell him? She'd always been a blunt and honest person. Maybe it wouldn't hurt for Joseph to see who she really was as she took her time to get to know him as well. "My thoughts often take a negative turn, and it's something that I have felt challenged to work on. My family used to tease me about being skeptical and sarcastic. But with the joy and positive nature of my parents around me all the time, I didn't think anything of it until after they were gone. I found myself spiraling in a negative direction. That's not who I want to be."

"I don't see you as a negative person."

"I'm glad. But you're not inside my mind." A new boldness overcame her. It felt good to share with him. "When I first came here, I was determined that life would never be good again. It was all my fault for my husband's death. I didn't think I deserved a second chance, and so I just needed to do my best to serve God in this filthy city and adjust to the situation. I guess I'd settled for thinking I'd be miserable the rest of my days and that was my burden to bear."

His soft chuckle made her feel lighter. "I can't tell you how many times I have had the same thoughts."

"Really?" The thought of this man next to her—a man so full of life and determination to change the world for good—having negative thoughts was a bit of a shock.

"Oh, definitely. I know I don't measure up to God's standards, and sometimes I'm overwhelmed by the evil around me, wondering how someone like me could possibly bring about any change. I know that I don't deserve a second chance, or a third or a fourth for that matter, but then I'm reminded of Christ paying the price for my sin, and I'm encouraged to keep doing what I'm doing."

"So you don't think less of me for having doubts and negative thoughts?"

"Not at all. We're all sinners, Olivia. All of us. And we all struggle. But your brother told me when I first came to know Christ that part of our job as a body of believers is to encourage and exhort one another. We're all going to feel beaten down at some point, and we're all going to lose our confidence. It's our job to help each other through the muck and mire."

"That's a good way to look at it."

"Why do you think it's so difficult for us to grasp that?" He steered her around a large mud puddle.

She laughed. "Probably because we're stubborn. Prideful. Selfish."

As his laughter joined with hers, he patted her hand again, a gesture that became special to her—almost intimate. She wouldn't mind one bit if he just kept his hand over hers.

They walked down the street for several long moments without speaking. Wagon wheels sloshed and rumbled through the muddy street, while men shouted at one another over the din and chaos. It was nice to walk in companionable silence while the world bustled around them. It seemed very. . .normal. Olivia allowed herself to think forward for a brief moment. What would it be like to be married to this man?

She looked away as heat crept up her neck. It was too soon to be thinking such thoughts, as nice as they might be. No. She needed to keep her focus on God first and seek His direction. Joseph might not even think of her in that way. It was best to guard her heart and mind. But Daniel had encouraged her to get to know their friend better. If she had his approval, that was a good thing, right?

"Penny for your thoughts?" Joseph stopped them again.

She turned her face back to him and looked into his eyes. "I don't think they're worth quite that much."

"I do."

As their gazes collided, Olivia felt like the air around them was suddenly sweeter. Cooler. Refreshing. She felt a blush rush up her cheeks, and she looked down at the ground hoping her bonnet would hide the telltale pink hue.

"Forgive me. I've embarrassed you." Joseph's boots aimed forward again, and he gently pulled her along. "I just realized that I don't know where we're going on this errand of yours."

Looking up and along the street, she couldn't help but laugh. They'd walked a good distance, and she'd completely forgotten what she needed to do. "Now it's my turn to apologize. It completely slipped my mind." She stopped and let go of his arm while she reached into her reticule. Holding up a piece of paper with her right hand, she took hold of his arm again. "I have a list."

"Well, I say it's time we tackle that list so we can get you back to the restaurant before your brother sends out a search party for us." He winked at her.

"That's a splendid idea." She wouldn't mind if they were going to pick up manure—she'd treasure every moment she had to spend with Joseph Sawyer.

CHAPTER 22

September was upon them, and the changes in San Francisco were almost as many as the ships that anchored in the harbor each day. Joseph looked out to the wharf. Changes for good couldn't happen overnight, but steady progress was all that they needed. And so far, they'd made good progress.

What amazed him the most was George's felicitous manner with him at the council meetings lately. He didn't balk at suggestions near as much as he used to. As soon as he'd seen the petition that Olivia had worked on for so many weeks, he opened the floor for the council to discuss what they could do in addition to the police. What would it take to put fire safety measures in place? Instead of closing the door on such discussions, it seemed Banister was now in favor. Many times, he'd offered to go to his employer for extra funding. All the members had nothing but praise for the head of the council. At this point, Joseph didn't care. He'd just keep an eye on things and see if he could find out what George was really up to. Someday the gentleman was bound to slip up. Joseph's gut told him that his instincts were correct. He just had to wait.

As Joseph walked up Market Street, he thought about other changes that were happening. The first brick building in town was going up. Several other large buildings and even a few large homes were under construction. Businesses were booming, and the influx of people continued to grow.

It was amazing compared to where San Francisco was just a year ago. Thinking back to that time, he found himself grateful again for his friendship with Daniel. He owed his friend his life. And through Daniel, he now knew Olivia.

Just the thought of her made him smile. Winding his way through the streets, he passed one of the large homes being built. Perhaps it was time for him to start thinking of building a home, a home in which he could raise a family. Olivia's face came to mind again. Would she be willing to stay here? Even if she got over the fact that he owned a gold mine, he wasn't sure she wanted to stay. But her brother was here, and he knew how close they'd grown. Maybe it wasn't such a crazy thought after all.

Redirecting his steps to the land office, Joseph decided he'd just have to step out in faith. He had plenty of money—that wasn't an issue—so he could purchase a piece of land in the best area he could find.

***

After leaving the land office, excitement built in his gut. This would be a nice project to keep his focus positive when other things tempted to bring him down. Checking his pocket watch, he realized that he'd better get home and change if he had any chance of following George tonight.

Pushing the thoughts of Olivia and building a house to the back of his mind, Joseph dressed in rags and made himself look as dirty as possible. He hardly recognized himself when looking in the mirror. He appeared exactly the way he'd hoped.

Thirty minutes later, he waited down the block from the building he'd seen George enter and exit numerous times. Knowing there had to be more going on than what met the eye, he'd realized a week ago that this was simply going to take patience. He'd attempted to learn how to be invisible, but with so many others crowding the streets at all times, he hoped he at least blended in. No one seemed to pay him any mind, so prayerfully, his plan was working.

Time passed slowly on the nights he'd set out to spy on George Banister, but he'd learned a lot. Three buildings had thick drapes drawn, and no one was seen going in or out. Where every other place seemed to bustle with activity, those quiet buildings were the ones that he watched the most.

The hour had grown late when a familiar figure slipped into view. George. A fancy carriage pulled up behind Banister as he walked up the steps to the building. Joseph waited. Who was in the carriage? And why did George go in alone?

A few minutes later, George exited the building with his arm around two smaller figures. Children? Their heads were down as Banister helped them into the carriage.

As the carriage started to roll down the street, Joseph joined the many people in the street and followed it. When they reached the edge of town, he tried to stay in the trees as much as possible. The sky was dark, so hopefully he could stay hidden. It wasn't long before the carriage turned down a private drive. Someone had gone to great expense to pave the driveway with bricks. As he snuck up the hill, he was a bit shocked by the massiveness of the home that was built there. Was this George's anonymous employer?

A row of bushes lined the drive as it went up to the door and circled back around. Joseph hid behind them, hoping he would still be able to get a glimpse of the happenings and be able to listen in.

George exited the carriage and dragged the others out. With closer examination, Joseph noticed ropes bound the children's wrists. They were definitely children. One was crying.

"We'll have none of that." George slapped the child's cheek and grabbed the collars of both kids, dragging them up the stairs to the ornate door. Once they were inside, Joseph sat back on the ground and seethed. Now that he'd witnessed this, could he go to the police? Would they need more proof? Even though Joseph didn't have any details, the children were clearly tied up and abused.

Lord, what do I do?

Silence greeted him while his stomach churned. He thought through all the ramifications and could only come to one conclusion. No matter what it cost him, he had to get to the truth and save those children, Dewei's brothers, and whomever else he could. It wasn't just his gut or his instincts anymore. It was real. And it had been happening right in front of them all.

Four days later, Joseph was no closer to having any proof than he'd been the night he'd seen George with the children. Either they were getting more careful, or nothing had transpired in those days. He'd gone to the police captain—Malachi Fallon—who was mortified to hear what Joseph had witnessed but admitted he'd heard rumors as well. With so much corruption and crime running rampant for so long, he and his sergeants and deputies had their hands full day and night. What the captain needed was more information. . .and time. Two things that Joseph didn't feel he had.

As he walked to the restaurant, he prayed for God to give him wisdom. The weight on his shoulders didn't outweigh the heaviness on his soul.

Every day he'd talked with Olivia and Daniel, and they'd prayed over the situation, but they hadn't come to any solid conclusions about what they should do. Discouragement seemed to hang over all of them. *God, what are we doing wrong?*

No answers came from heaven, and Joseph realized that God

knew the suffering of the people better than he did. It would all have to be in God's timing, not Joseph Sawyer's.

How fitting that they were studying the story of Joseph from the Bible today in their gathering. Sold into slavery by his own brothers, Joseph was saved by God for a purpose and a plan for His people. It had taken years for things to come around full circle, but in God's timing, all things had worked together for good.

Perhaps Joseph Sawyer needed to be a bit more patient and rely on God's timing and not his own. The reminder was a good one. Now if only he could remember that every single day.

As he entered the restaurant, he put on a smile and took a deep breath. Even though they were battling against evil in their city, he wanted to do something special for Olivia to show her that he cared as more than just a friend. They'd seen each other almost every day for months. He felt like they understood each other pretty well. It was time. Joseph had Daniel's blessing, and that encouraged him to move forward with his plan.

He took a seat at their regular table and waited for Olivia to come by. As she poured him a cup of coffee, she gave him a smile. "You look like you have something up your sleeve today, Mr. Sawyer." Her teasing tone made him widen his grin in return.

"You just might be correct, Mrs. Brighton."

She tilted her head. "Do tell."

"Oh, but I thought I'd speak to you about it after Bible study." He knew the taunt would make her take the bait.

Placing one hand on her hip, she narrowed her eyes and pointed the coffee pot at him. "You're going to come in here like the cat that swallowed the canary and then force me to wait all this time? That's not fair—or very gentlemanly, I might add—and you know it." She raised her eyebrows as if she was daring him to argue with her.

"Well, when you put it *that* way. . ." He drew out his words and took his time lifting his coffee cup to his lips and taking a long, slow sip.

"You are insufferable, Mr. Sawyer." Turning on her heel, she gave him another scathing look over her shoulder.

"Wait!"

She turned back around. "Yes?"

"I've planned a picnic."

"Oh?" Her eyes began to sparkle.

"For you and me."

Her face beamed. "Really?"

He nodded. "But I was hoping for a better time to invite you."

"Now is just fine." She sat down in the chair across from him and set the coffee down.

Realizing her intent, Joseph tried not to chuckle to himself. Instead, he leaned across the table and looked into her eyes, hoping that the depth of his feelings for her could be conveyed. "Mrs. Brighton. Olivia. I'd like to invite you to attend a picnic with me in two days' time. Your brother has already consented to give you the day off."

"Will wonders never cease. How did you ever manage that?" She shook her head. "I'm teasing." It was her turn to pause.

Joseph raised his eyebrows at her this time. "Well?"

"Well, what?" Her expression was all innocence and sweetness.

"I would request an answer to my invitation."

She sighed and looked around the room then out the window. Straightening the tablecloth with one hand, she grabbed the coffee and stood back to her feet with a grin. "I'm sorry for teasing. It would be my honor to accept your invitation."

"I look forward to it with great anticipation."

"Your expression is quite telling, Joseph Sawyer. So you should know"—she glanced around and then back at him—"I'm looking forward to it too." Her smile radiated joy across the room. In a flurry of skirts and apron strings, she left him sitting at the table in awe of her.

The feelings that flooded him were more than just a silly crush or even simple admiration. He admired her a great deal and felt very attracted to her beauty, but it was so much more. He wanted to give her the world. He wanted to spend every moment with her, wanted to know her thoughts, hopes, and dreams. He wanted to feel her touch, hear her voice, and bask in the warmth of her smile.

"You look deep in thought." Daniel's voice cut into his reflection.

"That I am." Joseph took a sip of his coffee.

"Oh boy. This sounds serious."

"It is." He aimed a grin at his friend. There was no denying it: he was in love with Olivia.

CHAPTER 23

The day had dawned bright and beautiful. Fall was in the air. The trees were just beginning to turn, and the ground had dried out from the many days of rain. It would be the perfect day for a picnic.

Olivia went to her wardrobe to see what she could spruce up today to look nice for Joseph. Even though she'd gone back and forth in her mind about whether she should allow herself to fall in love and marry again, her heart had finally won out. She *wanted* to marry again. She *wanted* to fall in love. She *wanted* it to be Joseph. He was the epitome of the kind of man she always thought she'd marry. Good, generous, intelligent, caring. And he loved the Lord.

Scanning her few articles of clothing, she rested her eyes on the blue dress. It was her favorite because blue was her favorite color. But sadly, it was becoming quite worn. Holding it up to herself, she looked at it in the mirror. Was this good enough? Was *she* good enough?

Even though her heart had made up its mind, she still had plenty of doubt. The biggest consolation she had, though, was that she'd known Joseph for months now. It would be October before they knew it. They'd become friends, and they saw each other every day. Most of her doubts stemmed from her hasty decision to marry Hezekiah. But this was different, wasn't it? She'd married Hezekiah the day she met him. She couldn't even compare the two situations.

She definitely couldn't compare the two men. Both were

handsome, but where Hezekiah was a dreamer and had never worked more than a few days at anything, always seeking his fortune, Joseph had stuck with his profession even though it was something she disliked. But why did she dislike it so much? Because of how the love of gold had turned men into frenzied fortune seekers? Or because it was Hezekiah's last venture? The one he'd spent all their money on then died before he ever saw a speck of any gold or profit.

She plopped on her bed and mulled it over. No matter the reason, she needed to come to terms with the fact that Joseph owned a gold mine, and he *wasn't* anything like Hezekiah.

The question now was, had she changed? Could she actually be a decent wife and helpmeet? She hadn't done a very good job the first time. How could she be assured that it would be different? That *she* would be different?

Tap, tap, tap.

She stood and opened her bedroom door.

Daniel stood there holding a large box wrapped in brown paper and twine. "May I come in?"

She put her hands on her hips as he entered. Knowing the look on her face was puzzled. "Of course. But what is this about?"

He laid the box on the bed. "This"—with a smile and wave of his hand—"is for you."

She felt her eyes widen. "Really? Whatever for? It's not my birthday. . ."

Her brother's face was a bit apologetic as he rubbed his chin with his fingers. "I've neglected to thank you for all you've done, Livvy. And I've worked you entirely too hard. It struck me again when Joseph asked if you could have the day off. So this is my peace offering—my gift to rectify all these mistakes on my part."

Her heart swelled with love for him as she reached forward and hugged him. "You didn't have to do anything. I should be thanking you for all you've done for me."

"Nonsense. Now open your gift. You'll need it today."

His comment puzzled her, but she didn't hesitate to untie the twine and rip the paper off the box. As she lifted the lid, a tiny gasp escaped her throat. It was a new dress!

Lifting it out of the box, she touched the beautiful, deep blue fabric. "It's lovely."

"I thought it would bring out your eyes. Mr. Lundry said it was the new style—not that I know anything about that—and recommended a few other items." He pointed back to the box.

Olivia glanced around the dress she was holding and saw petticoats and even a new pair of boots. She looked at her brother, who obviously was trying not to feel uncomfortable as a tinge of pink crept up his neck. The dear man. He had no idea the sad shape of her petticoats, and so this was quite the gift. She went to him again and gave him a big hug. "Thank you. It's perfect."

"Good. I'm glad." He clapped his hands together and backed his way out of her room. "I'll leave you to get ready for your picnic."

"Thank you, Daniel. For everything."

After he'd left, she closed the door and went to work changing her clothes. How wonderful it would be to wear a new dress, and one that was her favorite color.

Thirty minutes later, Joseph escorted her to a carriage and helped her into it. Her heart hadn't stopped racing since he'd first looked at her. The appreciation she'd seen there meant more than all the words in the world. He'd brought her a bouquet of flowers that she put in a vase with water, and then he offered his arm. Was this what real courtship was like?

The driver took them out into the country. Under a large cork oak tree, two chairs sat atop a lovely blue-and-white-checkered tablecloth.

Joseph extended his hand and escorted her out of the carriage.

"This is beautiful."

"I'm glad you like it. I was hoping for a perfect day, and I wanted you to be comfortable."

They settled onto the chairs, and Joseph moved his closer to hers and served her—such gallant and humble behavior. It made Olivia feel things she'd never really felt before. A memory washed over her. She'd been such a little girl at the time, but their father had been talking to Daniel about how to treat a lady. She might have been five or six at the most, so her brother had to have been a young man of fifteen or sixteen.

"A true gentleman takes on the servant role, Son. Just like Jesus did. God has given us the duty to be heads of the household, yes, but to be the head, we must humble ourselves. Just like Jesus—the King of kings and Lord of lords—who humbled Himself enough to wash the feet of His disciples. To be a man of God, you must remember to love as Christ loved the church—which is sacrificially."

The fact that she remembered the conversation was fascinating to her, because at the time, she hadn't understood it all. And it had been meant for her brother. But maybe Daddy had wanted her present as well so she would learn how to recognize a godly man.

"You look deep in thought." Joseph interrupted her memory.

She blinked and shook her head. "My apologies. Your actions just sparked a memory long forgotten. Or at least one I haven't thought of in a long time."

"I hope it was a good one." He filled her plate with cheese, ham slices, and crusty bread.

"It was." Looking into his eyes, she felt comfort. Peace. Protection. Things she'd never felt with Hezekiah. Not that he hadn't tried. And he had rescued her out of debt, which was a noble thing. Good grief. It was time she stopped comparing the two. She needed to look forward, not into the past.

She took the plate from him and thanked him. As they feasted on their luncheon, they chatted about everything from the weather to the price of a hairbrush. Conversation came easy, and they laughed about silly things they'd done as children and sobered when they talked about the needs of their city.

Her heart felt full and happy. This is what she'd imagined a relationship between a man and a woman should be: sharing every moment of life from the mundane to the serious, enjoying each other's company and opinions, participating in life together.

He poured her another glass of lemonade, and she sipped it slowly. The tanginess on her tongue was refreshing and cool.

"I hope this isn't too forward of me, Olivia, but I've brought you a gift. Or maybe two."

She had no idea what the protocol for gifts between unmarried people was, but she loved that he was so thoughtful. "You didn't have to get me anything. The flowers were gift enough." She gestured to everything around her. "And then all of this."

"But I wanted to." He gave her a shy smile as he handed her two boxes.

Lifting the first box, Olivia wondered what it could be. It was light, but the box was large. Opening it up, she covered her mouth with her right hand. Underneath the delicate paper was the exquisite blue velvet bonnet that she'd seen in the mercantile that day. "Oh, Joseph. It's. . .beautiful." She stumbled around for words. "But it was so costly!" Looking up into his eyes again, she got lost in the depths.

"I want you to have it. It will go beautifully with your dress." He leaned forward and reached one finger up to her cheek. "And it matches your eyes." Withdrawing his hand, he sat back in his chair.

She sat stunned for a moment, her cheek still feeling his gentle touch. Forcing her tongue to work, she tried to lighten the moment so she could catch her breath. "I had no idea it was a hat because of the box."

"That's because I asked Mr. Lundry to wrap it so you wouldn't know. I have the hat box back in the carriage if you need it."

"Thank you." She giggled. Here she was talking about boxes. "I will treasure this." Taking off her plain bonnet, she put on the new one.

"It looks beautiful on you." Joseph grinned. "Now, open the second one."

In the past few minutes, she'd completely forgotten about the other box in her lap. "Oh!" She opened the box and lifted the paper. It revealed a delicate, soft shawl. Almost the color of gold itself. "Oh, Joseph. It's so lovely." She lifted it up and felt the fabric between her fingers. "I've never felt anything so luxurious." Looking back up at him, she didn't know what to say. "I. . .I've never had gifts like these. Never."

He took the shawl from her hands. "May I?"

Lost in his gaze, she nodded.

Joseph stood and wrapped the shawl around her shoulders, his fingers brushing her arms. "In the gold territory of California, you outshine it all, Mrs. Olivia Brighton." He lifted her to her feet.

Staring into his eyes, she tried to come up with something to say, but words flitted away. Butterflies danced in her stomach, while her limbs tingled with delight at his closeness.

"May I?" The huskiness of his voice made her heart skip.

She gave him a slight nod, not entirely sure that she understood what he was asking, but she hoped it—

"Olivia." He whispered her name and put his arms around her waist. Then time stood still as he captured her lips with his own.

Never in all her years had she felt such fire inside of her and a longing for more.

Joseph pulled back and put his forehead to hers. "I've been wanting to do that for a while now."

Heat filled her face. "I'm glad you did."

He stepped back a pace and took her hand in his. "I must be honest with you, Olivia. I'd like nothing more than to kiss you again, but I shall refer to the manners of a gentleman and ask you to accompany me on a walk instead. Shall we?"

Thankful for his good judgment, Olivia smiled. "I'd love to."

As he led her down the hill, she couldn't keep the smile from her face. She wanted him to kiss her again. And soon.

CHAPTER 24

The afternoon had been so absolutely perfect, Olivia felt like she was floating. It didn't even matter that her new boots needed breaking in and her feet were sore. It didn't matter that she needed to do a million things tomorrow. It didn't even matter that horrible things were going on in their city. Tonight she just wanted to revel in the feeling of. . .love. Yes, she was in love. She put a finger to her lips. When Joseph had kissed her, she thought she was on her way to heaven.

Sitting on the settee in their parlor, she unhooked her new boots, and memories of the day washed over her. She'd felt a little guilty at first because she'd never found much pleasure in marital intimacy with Hezekiah. She didn't even feel much excitement when he kissed her, they'd gotten married so fast. But she figured that would come with time.

Now she knew it was *very* different than what she'd imagined. Something had been ignited within her, and it made her heart feel like it might burst. Now that she had a taste of love, she longed to get married again. Everything seemed so much brighter now. She couldn't wait to see Joseph again. And to be honest, she couldn't wait until he kissed her again, a thought that followed her around and made her blush.

With a sigh, she went to her room to put away her new bonnet, shawl, and boots and to change out of her new dress. Joseph had complimented her several times, and it made her feel like she was a queen.

Pulling her nightdress over her head, she decided to snuggle in her bed with her mother's journal. It would be a couple of hours before Daniel was done in the restaurant. That would give her a lot of time to soak in her mother's words. She'd only had the chance to read a few entries before now, and she longed for more. Instead of hurting her heart—which she had expected because it would remind her of the loss of Mama—the journal had helped to bring her healing. It made her feel like she'd gotten to know her mother just a little better, and she felt connected to her in a way she hadn't before.

She opened the leather-bound book and picked up at her bookmark.

March 28, 1829

Our beautiful baby girl was born yesterday. God has so greatly blessed us. For so many years, I thought I wouldn't be able to have more children, and then we were given a precious daughter. I spent most of yesterday sleeping (as the birth wore me out) and, when I was awake, praying over this new gift from God. We don't live in easy times, and life out here is especially hard. There aren't many white people and certainly no other children. The Mexicans are good people but shy away from us still after all these years. But Daniel has already claimed protection over his baby sister. He loves to hold her and talk to her. I pray that they have a close relationship.

Horatio is out visiting some of the sick in the village today. His face when he'd discovered I'd delivered a girl was one of pure joy. He looked so out of place—his big hulking frame holding our tiny little baby—but it also looked so right. I love that man so much. I pray every day for each of our children's future spouses. That they would know true love like their father and me. And that they would wish to serve the Lord with all their hearts.

I'm still quite weary and need to feed our little one. Prayerfully, tomorrow we will settle on a name for our little princess.

Olivia set the book down in her lap. Her parents had always shown her love—they'd been so very dear to her—but reading Mama's words that were all about *her* at the beginning of life. . .it made her want to cry.

"Oh, Mama. I miss you." She closed her eyes and talked to the room. "I wish you were here to talk to about so many things. I wish you could be here to see me get married and to have children. You would have made the best grandmother." The thought made Olivia smile. "But I'm sure Daniel will be a wonderful uncle someday."

She wished she could thank her mother for saving the precious treasures in the box. Especially the journals. Nothing could ever replace such prized documents. She'd learned so much about herself and her relationship with God while she'd read the testimonies on the pages.

Closing the book, she sat up on the edge of the bed and threw the covers off. She couldn't allow the legacy to die. She should go to the mercantile tomorrow and purchase her own journal and start recording her thoughts about what she was learning, just like Mary Elizabeth and Faith. She could write about all that she'd already been through and how she'd overcome her negativity and fear. As the days went on, she could write about her own family and how God saw them through the tough times.

Impassioned with her new challenge, thoughts raced through her mind. Why should she wait? She went to the desk and pulled out a piece of paper. Dipping her quill into the inkwell, she wanted to get all her thoughts and feelings from the day recorded so one day future generations could read about Olivia Livingston Brighton and Joseph Sawyer.

The man sat at his desk and watched Banister enter the room. He steepled his fingers and waited for George to approach.

"Good evening, sir."

"And to you, Banister."

"You sent for me?"

"Indeed." He stood. "I think that very soon it will be time for me to reveal myself as the great benefactor of the city."

Banister raised an eyebrow.

"I've commissioned two grand hotels to be built and also a very stately brick building that I will eventually donate to be used as the city hall. Let's keep my identity a secret for right now, but we can get the word out about how I (the anonymous patron) want to see the very best for our city and think it's only reasonable to help establish good and decent businesses all the while supporting the needs of our government. I'll even pay for substantial ads to be placed in the large newspapers across the country, inviting good and decent folk to come to San Francisco and build businesses. What if we were to offer. . . let's say fifty dollars to each businessman to come here and start up a legitimate business that I approve? We need banks, we need laundries, we need hotels, restaurants, lumberyards, mills, dairies, grocers, you name it."

"That's extremely generous, sir." Banister nodded. "And would make you even more of a mystery and fascination for the people. Everyone will want to know who the benefactor is. They'll all worship this man before they even know who he is." A slow smile spread across his face. "It's a genius plan."

"And let's not forget it will show my *heart* for making this city great. All the while, we have three other buildings being built to help accommodate our *other* businesses. No one will be the wiser."

"Very good, sir."

"Then, when the time is right, I'll show myself—humbly of course—and perhaps even become a senator once California gains her statehood. I can be beloved in the people's eyes. Doing good at every turn. There will be no need for anyone to suspect anything else."

Joseph sat back in the carriage and thought back on the day. He didn't want to wait any longer. Why couldn't he just declare himself to Olivia? He shook his head and chuckled to himself. Probably because it would scare her away. It had taken months for them to get to this place. And just because he knew that he wanted to spend the rest of his life with this woman didn't mean that she felt the same way. Yet.

That's why they always said that patience was a virtue. Whoever *they* were. He'd heard it quoted hundreds of times. Maybe he should pray for it, because patience was not his strong suit.

The carriage rocked over the rough road, but Joseph didn't mind. The driver was going to drop him off at home, where he planned to write Olivia a letter. Maybe over time, he could woo her with not only his presence but with his words. Daniel was already quite supportive of the relationship, and Joseph hoped that by this time next year he could be married. When his new house was finished, he'd show it to her and get her input on furniture and decorations. He wanted her involved in every area of his life. It was so exciting to be in love!

The carriage rolled to a stop and he hopped out. "Thanks, James."

The driver waved and turned the carriage back into town. Pretty soon Joseph needed to purchase one of his own because he hoped to be able to take Olivia out more often.

He took the steps two at a time up to his door, but then his heart sank as he went to put the key into the lock. Another note was tacked to the door. Joseph closed his eyes as he tore it down. Perhaps it wasn't what he feared. But as he opened the paper, his heart sank:

Told you to watch your back.

You didn't listen.

Now you have a decision to make.

Or we'll go after the pretty little waitress.

Wadding up the paper in his hands, Joseph wanted to hit something. Who was threatening him? George? His employer? Someone else?

There was no question that he'd messed up somewhere. And now he'd put Olivia at risk. What was he supposed to do? Put her in danger by continuing to court her? Or stay away and risk hurting her and their tenuous relationship? His gut told him that this could very well be the end of his dreams. Normally, a man who didn't scare, Joseph didn't like idle threats. But this time was different. This time they'd involved Olivia.

He unlocked his door and stormed in. One thing was certain, he needed to change his disguise. Perhaps even rent a room somewhere else so that when he was done watching the happenings on Pacific Street, he could return there.

As he mulled over all his options, Joseph couldn't bear the thought of not spending time with Olivia anymore. But he also didn't want her in danger because of him. Then again, if he wasn't around her, he couldn't protect her. Maybe he needed to let Daniel know so that they could figure out a plan.

And the police. Joseph should bring the note to the police captain.

Nodding, he hoped he was making the correct decision.

Lord, I need Your wisdom and guidance because I have no idea what to do. I love Olivia, and I don't want her hurt. But I also know more is at stake. We don't know how many lives are in danger. Help us to figure this out. In Jesus' name I pray, amen.

CHAPTER 25

After he'd sent a note to Daniel, Joseph went to the barn behind the restaurant and waited for his friend. It didn't take long for Daniel to appear, and Joseph told him everything about the notes and his concern for Olivia.

"Has anything else happened other than the notes?" His friend crossed his arms over his chest and paced the floor.

"No."

"So no action has been taken on them?"

"No. Not yet."

"Do you have any idea who would write them?"

"It's not George, even though he would be my first guess. He's never seen me when I've been following him. And I know George's handwriting from the city council meetings." He pointed to the wrinkled paper in his hand. "This isn't it, but that doesn't mean that it isn't someone who's working for him. Like that big man who basically accused me of snooping that night in the alley." He sat on a bale of hay. "Should we tell Olivia?"

Daniel shook his head. "I'm not the best person to be giving advice, because she's my sister and my first instinct is to lock her up so she can't be hurt. We both know that I can't do that. I think our best bet for right now is to continue as normal, but one of us should try to always have an eye on Olivia. She already never leaves the building without one of us and is well aware of the dangers of San Francisco. I don't think it would change what she'd be doing anyway. The only difference I can think of is in the dining room. I don't often keep track of her in there when it's so busy. If you don't mind spending more time here during meal times, that might help us protect her."

"I can do that. I want to spend more time with her anyway." Joseph nodded. "And in the meantime, I've already decided to rent a room somewhere else. I'll change my disguise and be more careful. I'm going to take the notes to Captain Fallon and see what we can do. But the man's hands are probably too tied up with everything else he has to deal with. Crime is rampant across the city, as you well know."

Daniel let out a long sigh. "I'm sorry that all this is happening. I wish we could just snap our fingers and clean up the mess in this town, but we can't. And I know you'll do your best to protect Olivia. I will too. But we also know there are a lot of other lives at stake." He ran a hand through his hair. "This scares me, though. It makes me worry for my sister and for you."

"But God is bigger than all this. We know that. I have to keep telling myself that. Otherwise, I'd be on the next ship out of here. I just couldn't bear for anything to happen to Olivia."

"I know you care for her, Joseph. That makes me happy, and it also helps me feel a bit safer, because at least two of us are working to keep her safe."

"I do care for her. A lot. In fact. . .I love her."

Daniel's eyes widened. Then he walked over and slapped Joseph on the back. "That makes me *very* happy. Now don't let me down. And don't let anything happen to my sister. I'm relying on you."

Olivia walked toward a table where an absolutely stunning woman sat. Her pink dress was made from shiny satin and was covered in ruffles of lace and other frills that Olivia had never seen. The matching hat was a masterpiece all its own.

Feeling a bit frumpy in her worn day dress and apron, Olivia smoothed the skirt and headed for the table to take the woman's order. It had been ages since she'd been around another woman.

Charlie thrust a hand toward her as she passed. When she stopped, he motioned her close. "Don't you know who she is?" His whispered words were raspy and harsh.

Olivia frowned. "No. Should I?"

"She's a madam! You can't go near her. She shouldn't even be in here."

Olivia felt her eyebrows rise at the revelation, but Charlie could be wrong, couldn't he? "She's a customer, and I don't know anything about her occupation. I think I should give her the benefit of the doubt, don't you?"

Charlie crossed his arms over his chest. "No, I don't."

"How do you know who or what she does anyway?"

He sputtered for a moment and then narrowed his eyes. "Everybody knows who she is. I was just trying to warn ya. I wouldn't want yer reputation sullied."

She softened her expression and gave him a smile. "I appreciate you looking out for me, Charlie, but I don't think it's a problem. We don't judge our customers." She patted his arm and walked away.

"Maybe you should." His muttered words followed her.

While she'd never had to deal with anyone of that profession before, this wasn't exactly a situation that she'd ever discussed with Daniel. What would he think about this? He had gone to check on the restaurant that was under construction, and she wished he would hurry back. Not that she was worried about handling the situation, but she couldn't stand to think that she might bring embarrassment to him by not doing it correctly. Would they lose customers if they served this woman? Of course, the rules of society didn't matter much in San Francisco. People did pretty much as they pleased.

Olivia shot a prayer heavenward. It didn't matter what people thought. She was supposed to love her neighbor as herself. Jesus commanded it. The best thing she could do right now was treat this woman with respect and show her God's love. With a nod to bolster herself, she walked straight up to the table and pasted on a smile. "Good morning. What can I get you today? Our special is roast beef."

The masterpiece of a hat lifted, and Olivia noticed red-rimmed eyes. Her heart ached for this woman—whoever she was.

"I'll take the special. And some coffee, please." She lowered her head back down.

"Of course. I'll be right back." All the way to the kitchen, she debated what she should do. The woman was obviously troubled. And if Charlie was correct and the woman was. . .well. . .an actual madam, then what could Olivia possibly do to help her? She knew nothing of that world.

When she had the woman's plate in hand, she grabbed a coffee pot and went back to serve her. "Here we are." She placed the food in front of the guest and poured a cup of coffee. As she stood there, she searched for words to say. "I'm Olivia," she blurted out.

Those red-rimmed eyes looked up at her. A slight smile lifted the woman's lips. "I'm Julia."

"It's nice to meet you, Julia. Can I get you anything else? Perhaps a piece of pie?"

Julia blinked several times. "I'm fine for now. But thank you."

"Are you sure? We make the best pies in the city." For some reason, she felt she couldn't leave just yet. But how did she keep the woman talking?

"I've heard that." Julia looked down to her plate and then back up. "Apple pie would be lovely. Thank you."

Not knowing what else to do, Olivia went back to the kitchen to fetch the pie. Plenty of other tables needed her attention, but she felt such a prodding to speak to Julia, and she had no idea why. Grabbing a plate of apple pie, she headed back toward the dining room. *Lord, help me, because I don't know what I'm doing, but I definitely feel You're nudging me.*

She delivered the pie and smiled at the woman. "Your dress is beautiful."

"Thank you." It was almost a genuine smile.

"Did it come from a store here?"

"No." Julia looked down again. "It's from New York."

"Well, it's lovely and it looks wonderful on you." Could this conversation be any more awkward? Olivia sighed. *What am I supposed to do, Lord?* No answer came. "Let me know if you need anything else." At least she'd tried. She turned to go.

"Olivia?"

She looked back. "Yes?"

"Why are you being so nice to me?"

The question completely took her by surprise. "Well. . .I believe God tells us to love everyone."

"But surely you must know who I am? What I do?" She cast a glance around the room. "Everyone else in here seems to know, and they've all given me quite the stares as we've been talking. It's almost as if they're trying to protect you from me. They don't want you tainted by merely talking to me." The edge in her voice on the last words made Olivia want to throw her arms around the woman and hug her. So much bitterness and pain.

"I don't care about what you do, because God loves you no matter what, and I'm going to do the same." Olivia took a chance and sat down in the chair across from the gorgeous Julia. "You're not a disease. I don't scare away that easily."

Julia let out a half laugh. "I'm glad. I'm sorry to be so prickly, but I don't know what I'm doing. I just came back to the city after traveling for. . ." She let the sentence hang. "It doesn't matter. What matters is that I heard you had a Bible study here."

"We do." Olivia perked up at that. "We'd love to have you join us. We meet every day after lunch."

"You'd allow me to come?" The shock on Julia's face was astonishing. Had people really treated her that horribly? "You mean, you wouldn't be ashamed to have me here?"

"No." She could say that with all sincerity. If this woman wanted to know more about the Bible, that was exactly what they'd set out to do. Teach the Bible. "Not one bit."

"Are you sure the men won't mind?"

"No, they won't mind. I'm sure of it."

"Can I come today?"

"Of course." Olivia smiled. "Why don't you stay until then? You can take your time eating lunch, and I'll come over and check on you as often as I can."

"I'd like that."

"Good. Well, I better get back to it." Olivia stood and walked away.

Over the next hour, she'd dashed around faster than she ever had not only so she could check on Julia, but because everyone in the restaurant seemed to be curious about why they were serving a lady such as she in Livingston's.

After fumbling around with explanations at the first few tables and becoming quite aggravated with the attitudes of some of the men, she resorted to quoting scripture to them. And it wasn't a complimentary verse either. It made them all hush up quite rapidly.

Charlie was still hanging around, sitting at his table with his arms crossed. She filled his coffee cup again and gave him a smile. "What has you so brooding, Charlie?"

"I don't like it, that's all."

"What don't you like?"

"That woman. She shouldn't be in here."

"And *you* should?"

"Of course." The look he gave her showed he was offended she'd even ask it.

So she decided to tell him the same thing she'd told the others and hoped he would still come back. "You know, Charlie, the Bible has some great advice on this. 'He that is without sin among you, let him first cast a stone at her.'" She watched his face.

He softened a moment. "I still don't like it, but I respect your opinion." He stood and nodded at her then left.

Olivia glanced over at Julia—the woman had been watching. She hadn't heard that, had she?

"Livvy." Daniel's voice made her turn around.

Relief washed over her. "I'm so glad you're back. I need to talk to you right away."

He smiled. "If it's about the fact that you've been serving and talking to a local madam at lunch today, don't worry. I've already heard all about it."

Chapter 26

After Bible study, Olivia sat at the table with Julia while Daniel and Joseph took a few of the younger men off to pray in the corner. She'd shared a Bible with the woman and now watched as Julia seemed glued to the page.

"That verse that you quoted to the men. Did Jesus really say that?"

It made Olivia smile. "He certainly did. Let me find that passage for you." As she turned the pages to John 8, she prayed for the right words. "Here it is."

Julia read the chapter and looked up at Olivia with a slight grin on her face. "You would stand up for me like that?"

"It's what Jesus did."

The beautiful woman leaned back in the chair. "You sound like the missionary I met."

"Is that why you came today?"

Julia nodded. "I told you I just came back from traveling—which is true. On the ship on the way back, I met a man who was a missionary. He was going to South America, and he sought me out every day even though he found out what I was. He said he didn't care, and he couldn't leave until he'd told me about Jesus."

The missionary sounded like someone Olivia would like to know. It made her smile. "And did he?"

Julia laughed. "Did he ever. He talked to me about Jesus for the next two weeks. Most of the time, I tried to ignore him, but after a while—when everyone else on the ship was shunning me—his words started to sink in. I even prayed with him and asked Jesus to take over my life."

"Julia, that's wonderful!"

"You can imagine what this means for me, though. My business. All my girls. I talked to him at length about what I should do, but it's a lot more complicated than just stopping. Does that make sense?"

"It does, I think. It's because you feel responsible for your. . . employees."

"Yes, I do. So James—the missionary I told you about—he told me to find a church or small group of people that studied the Bible. He made me promise that I would do it the first day I was back so that I wouldn't get sucked back into my old lifestyle." Julia wrapped her arms around her middle. "But I tell you, I don't know if I can do it. I *want* to change and turn my life around, but you don't understand how difficult this will be. If I hadn't made myself walk to the church this morning—all because I'd made James a promise—I wouldn't have seen the sign posted about the study here every day. And then when I was walking here, I thought of at least a hundred different excuses why I should turn around and quit. Then once I was here, I was pretty sure that you all would get rid of me as quick as you could. Your customers definitely didn't appreciate my being here."

Olivia smiled at her new friend and leaned forward to pat Julia's knee. "But you're here. And we want you to be here."

"Yes, we do." Joseph walked up beside the table and laid a hand on Olivia's shoulder. "It's amazing what God can do in our life when we give it over to Him."

Julia blinked at the tears forming in her eyes. "I still can't believe you all are being so kind to me."

"We want to be your friends." Olivia felt tears sting her own eyes.

"And we want to help you in whatever way we can." Her brother had joined them and sat in the chair next to Julia. "So let's make a plan. What do you need to do to take care of your employees and let go of your former life?"

<hr>

Three weeks had passed, and nothing had changed, at least not where the slave trade was concerned. Joseph was beside himself. Oh, he loved spending time with Olivia, but she'd noticed that he and her brother had been hovering. A lot. He'd told her that he just wanted to be with her as much as possible while he had the time. She'd smiled and kissed him on the cheek, but it didn't stop the churning in his gut.

He regretted not telling her the truth, but he didn't want her to worry too. Besides, she already had to be on guard all the time in San Francisco, especially now that she'd helped Julia basically dissolve the biggest brothel in town. Word had spread like wildfire, and several of the customers made their displeasure known to her. It hadn't stopped some of the girls from starting up a new one, but at least they'd helped several of the ladies travel back to their families or start over with a new, respectable business of their own.

If only all of this were over. If they could catch the ringleaders, the people being held could be saved, and he and Olivia could go on and be happy.

Patience.

That word kept pummeling him.

As he sat in the restaurant and watched Olivia navigate her way between tables, carrying multiple dishes, he tried to get his mind off the threats.

Daniel sat down in the chair next to him. "Any word?"

"Nope. Nothing. But I am meeting with Captain Fallon today. He sent me a message this morning."

"Maybe it's good news." Daniel stood up. "This place is growing so fast, we can't keep up. I can't imagine how Alcalde Geary is doing, not to mention the police. Look, I have to run, but let me know what the captain says." His friend patted him on the back and headed toward the kitchen.

Joseph pulled out his watch. It was about time for him to head to the police office on Portsmouth Square. Scooting his chair back, he stood and looked around for Olivia. She was headed in his direction and smiled.

He loved looking into her blue eyes. When he was close enough, he took her hand for a brief moment and squeezed it. "I have a meeting with Captain Fallon. I'll be back for dinner."

She gave him a nod, her smile making his heart do unusual things. "I'll be praying for you."

He lowered his voice. "I'd like nothing more than to kiss you right now, but I don't think we want the spectators."

She covered a light laugh and then lifted her chin. "Well then, I guess I shall just look forward to the next time we have the opportunity."

He winked at her.

She turned and went back to work.

Joseph breathed in deeply. What he wouldn't give to be married to that wonderful woman already. Shaking his head, he knew he'd better get his mind focused, and he left Livingston's Restaurant.

The ride to the police office was brief. Joseph dismounted and tied his horse at the hitching post. Maybe today they'd finally make progress. He swung open the door and headed for Captain Fallon. "You sent me a message?"

"I did." Fallon grabbed his arm and pulled him over into a corner. He looked around the room and spoke in a hushed tone. "I've found a way to get the proof that we need, but I need a man for the job. . . ."

The captain grimaced. "I need *you* to do it."

Joseph let the weight of it sink in. It only took him a second to think it through. "I've already been doing what I can—I'm glad to help with anything you need."

"Well, it'll mean leaving immediately. You'll have to change your appearance and go by a different name. I've got a friend down at the docks who can get you a job. He says the witnesses and proof are there. But there are tons of men looking for work, so it'll look suspicious if he doesn't fill it right away." The captain looked at his pocket watch. "You've only got about an hour. You can't let anyone know what you're doing or where you're going. It's the only way we'll keep this a secret. Son, I know it's a lot to ask, but I need someone to get inside and get the proof we need. Everything needs to look normal. Tell your foreman that you're on a business trip or something."

A million different thoughts exploded in his mind, but the one first and foremost was Olivia. What would she think? How could he possibly leave without saying goodbye? At the same time, he knew he had to do this. It was the only way.

He nodded at the captain. "I'll get it done. Just tell me where to go."

The police captain gripped his hand and shook it. "Thank you." He whispered the man's name in his ear, and Joseph ran outside, got on his horse, and raced home.

With so little time, his mind went through all the scenarios. How could he accomplish all this? When he made it home, Dewei was on his front porch. Joseph sent a prayer heavenward. He needed an ally. But how could he tell him without actually *telling* him?

He nodded at his foreman as he hurried inside. Dewei followed him silently.

Joseph turned on his heel. "I need your help."

Dewei nodded. "Anything."

"Will you help me shave off my hair?"

The man's eyebrows rose, but he nodded.

As Joseph looked through all the items he'd purchased for disguise, he landed on a couple things he hadn't worn yet, things that looked like someone at the dock would wear. He found a round knit cap that reminded him of what he'd seen sailors wear. He threw a few items in an old potato sack and then sat down so Dewei could shave his head. What else could he do to change his appearance?

"You grow beard and mustache." Dewei was nodding as he shaved Joseph's head.

How the man knew what he was thinking, Joseph would never understand, but he appreciated the man's astuteness. He looked at himself in the mirror and realized it wouldn't be too hard for him to do that. It would take a few days to fill in, but he always looked scruffy by the end of the day anyway. He'd just have to keep his head shaved.

"How's the mine?"

"Very good. Came here to inform of new vein. Lots of gold. Very good. Will need to build new tunnel."

Exactly what he needed. He could have Dewei go to the restaurant and tell Daniel and Olivia about the mine's new prosperous find and that Joseph was needed there as the new tunnel was built and work increased. Then he could ask his man to help spread the word so people would understand Joseph Sawyer's disappearance. It would hurt him in the long run because very few people knew that he owned a mine, but it would be his cover for now. And he needed that more than anonymity. He could deal with the fallout later. Now he just needed to write a note to Daniel for Dewei to deliver. He couldn't give details, but perhaps he could at least give a hint.

Dewei finished with the shaving, and Joseph turned to him. "Thank you, my friend. I can't tell you what I'm doing, but I need your help. First, you'll need to go tell Mr. Livingston and Mrs. Brighton about the mine." As he filled in the details, Dewei nodded and responded with his customary "Very good."

"I'm going to write a note for you to deliver to Mr. Livingston when Mrs. Brighton goes back to work so she doesn't see."

His man nodded.

"Then I'm going to need you to hire more men. Not to work the mine at this time; we'll deal with that later. But for security, because once you tell people around town, there are bound to be some problems. Can you handle that?"

Another nod. The man lifted his chin. "You go help family. . . brothers?"

Joseph wiped a hand down his face. "Yes. But you cannot say a word to anyone. I can't tell you where I'm going."

"Very good." Dewei bowed. "I do everything you say."

"Are you sure you understand everything?"

His loyal foreman repeated everything in precise detail.

Joseph gripped the shoulders of the man who'd worked for him tirelessly. "Thank you. I know I can trust you to take care of things." He ran over to his desk and penned a note for Daniel:

Our project has come to fruition. I will be busy with this new job. Please pray that we find all the treasure that we can. The wharf is beautiful this time of year.

Having no idea if Daniel would pick up on his clues, Joseph didn't have time to rethink the matter. He folded the missive, poured on the wax, and sealed it. Handing it to Dewei, he sighed. "Please get my horse from the police office at Portsmouth Square later today. I'll have to leave him there."

With that, Joseph left out the front door.

Olivia stood up from the table and stretched. Today for Bible study it had just been she, Julia, and Daniel, but it had been good. She'd missed Joseph's presence, though. All her brother had told her was that he'd had a meeting with Captain Fallon. As she picked up her Bible, a Chinese man walked up to her and bowed. The man's appearance was immaculate. Black hair with silver shining through especially at his temples. Not tall or broad in stature, but his eyes held wisdom. Could this be Dewei, Joseph's trusted foreman?

"Dewei." Daniel walked back over to them. "It's good to see you again."

"Mr. Livingston." The man bowed again. "Mr. Sawyer sent me with news."

"If you all will excuse me." Julia squeezed Olivia's hand. "I need to get to the bank."

"Will you be back for dinner?" Olivia gave her friend a smile.

"Of course." Julia waved and left the dining room.

"Would you like to have a seat? A cup of tea?" Daniel offered to Dewei and gestured to the table.

"No. But very good, sir." Dewei stood with his hands clasped in front of him. "Mr. Sawyer's mine very prosperous. Very good. New gold found. Will take very long time to build new tunnel."

"I don't understand." Olivia furrowed her brow.

"He be busy. Very busy for long time. He wanted me to let you know so you do not worry."

"You mean he won't be coming around for a while?" Daniel leaned back and crossed his arms over his chest.

Dewei nodded. "Very good. Yes."

Olivia didn't understand why this man was telling them these things. Why couldn't Joseph? Didn't he have plenty of workers to handle all this? Wouldn't he want to share this exciting news at least with *her*?

Daniel's brow furrowed. "Are you telling us that Joseph sent you to tell us that we won't see him for a while? Not at all?"

"Very good." The small man nodded again. "Mr. Sawyer very busy."

Olivia turned her back and walked toward one of the windows. Something didn't set right with her, and frankly, it hurt that Joseph didn't bring them the news himself. What did it mean that they wouldn't see him for a while? Couldn't he work a few days at the mine and come back every once in a while? Why did he have to stay there? As she turned back around to voice her questions, she noticed Daniel nod and put something in his pocket. Had Dewei given him some other clue?

"Thank you for coming." Daniel bowed and then Dewei bowed.

The man quickly left the dining room.

Her brother gave her a smile that didn't quite reach his eyes and shrugged. "Well, I guess we'll see Joseph soon." He walked away, and Olivia could only stare after him—all her questions left unspoken.

What wasn't Daniel telling her?

CHAPTER 27

The floor underneath her boots creaked and echoed as Olivia paced back and forth in their parlor. For weeks, she hadn't seen Joseph or heard a word from him. It was already December. It should be a time of celebrating Christ's birth. A time for church, carols, and baking goodies for Christmas treats. But no. The longer Joseph was gone, the more her worry grew.

It didn't help that Daniel had been tight-lipped on the subject. He'd continually tried to convince her that sometimes business had to take the forefront, especially when it was as crucial as this was. Whatever that meant. What did her brother even know about gold mining?

She rubbed her forehead as she made another pass on the floor. Her biggest problem was that she'd really come to care for Joseph Sawyer. But as each day went by, she began to increasingly doubt his care for her. Then that ugly negativity and anger would rear its head, and she'd think that he was just like all the other gold diggers. He might have put on a good facade for a while, but as soon as his gold called, he answered. She let out a huff. Maybe this was for the best. If the man was only caught up in making money then he wasn't the man for her. Maybe she should put all thoughts of Joseph Sawyer out of her mind.

Which should be easy to do. Daniel's other restaurant was finished. As of tomorrow, she was officially the manager of Livingston's

Restaurant. She'd have plenty of things to keep her busy and keep her mind off a handsome blond man with brown eyes. If only she could convince her heart of that.

Over time, Joseph had gotten used to the stench of the docks and all the workers who didn't seem to care about bathing. Ever. Well, at least he'd gotten to the point where he didn't want to throw up every thirty minutes. He'd built some good relationships with the workers and gained their trust and comradery. But so far, no proof. No evidence. No witnesses.

"Borden!" his boss called for him. Joey Borden had become his alias. At least Joey helped him recognize when he was being called since he'd been called that as a kid.

"Aye!" He walked over to the man. He'd been working on his dock accent and had it down to a science. But man, he would be so ready to get back to his real world. . .and take a bath.

"You and Lucky over there need to deliver this pile of crates to this address." The boss handed Joseph a slip of paper.

"Sure thing, boss." Joseph—Joey—smacked his State of Maine Pure Spruce Gum like all the other dock workers. Ever since a ship from the Northeast had come with this new invention, all the men had taken it up since they weren't allowed to chew tobacco and spit while they worked. Joseph didn't mind too much because at least it helped the smell.

He and Lucky loaded the crates into a wagon and took off for their delivery. Each time he'd been called out for a job like this, Joseph hoped that he would see or find something—anything—that would help the police, but so far. . .nothing. When they arrived at the address, they headed for the back door, where most people wanted their deliveries. This wasn't a building he was familiar with, but his senses went on high alert. Every window had dark drapes just like the others on Pacific Street.

"Let's get 'em unloaded." Lucky was a hulk of a man and started with the heaviest of the load. "I'll hand 'em down to you, Joey."

"Gotcha." He smacked his gum again.

When the last of the crates were unloaded, he went and knocked on the back door. It flew open. A man at least twice his weight blocked the door and scowled at him around the cigar between his lips.

"We got a delivery." Joseph tried to sound nonchalant.

"Wait there." The man pulled the door closed, but it didn't latch and slowly inched open. Inside, a mound of people were huddled, chained together, some half-naked, and fear all over their faces. Joseph looked back at Lucky. The man's eyes were wide.

Joseph had to think fast. They had two witnesses. He closed the door and waited for the man to return, hoping the man wouldn't know they'd seen anything. If they could successfully make the delivery and hightail it to the police office and *if* he could convince Lucky to testify, there was a chance that those people could be saved tonight.

The door opened again, the man filling the doorway. "Leave it there. We'll take care of it."

Joseph shrugged. "Hey, if we don't havta haul it in, that's less work for us." He handed the man the page to sign for the delivery. The man scribbled his name and then slammed the door again. This time, Joseph heard a lock click into place.

He ran back to the wagon. "Lucky."

"Yeah."

"You saw that."

"Yeah."

"We gotta do something about it."

The big man just sat there.

"Please, Lucky. We gotta do something, and we gotta do it now."

It took a few minutes to convince the big man to help, but Joseph finally did it. They went straight to Captain Fallon, where they gave their testimonies about what they had witnessed, and Fallon dismissed Lucky and thanked him for his service to his city. The dock worker lifted his shoulders a bit and walked out of the station with his head held a bit higher than before. Maybe this experience had done the man some good. Maybe he would come forward again if he ever saw something like this.

Fallon sat on the corner of his desk and motioned Joseph closer. "We'll check this out right now. Come by tomorrow with a delivery of something—I don't care what—just find an excuse to get here, and I'll let you know what happened."

"Yes, sir."

"And Joey?" The captain used his alias. "If you can, find a way to take a bath."

"Yes, sir."

Olivia walked down the busy street beside Julia, with Daniel not far behind them. One thing she'd noticed since she and Julia had become friends was that the men wouldn't speak to either of them when they were together. While it made things *feel* a bit safer, it didn't help her feel any more comfortable. But she really didn't care. Julia was a child of God and forgiven. She'd given up her former life and sincerely wanted to do good. Not that many people believed it. At least not yet. But there had been several positive comments about her brothel being gone. Would she ever be known as anything other than a madam?

If Olivia had anything to do with it, she'd see to it that things changed. They'd had an influx of families arrive recently. There were men wanting to start businesses who came with their wives and children. That had to make a difference. At least Olivia hoped so.

Daniel stepped up next to them. "The curtains look great in the restaurant by the way."

"Thank you." It had taken her a lot longer than she'd expected to hand-sew curtains for every one of the large windows. Then she'd had to sew ones for the new restaurant as well. "I'm glad that project is done. It's a good thing Julia helped me or I might never have finished."

"Well, they look great. The customers talk about them a lot." He shoved his hands into his pockets. "So. . .how are you doing with Joseph gone?"

Exactly the topic she didn't want to talk about. "I'm fine."

"No, you're not." Julia leaned around her and spoke to her brother. "She misses him a lot."

"I know she does. She's in love with him." He nodded.

"And she used to talk about him all the time."

"I know. Joseph this and Joseph that. I kinda miss it." Daniel looked amused.

"I'm standing right here in the middle of you two, so there's no need to talk about me like I'm not here."

"I'm sorry for teasing, Livvy."

"We're just concerned about you." Julia turned toward her and put a hand on her hip as she walked.

Olivia came to a stop in the street. "Must we discuss this now?"

Daniel sighed. "Sorry."

Julia didn't say a word.

They all started walking again. For several moments, the lack of conversation stretched over them until Olivia couldn't take it anymore.

"I don't understand why I haven't heard from him. I thought he felt the same way about me that I felt about him."

Her brother patted her arm. "He does, Livvy. I know he does."

"Well, I'm glad *you* know that, but it's not so easy for me. I've never been in love before."

Julia gasped next to her. "But I thought you were a widow?"

With a sigh, Olivia shook her head. This was not a good time for her to talk about the past, not when she'd worked so hard to let it go. "It's a long story."

"Maybe another time then." Julia fiddled with the string on her reticule.

"Livvy, it seems like you're holding something back from us. I thought we decided that we were all in this together? Don't you remember at Bible study the other day?"

"That's when we were talking about our city and all the changes. It had nothing to do with Joseph and his absence."

Julia stopped and put both hands on her hips. The look she gave Olivia was quite severe. "I can't believe you would stand there and say that after all we've been through together the past few weeks. All the things you've had to endure because you took in a scorned woman. Me! How dare you belittle our friendship like that."

The scolding hit her straight in the heart. It was true. They deserved her honesty. "I'm sorry. I just didn't want to put it into words because it hurts too much." She looked at her brother and saw his concern for her etched on his brow. "And I didn't want you to be hurt either. But if you want to know the truth, I've been asking God to remove my feelings for Joseph if it's His will."

"Whatever for? The man loves you." Daniel's voice held disbelief and a bit of shock.

"It's just been so long. And I'm beginning to think that he's just like all the other gold miners. He doesn't care about me at all. Maybe he never did. Just the gold."

CHAPTER 28

Joseph carried a crate of soap on his shoulder. The only excuse he could find was that the police captain needed soap and a shipment had just come in. His boss didn't seem to care or suspect a thing. But as he walked up the hill to the office, his stomach churned. Were they able to rescue all those people? And even if they had, there were probably a lot more hidden in other buildings around town. Or did the police arrest the men working at the building and get them to give up their boss? That would be too easy, but it sure would be nice if it were true. Joseph missed Olivia more than he could say.

And he missed his bed. And clean clothes. And a clean-shaven face. He'd kept his bald look and grown a mustache and beard while he'd been working at the docks. He doubted anyone would recognize him, because he didn't even recognize himself in the mirror.

Prayerfully, Dewei had gotten the message to Daniel and Olivia and then the note to Daniel. He had no idea, though, if his friend would understand the message. If something happened to Joseph, would anyone know? He should have given his friend some kind of clue to a timeline or when to look for him, but he hadn't.

One of the sergeants opened the door for him as Joseph approached.

"I got some soap for the captain."

"Right this way." The man led him to Fallon's desk.

"Got your order, sir." He let the crate thump on the floor. He held out the paper for Fallon to sign.

The captain came close and signed the page. "The building was completely empty. We've got nothing to go on." He let out a long sigh. "I'm sorry."

His stomach plummeted. This was not how it was supposed to go. They'd seen it with their own eyes. How did they empty that building so fast?

Joseph tried to keep a straight face. "I'll keep at it, sir." Discouragement flooded his being as he turned and walked out of the building. At this rate, he might never get to go home. But he had to keep trying. He'd promised Dewei. And he'd seen it for himself—people chained up, starving, and in fear.

As he walked back to the docks, he jammed his hands into his pockets. His shoulders slumped with the weight of all that had transpired, and he had no way to do anything about it. Spying was an awful business. It took stealth, diligence, and patience. Too much patience. He wasn't sure how much more he could take.

A shove from behind pushed him down the hill. He rolled and tried to stop himself, but someone jumped on top of him and threw a bag over his head. Then something heavy hit the left side of his head. Everything went black.

Beads of sweat ran down Olivia's back. Being the manager was wonderful some days and horrible the next. Today, cook had needed help in the kitchen when one of his workers fell ill. Olivia had done all she could to keep up and deal with the heat from the stoves and ovens at the same time. How did Daniel manage this?

Two hours later, the lunch rush was over, and Olivia raced up the stairs to change her clothes. She was basically soaked through. She had to find something cooler to wear if she was going to survive the day.

Footsteps sounded on the stairs, and she prepared for a knock on their home door. Scurrying around, she threw on a clean dress and went to the door, but it swung open and Daniel stood there—his face ashen.

"What is it? What's wrong?" Heart racing, she stepped back to allow him entrance.

Her brother came forward and gripped her hands. "Dewei is here to see us."

"Oh no!" Sobs choked her throat. "Not Joseph. . .please tell me. He's all right, isn't he?"

He led her to the settee. "Wait here for a minute." He went to his room and returned with a note. "I don't know what's happened. I'm pretty sure that Joseph was spying for the police. Read this. Dewei gave this to me that day he came to see us to tell us about Joseph's mine." He handed her the paper.

Our project has come to fruition. I will be busy with this new job. Please pray that we find all the treasure that we can. The wharf is beautiful this time of year.

It didn't make any sense to her. "What does it mean? And why didn't you tell me about it?"

"Because Dewei told me it was very private. As to the meaning, I'm not entirely sure, but I was hoping that the project is about the slaves and children we'd heard rumors about. Busy with the new job could allude to the mine, but I don't think so—I think that was to throw anyone else off if they saw the note. The new job is most likely what he's doing for Captain Fallon. Remember, the day he left—the day Dewei came to see us—he had a meeting with the captain." He let his finger slide down the writing. "I'm assuming *treasure* means people. But again, he was trying not to give anything away to people who might see this. And the only thing I can figure for the last statement is that the something has to do with a job down near the water. So if we don't hear from him, maybe go look for him down at the docks?"

"So you're saying you don't think he's at the mine?"

"No. I'm positive he's not at the mine."

Her heart unclenched. Relief over why he left engulfed her, and then it was replaced by worry and fear. If he wasn't at the mine and Daniel's assumptions were correct, that meant that Joseph was in a lot of danger.

"Are you okay with me bringing Dewei up here?"

She nodded and wiped a tear that streaked down her cheek.

In a moment, Daniel returned with Joseph's foreman.

The man bowed. "Need your help, please."

"Of course. Anything we can do." She offered him a seat.

The man sat on the edge of the cushion. "I follow Mr. Sawyer often at the docks. He no tell me what he do, but family"—the man pointed to his chest—"Dewei's family Mr. Sawyer try to save." The man let his chin drop for a moment then lifted it and looked into her eyes. "Three days ago, Mr. Sawyer disappear."

She put her hand over her mouth.

Daniel put a hand on her knee. "Do you have any idea what happened to him?"

Dewei looked back and forth between the two of them. "Saw someone hit his head and drag away. Was too far away to follow. When Dewei catch up, they gone."

❧

"I don't know what to do, Livvy. I feel completely helpless." Daniel paced in the parlor while she tore apart a pillow that had started to fray. Five days had passed since Dewei's visit. Nothing could ease the ache she felt in her heart. Christmas was two days away, and Joseph was missing.

Oh, Lord, please keep him alive and well.

The prayer had become her constant because she didn't know what else to do. Daniel had visited Captain Fallon, but there was no news. Sadly, the police chief believed that the reason Joseph was taken was because there was someone on the police force who had been bought by whomever was behind the slave ring. He'd told them that he'd suspected it for a while and didn't think that anyone had overheard his conversation with Joseph, but he couldn't be certain.

"Is there anything else we can try?" She knew it was grasping, but she had to ask.

"I don't know. I've been wracking my brain, and Dewei has searched high and low for answers. The only thing that we can figure is that someone got wind of Joseph spying for the police. I take comfort in the fact that they didn't kill him right away, so hopefully they don't know who he is either."

She stood to her feet, threads and pieces of fabric littering the skirt of her dress. "I can't just sit here anymore. I can't. Oh, Daniel. . . What will I do if something happens to him? I never even told him how I felt."

Her brother wrapped his arms around her. "We've got to trust in the Lord, Livvy. He knows what Joseph is going through right now, and I have confidence that He is lifting our friend up."

Knock, knock.

Daniel went to the door. "Who is it?" He spoke through the wood.

"Julia."

Daniel opened the door and let their friend in. But it wasn't just her. Behind her hid a small figure. When the boy looked up into Olivia's eyes, she sucked in a deep breath. The boy from the alley! He looked so much worse. Skin and bones, his cheeks hollow, and his arms covered in bruises.

Olivia opened her arms and knelt in front of him. "You found me." Gingerly, she hugged the boy. Keeping her hands on his shoulders for fear he might run away, she leaned back an inch or two. "Are you all right?"

He nodded and bit his lip.

"He's been through a lot. I helped him escape this morning, and we've been hiding ever since." Julia's shoulders shook as she inhaled. "I've never been so scared. You should see the brutes that are after us." She placed a hand on the boy's head. "But this little man, he knew exactly what to do. He said we had to come here."

Olivia couldn't help but smile. "I'm so glad you remembered." Standing up, she took his hand and led him over to the couch. "You're safe here."

"I don't know about that." Julia shook her head. "You see, we didn't just escape. He knows where they took Mr. Sawyer."

CHAPTER 29

Everything tilted around him. Joseph tried to open his eyes, but only one would work. The other must be swollen shut. At least his head didn't pound like it had been. He had no idea how many days he'd been here, but he was almost thankful for the time he'd been unconscious. Attempting to sit up, he felt the room sway even more. Then he realized it wasn't the room. He was on a ship, and it was rolling with the waves. Were they out to sea?

He lifted his right hand and felt the weight of the chain. It was too dark to see, so it must be night or he might be deep in the hold of the ship. Either way, his eyes would have to adjust to the dark.

If he'd thought the smells were bad working at the docks, he'd been gravely mistaken. Now it smelled like he was in a sewer surrounded by rotting fish. His stomach attempted to heave, but he held it at bay, not that he had anything in his stomach to give up. This would probably be the end of him.

Surprisingly, he was at peace. Thanks to Daniel, Joseph knew that his heart was right with God. He'd wished he could have spent one last day with Olivia and told her that he loved her, but it wasn't meant to be, and he needed to accept that. He'd done what he thought was right—he'd tried to help those less fortunate.

Breathing slowly, he closed his eyes again and laid back on the hard wood underneath him. If it was his time to go, he was ready. But he wanted to pray for all those people to be rescued. He might have failed, but there were others who knew and who would continue to search for answers. *Thank You, Lord, for what You're going to do. Thank You for letting me serve You. God, thank You for saving me. Please keep Daniel and Olivia safe. If my life needs to be a sacrifice for You, I'm ready, but please save those people. Many of them may not know You, so they're not ready to die.*

Joseph continued to pray for everyone he knew, for every business, for every ship, even for the ones who were behind the heinous crimes. He didn't want to go to sleep and have it just be over. If it was his time, he wanted to go out talking to God.

The man stood at the edge of the crowd while George stepped up to the platform they'd built in the town square. Notices had been plastered around the city for a week, talking of the gathering that was to happen on the night before Christmas Eve. A lot of people had gathered, and that made him lift his chin a tad bit higher.

"Ladies and gentlemen." George cleared his throat and paused. "It is my honor and privilege as head of your city council to introduce to you the man who has been our great city's benefactor for many months. My employer has wished to remain anonymous for all this time because he is a humble and giving man. But as we journey toward statehood, many prestigious government officials in our fine country have asked for his assistance and desired that he consider the possibility of serving our country in an official manner."

The crowd applauded, and murmurs were heard throughout as people looked over their shoulders to see who it could possibly be.

A smug smile lifted his lips. The event was playing out just as he'd hoped.

George held up his hands to silence the crowd and continued.

"Not only is this generous man donating money to fund so many of our city's services, but he is in the process of building a home that can be used for orphans and widows. Another magnificent building that he has had under construction, he'd like to donate to the city for public offices and possibly even to be used as a courthouse. And while this man has already done so much more to improve our lives here, as a token of his generosity, he has a Christmas gift for each one of you to tell you that he knows how much many of you have labored and suffered." George waved at some men. "If our ushers would come forward, they will hand out the gifts to each one of you."

The crowd hushed as they watched the ushers open their burlap sacks and give crisp one-dollar bank notes to each person. Gasps soon traveled the area as awe spread through the people. It was going exactly as he'd planned. Who wouldn't love him now, especially as he'd given them all money? A lot of money.

"It is now my great honor to introduce you to Mr. Horace VanCleeve."

Thunderous applause and cheers greeted his ears as he made his way to the platform. He held up his hands and bowed humbly to them, nodding along the way. When he reached the stage and looked out at everyone in front of him, he knew he'd accomplished his goal. The city was now his.

Olivia sat on the settee with a small boy curled up in her lap. The lad had been asleep for a long time after she'd helped him take a hot bath. She'd had to change the water two times because he'd been so dirty, but he didn't seem to mind. The warmth probably felt good since he'd told them he'd always been cold. The child had only been able to manage a few bites of bread and a cup of water, but she remembered reading somewhere that malnourished people needed to eat very small amounts at first.

She looked across the room and watched Julia. The woman had risked her own life to help this boy, knowing that she would be dead if they ever caught her. But she said that if she'd learned anything in their Bible study, it was that she had to do the right thing. She was ready to follow God no matter the cost. Even in sleep, the woman was breathtakingly beautiful. It broke Olivia's heart to think of all she'd had to endure, but she praised God for how they'd made it this far. Oh, what she wouldn't give to see her friend flourish in her new life. As it pressed on her heart, Olivia lifted it up in prayer. *Lord, please give her a beautiful future full of love and hope. Thank You for all You've done in her life.*

What an amazing God they served. The sacrifice that was made for them all. . .the unconditional love, the forgiveness, the joy. There was so much to be thankful for. Now if only Daniel would return with Joseph, her Christmas would be perfect.

He'd left hours ago, following their young charge's description of the ship he'd seen Joseph being dragged to. She looked down at the boy. If he didn't tell her his name in the morning, she would just have to give him a new one.

As weary as her body was, she felt unsettled and didn't feel comfortable going to sleep. She needed to guard her charges. Daniel had locked the building up tight, but that didn't mean someone couldn't still get to them.

Determination filled her. Not on her watch.

Something jolted her awake. The lanterns had gone out, and her neck was stiff from sitting upright and falling asleep. She had no idea how long she'd dozed off, but her two charges were still fast asleep. As clarity came to her senses, the distinct smell of smoke drifted in the air. Shifting the boy off her lap, she stood and went to the window, pulling the curtains back. An orange glow filled the sky. It wasn't the sunrise.

"Fire!" A shout was heard down in the street followed by another and another.

Olivia went to Julia and shook her shoulders. "Julia, wake up."

The woman blinked up at her several times. "What is it?"

"There's a fire. We've got to get you out of here."

She went to the boy and laid a hand on his cheek. "Wake up, sweetheart. I need you to wake up."

He sat up straight and looked around him.

"I'm sorry to wake you, but we don't have time. Let's get you somewhere safe." Grabbing his hand and Julia's, she led them out the door and down the back stairs. When they reached the outside, thick smoke filled the air, but there weren't any flames close to them as far as she could see. That was a good sign at least for now.

She whisked them to the barn they kept behind the restaurant. "I want you both to get on one of these horses." She saddled Buttercup as quickly as she could and handed the reins to Julia. "Cover your face and hair with your shawl; it will keep the smoke at bay and also keep you hidden." Leaning down to the boy, she pulled a handkerchief out of her pocket. "Cover your nose and mouth with this, and it will help you breathe."

She hugged Julia. "I want you to leave now, get out of town before it gets worse." Giving her directions to the tree where she'd picnicked with Joseph, she smiled. "Wait for me there. I just need to grab a few important things out of the restaurant and house. Then I'll saddle the other horse and join you."

"Promise me, Olivia? You won't try to fight a fire or rescue anyone else on your own?"

"Yes, I promise. Now hurry."

When she was certain they were headed to safety, Olivia ran back to the restaurant building, which also held their home. When she looked to her left, however, she noticed that the building next door was already on fire. How had it spread so fast?

She knew that she needed her mother's trunk, the ledgers for the restaurant, and the money box. As the manager, that would be the best she could do. Everything else could be replaced if they lost it all. Covering her face with her sleeve, she raced up the stairs.

CHAPTER 30

Joseph. . .Joseph, wake up." A voice broke through the fog in his mind and brought him awake. He knew that voice.

"Daniel?"

"Sadly, yes, it's me, my friend."

"What are you doing here?"

His friend's chuckle was accompanied by a groan. "Well, you see, I came to rescue you."

"Are you hurt?"

"Oh, they roughed me up pretty good, but I'm in better shape than you are."

Shouts and cries were heard all around them. Joseph tried to focus, but it was so dark. "What's going on?"

"The city's on fire. At least that's what I think. I keep hearing shouts of 'fire.'"

The stench of smoke drifted over him. "Where's the guard?"

"I think he's asleep."

"Let's wake him. Maybe we can use this to our advantage." Joseph didn't have a plan, but at least it was an idea to start with.

"Help! Help!" Daniel started shouting.

Joseph joined in. "Help! Help!"

Before they knew it, shouts and cries were coming from all over the place.

A startled cry in the corner alerted them that the guard was awake. "What's happening? Is the ship on fire?"

Joseph used his most soothing voice. "It seems the city is on fire, sir. If the flames reach this ship, we don't have much chance of survival."

The man stomped around with panic in his voice. "I can't swim. I don't want to die!"

"I understand. I can help you. I know how to swim."

"No. We can't leave the ship. We can't." The man was working himself up into a frenzy.

"Sir, please listen. I can help you. I can. I promise you."

In an instant, an orange glow lit up the hold.

"The ship's on fire! I don't want to die!" The guard backed himself into the corner.

Joseph kept his tone soft and calm. "Please. Release me, and I'll help you off this ship. I promise."

The man's eyes had turned wild. "I don't want to be burned alive."

"So help us, and we'll help you," Daniel supplied.

The man ran over and unlocked their chains.

Joseph searched and didn't see anyone else. "Are there more?"

"You promised to help me!" the man screamed.

But the wails grew in sound. Daniel followed the sound and lifted a hatch. "Oh, Lord, have mercy on us all."

Joseph staggered over and looked down. Hundreds of men, women, and children were huddled down there. His body shuddered. Yelling at the guard, he held out his hand. "Give me the keys! Now!"

The guard handed them over. "Don't let me die."

"I won't unless you don't help me rescue these people."

The man bolted into action. Between the three of them, they helped everyone out of the hold, but the flames were closing in and the smoke grew so thick, they couldn't breathe.

Joseph didn't know where the strength was coming from, but he helped get everyone off the ship. Even the guard. With the ship anchored only a few yards from the dock, the people were able to make a chain to safety for those who couldn't swim.

The guard collapsed in a heap on the dock and began to sob. "Thank you. I'm sorry. I'm so sorry."

Daniel leaned over the man and spoke to him in a hushed tone.

Joseph checked to make sure that no one was left in the water. The emaciated group of prisoners blinked against the brightness of the fire. How long had they been kept in the utter darkness? His heart clenched to think of what could have happened. Every muscle in his body ached. Most of his bruises were healing, but he'd been chained for far too long. When he looked back to his friend, Daniel was praying with the guard. It made Joseph's heart swell.

A loud roar reached his ears, and he turned toward town. "Daniel, look!"

Before their very eyes, San Francisco looked as if it were hell itself. Flames shot into the night sky, giving it an eerie glow.

His heart sank. "Olivia! I've got to find Olivia."

The two friends raced into town as fast as their legs could carry them. Bucket brigades were hard at work, but the fire was spreading quickly. *Oh Lord, please let her be safe!*

Grabbing the ledgers she'd been working on in her room, Olivia stuffed them inside her mother's trunk. Now where had she put the money box? The temperature had risen significantly in their living quarters, and she feared the fire would be upon her at any moment. Why was it that she couldn't think clearly in a moment of chaos?

Lord, help me. Please.

She thought through and retraced her footsteps from the night before. Snapping her fingers, she remembered tucking it under the bed when she'd given the boy a bath. Crouching down on the floor, she reached for it and got hold of the heavy box, but when she stood up again, the smoke was much thicker. Not a good sign.

She'd just made it to the parlor when flames engulfed the door. That was her exit. Blocked. The orange beast licked at the wall. Olivia backed up and headed to the window that was the farthest away from the fire. The smoke choked her as she moved. She grabbed her apron and covered her nose and mouth, not that it could do much good. She needed fresh air and an escape.

When she made it to the window, she couldn't get it open. Tugging with all her might, she still couldn't get it to budge. She ran to another window. Same thing. Then she ran to Daniel's room and tried. Then her own room. None of the windows would open. How could this be? Was she to die here in the flames?

Tears squeezed from her eyes as the smoke seeped through her apron and burned her lungs. Dragging the small trunk and money box back to the farthest window, she thought about trying to break it. Could she do it? She took the pillows and a blanket off the settee. She pressed her face to the glass and looked to see if there was anyone who could help her, but people were running away from the fire. No one was there to quench the flames with water. No one was there to rescue her.

Looking down, she realized she would probably break a bone or two in the fall. It was a long way down from this window. The first floor had ceilings that were at least twelve feet tall. Even if she were able to lower herself from the windowsill, that would be quite a drop. But that was better than burning alive, wasn't it?

First she needed to break the window. When she looked back into their home, the flames were only feet away from her. Time had run out. Picking up the money box, she threw it at the window and hoped it would break the glass. As the window shattered, the fresh air through the window fanned the flames into a fireball around her. She picked up the trunk and heaved it out the window too. Then she threw the pillows and blanket. Covering the shards the best she could with her apron, Olivia climbed over the ledge and scooted her legs out. As she looked down, she wondered if there was any way she could land on the pillows rather than on the hard trunk. She'd have to leave that in God's hands—there was no time to worry. Her hands stung with the heat as she held on to the sill. It was now or never. With a deep breath, she let go and plummeted to the ground. Her feet slipped out from under her and she rolled onto her back with a thump. The air knocked out of her, she tried to assess the rest of her body, but the jolt had sent a searing pain up through her legs and she couldn't tell if she was all right or not.

"Olivia!"

Unsure whether she was dreaming, she waited for her name to be called again. That sounded like Joseph's voice. Could it be?

"Olivia!" Footsteps pounded closer.

Finally her lungs relaxed, and she could take a deep breath. She closed her eyes for a moment and inhaled again. Was Joseph really here?

"Oh Olivia. Are you all right? We've got to get you away from the building."

As she opened her eyes, the most beautiful sight was before her—*Joseph.*

"You're alive!" She gripped the sides of his face as he lifted her to her feet.

"Yes, I am. Thanks to your brother and our little friend and a guard that had a change of heart at the last minute." He pulled her away from the building.

She couldn't wait any longer. Pressing her lips to his, she kissed him with all the love she'd held in her heart. "I love you, Joseph Sawyer."

A tap on her shoulder interrupted her moment with the man she loved. Daniel was there holding the two boxes she'd risked her life to save, a mischievous grin on his face. "You didn't have to save the money box, Livvy. It's just money. You're far more valuable than that."

"I'm glad you think so."

"Don't mind me. Carry on." He blinked at her, an innocent expression on his face.

Reaching over to swat at his arm, she stopped and put a hand to her backside. "Ow."

"Are you all right?"

"Are you all right?" The two most important people in her life asked at the same time.

Lifting her arm again, this time Olivia followed through with the playful smack to her brother's shoulder. "I'm fine, you stinker." Even though he'd interrupted her moment with Joseph, she was so thankful to be alive and with both of them. "It's just too bad you didn't get here a few minutes sooner. You could have cushioned my fall."

Joseph walked down the street holding Olivia's hand in his own. The devastation was more than he could have ever imagined. So much loss. The rumors had stated that it was over a million dollars in damage. The amount was staggering and beyond his comprehension. Could it all have been prevented if he'd pushed harder to get fire safety measures in place? It was something that burdened him, but he'd never know the answer to that question. Hopefully, now the council would make it their top priority.

As they reached the square, a crowd had gathered. George Banister stood on the little platform. He held up a hand. "Ladies and gentlemen, our city has suffered a great loss...." He continued his little speech while Joseph scanned the crowd for Captain Fallon. After Joseph had made sure that Olivia, Julia, and the boy were safe and all right, he'd gone straight to find the captain with Daniel. They'd laid out all the evidence before the police chief and had three witnesses who testified that one Mr. Horace VanCleeve was behind the slavery ring. As the morning dawned, Captain Fallon had found more than five hundred people who had been held in chains and forced to work as slave labor. One of VanCleeve's employees—a man named Randy—had been caught trying to hide evidence, and once he was confronted with the possible consequences of his actions, it didn't take long for the scoundrel to turn on his employer. He provided more evidence and even confessed to writing the threatening notes posted on Joseph's door.

It had taken Joseph another hour to find Dewei's brothers, but he'd done it. His foreman had cried and wrapped his arms around his family. Joseph told him to take them to his home and feed them, clean them up, and for everyone to get rest.

Weak as he was, Joseph felt renewed by the fact that people had come together. It was a good start for them to turn their city around.

George was still on the stage blathering when his employer joined him. As soon as the man opened his mouth, a circle of men surrounded the platform.

Captain Fallon moved forward, one of his own deputies tied up at his side. "Mr. VanCleeve, as captain of police in this fine city, I'm here to tell you that you are under arrest for a whole slew of crimes. You too, Mr. Banister."

VanCleeve sputtered. "You are gravely mistaken, Captain Fallon. I am this city's benefactor—"

"We have witnesses and all the proof we need, Mr. VanCleeve."

Banister and VanCleeve tried to argue, but the sergeants took care of the men on the stage in quick order. Fallon handed off the deputy who had been VanCleeve's informant to a couple other deputies and stepped up. "Ladies and gentlemen, I'm sorry to tell you such grievous news, but there's been some downright evil practices going on in our town. We won't allow this to continue. This is our city. Our home. You have my word that I will do everything in my power to clean up this city."

The alcalde, John Geary, stepped up beside the captain. "Thanks to our hardworking police chief, we've dissolved the slavery ring that had infested San Francisco. There's still much work to do on so many fronts, but we're committed to the job. And even though our city has been devastated by fire, we're here to tell you today, that together we will rise from these ashes and make our city great—a golden light for thousands of people who seek a better life."

CHAPTER 31

*January 1, 1850,
San Francisco*

Their small group of wedding guests gathered in the church that had miraculously survived the fire with only a few burn scars on the outside. Olivia looked around with a full heart. She'd married Joseph Sawyer today, and she couldn't have been happier.

Luke, the boy she'd rescued in the alley, came up to her and placed his hand in hers. "Will you be my family now?"

Crouching down beside him, she wrapped him in a hug. "I would love to be your family. Always and forever."

"Me too." Joseph rested a hand on the boy's head.

Love for this man rushed through every vein in her body. How had she been so blessed?

Looking back to Luke, she stood up. "Did you know that there is a long line of Lukes in my family?"

"Really?"

"Yep. I'll have to tell you about their stories one day, because they're your family now too."

The grin that spread over his face melted her heart.

Julia came over and took Luke's hand. "This sweet little guy and I are going to have so much fun while you two take your wedding trip."

"Hey, what about Uncle Daniel?" Her brother tousled the boy's hair. "I thought we were going to have all kinds of adventures together."

Julia giggled. "As long as you behave yourself, Mr. Livingston, we might allow you to join us."

As the trio walked away, Luke beamed a smile back at her over his shoulder.

"I've been waiting for this moment, Mrs. Sawyer." Joseph's strong arms wrapped around her waist.

"Oh, have you now? What moment is that?"

"The moment I can have you to myself and do this." He lowered his head and kissed her.

Heat filled her face at the passion he ignited within her. When he pulled away, she couldn't help but fan herself with her hand. "Mr. Sawyer, you have my permission to do that as often as you like."

"I like the way you think." He took her hand and tucked it into the crook in his arm and pulled her close to his side as he walked toward the door. "There's something I'd like to discuss with you, sweetheart."

"Of course."

"What do you think of opening a store of our own here?"

"What about the mine? And what kind of store?"

"Any kind of store you'd like. I'm actually thinking of opening several. As to the mine, I've already sold it. I've made plenty of money and would like to help Dewei and his brothers bring the rest of their families over one day and work for us or Daniel. They are hard workers and deserve the chance and opportunity of freedom in America." He pulled her closer and kissed the tip of her nose. "Besides, the gold I was searching for was not in a mine. I found it in you, my bride."

His words made every nerve ending in her come alive. This man was hers. He loved her. Found her more valuable than gold. And he loved God. Was there anything more precious?

Standing on her toes, she kissed him again with all the desire and love she held for this wonderful man.

He wrapped his arms around her as he deepened the kiss, and a pleasant moan escaped his lips. "I love you, Olivia Sawyer."

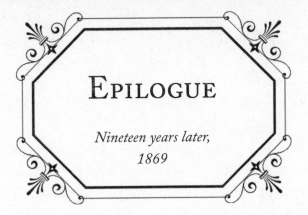

EPILOGUE

Nineteen years later,
1869

Olivia Sawyer looked out the window at her children playing in the yard. The Lord had blessed them with eight beautiful precious lives, and she thanked Him every day. God was indeed the God of second chances. She'd never forget how He'd changed her life from negativity to joy.

The clock in the hall chimed. Daniel and Julia and their family would be arriving in about an hour. She had just enough time before dinner to write in her journal. The beautiful box from her mother sat next to her chair where she embroidered, read her Bible, and cuddled with her children. Opening it up, she pulled out the stack of journals. Running her hands over each cover, Olivia prayed that she could pass on a legacy of faith to their future generations. Just like Mary Elizabeth Lytton and Faith Weber. She pressed the priceless, fragile books against her chest.

"What are those, Mama?" Emma—their thirteen-year-old daughter—stood by her chair and placed her hand on Olivia's shoulder.

She'd always kept the books buried deep in the chest so sticky little hands couldn't get to them, and the children knew never to open the prized box. But it was time. Time for her to pass on her heritage. "These are journals of my great-grandmother and my great-great-great-great-great-*great*-grandmother."

Emma's love of books and writing had joined with her sweet and quiet spirit. The look of awe on her face made Olivia smile. "How old are they?"

"This one is from 1620." She reverently held the cracked leather volume. "And this one"—she held up the other—"is from later in the 1700s."

"That's a long time ago."

"Yes, my sweet Emma, it is. But when I was going through one of the hardest times of my life, these two journals—written by women in our family all those generations ago—they encouraged me and helped me to fall in love with your father."

"Really?" A smile spread across her daughter's face.

Olivia nodded.

The front door swung open, and Joseph stepped in. "Well, there's two of my beautiful ladies."

Olivia stood and went over to hug the man she'd loved for close to twenty years. "You're home early. What a lovely surprise!" She kissed him full on the mouth, and Emma giggled.

"Mama was just telling me about how she fell in *love* with you." Their daughter's syrupy voice teased.

"Oh, she was now?" He pulled Olivia closer and kissed her forehead. "Did she tell you that I fell in love with her a *long* time before she fell in love with me?"

Raising one of her eyebrows, Olivia gave him what she hoped was a fierce look. "Now, now. It wasn't that much time before I fell in love with you."

"Oh, it was torture, I assure you." Joseph sat on the sofa, and Emma cuddled up next to him, all ears, waiting for what he would say. Olivia placed the books back in the trunk as he told his tall tale of romance. It made her smile that this man loved her so unconditionally. Even with all her flaws.

The life they'd built together in San Francisco was beautiful. After he'd sold the mine, Joseph had built several stores throughout the city, which had grown in number over the years. Just as he'd promised, the first one had been hers—a millinery shop. With lots of blue hats. Known for quality merchandise and fair prices—even when the competition was charging outlandish prices—the Sawyer businesses had thrived. The Lord had blessed them abundantly. More than she'd ever imagined.

As he finished telling Emma his tale, Olivia thought back to that tumultuous time at the birth of their city. Her husband would always be her hero—not only for loving her and coming to rescue her when he'd almost died himself—but for saving hundreds of lives by putting his own life on the line. She'd regaled their children with the story of his spying, capture, and survival many times, hoping that they would pass it on to future generations because their family—and the world—needed more examples of faith and strength. It needed more men willing to sacrifice everything for the good of those around them. It needed more men who followed God with their whole hearts. The world needed more men like Joseph Sawyer.

Her heart swelled with pride. The legacy they would leave behind was beautiful because God—in His infinite wisdom—had joined the two of them together.

"What are you thinking, my love?"

She gazed up into his eyes and wrapped her arms around him. "About how I have loved being your bride all these years and how that love continues to grow each and every day."

"The feeling is mutual." He closed the distance between them and captured her lips in a passionate kiss.

As the sound of Emma's giggles floated over her, the rhythm of little feet running toward them made Olivia grab onto her husband even tighter. "Brace yourself," she whispered against his mouth. "We're about to be overtaken by our brood."

"Oh, I think we can handle it." He pulled her tighter against him and picked up where he had left off.

Note from the Author

The Gold Rush of 1849 is something that most of us have heard a lot about, but perhaps we don't know many of the actual facts. Over time, there's a tendency to glamorize certain aspects of history while ignoring the truth of what really happened. I found that to be the case about so much of what I *thought* I knew of 1849 San Francisco.

So it's a good thing I love research. While I was researching for *The Golden Bride*, I discovered so much more than I'd ever anticipated. And just like all my other historical novels, I love to give you a note at the end with the chance to look up some of the interesting things for yourself should you wish to further explore our great country's history.

Many things about this point in history are pretty dark. So to keep the story from depressing or disgusting you, I only touched on some of these aspects briefly. But like all our history, it's important that we know the truth of what happened. I know how enlightening it has been for me to understand so much more of what went on during this time period.

If you'd like to know more for yourself, a lot of wonderful resources are online and of course there are many books. One of the books that I found fascinating was *Historic San Francisco: A Concise History and Guide* by Rand Richards. A wonderful map from the time period can be seen here: www.davidrumsey.com/luna/servlet/detail /RUMSEY~8~1~1934~190050:Official-Map-of-San-Francisco, -Comp.

I always try to include a little bit about what was real and what was not. The schoolhouse on Portsmouth Square was indeed the police's first office. Built in 1847, the one-room schoolhouse was at Clay Street. Because all the students—and the teacher—had headed off to find their fortunes as soon as gold was discovered, it was the logical solution given that population growth overwhelmed the city structure so rapidly. There's a ton of information at sanfranciscopolice.org/sfpd-history that helps to give an even greater glimpse into what they dealt with to get things under control in the exploding city.

The mention in *The Golden Bride* of the fire that burned down the Shades Hotel was the first of many fires to plague the city. It indeed happened in January of 1849. When the *Philadelphia* burned in June of that same year, it was only another reminder that if they didn't do something about it, their city could be gone in a flash. In fact, there were six fires in addition to this that were called *great fires* in the first two-three years. The next fire would be the first great fire. It was a horrifically destructive fire—which was the fear of many—and is just like the one in the story on Christmas Eve. More than a million dollars of property was destroyed in just a few hours. And all three of these fires were in the crazy year of 1849 in the midst of the crime, filth, and population boom. The more I researched about the history of San Francisco and what we now call the Gold Rush, the more I realized that I needed to include one of the city's greatest nemeses: fire.

Real people included in the story: Military Governor General Bennet C. Riley (California was a territory at the time); the first alcalde and then mayor (in 1850 once California became a state) of San Francisco, John Geary; and San Francisco's first police captain, Malachi Fallon. Please note that I created their personalities for the story.

My city council in *The Golden Bride* is fictitious. There was indeed a city council, but I created mine for the sake of the story and so as not to take anything away from the real individuals who served.

The crime, filth, shacks, tents—it was all real. And probably so much worse than we can imagine. All in all, the original San Francisco is nothing like the prestigious and world-renowned city of San Francisco of today.

John Geary's speech in chapter eighteen is taken from sources that quote his speech. I was impressed by his words and his heart to tackle the massive duty before him. You can see parts of it here at this link: www.foundsf.org/index.php?title=Mayors_1850–1897

A lot of readers ask about my favorite snippet of history that I learn while doing research. Most of the time, it's something that I used in the novel—for instance in *The Patriot Bride*, I used Benjamin Franklin's love of air baths—but this time, I didn't use my favorite fact in the story but want to pass it on to you.

Did you know that San Francisco expanded its shoreline out into the sea and some areas of the city are built upon landfill? And not just landfill, but sunken ships! Somewhere in my memory, I recalled hearing that notion. But I had no idea how much or where until I started my research. Since it was fascinating to me, I thought I'd include a little peek for you into this interesting piece of history. Check out the map at the link listed to see for yourself news.nationalgeographic.com/2017/05/map-ships-buried-san-francisco/.

It has been a pleasure to share with you another story in the Daughters of the Mayflower series. Thank you for traveling with me.

I couldn't do this without you.

Enjoy the journey,
Kimberley

ACKNOWLEDGMENTS

It takes so many people to put a book like this into your hands. Each time, I'm amazed and grateful.

But this time, I feel like I need to pour out my gratefulness in truckloads full because life just threw some crazy punches. I had a cross-country move and a horrible five-week-knock-me-flat illness that threw the schedule topsy-turvy.

So the team at Barbour needs a huge round of applause. (And probably a whole lot of chocolate from me.) Becky Germany—thank you. Those two words are not enough and will never be enough. Faith, Shalyn, Liesl, Krista, Bill, and everyone else there who makes up the incredible team—thank you.

Becky Fish. Wow. You deserve an award for this one. Thank you. What a joy it has been to work with you again.

My critters: Darcie Gudger, Becca Whitham, Kayla Woodhouse. I love you all. Thanks for cheering me on.

Tracie—thank you again, for all your insight and brainstorming.

Jeremy—my hero, the love of my life, and the best husband in the whole world. I love you more.

Thank You, God, for the opportunity to share Your story once again. It's all for You.

And to my readers, thank you. Thank you. Thank you.

Kimberley

ABOUT THE AUTHOR

Kimberley Woodhouse is an award-winning and bestselling author of more than fifteen fiction and nonfiction books. A popular speaker and teacher, she's shared her theme of "Joy Through Trials" with more than half a million people across the country at more than 2,000 events. Kim and her incredible husband of twenty-five-plus years have two adult children. She's passionate about music and Bible study and loves the gift of story.

You can connect with Kimberley at: www.kimberleywoodhouse .com and www.facebook.com/KimberleyWoodhouseAuthor